"CRAWLED INTO
TO HIDE, DID YOU, KAREN?"

He didn't give her a chance to answer before he roared on. "Funny, I didn't take you for a quitter. I thought you were the type to face things head-on!"

"Brick," she pleaded, "please understand. This can't continue. I need the respect of the community. The support of my men."

Suddenly she felt two broad, male hands on her waist. "None of that's going to keep you warm at night, Karen. None of it's going to put out the fire burning deep inside you."

Then his lips claimed hers. It took all her strength to wrench herself away.

"Listen to me carefully," she said coldly, through her misery. "If you ever touch me like that again, Lieutenant Bauer, *I will have your badge!*"

For Betty Cook, who's always there to lend a hand

Special thanks and acknowledgment to Suzanne Ellison for her contribution to this work.

Special thanks and acknowledgment to Joanna Kosloff for her contribution to the concept for the Tyler series.

Published 1992

ISBN 0-373-82505-6

BLAZING STAR

BLAZING
STAR
SUZANNE ELLISON

Harlequin Books

TORONTO • NEW YORK • LONDON
AMSTERDAM • PARIS • SYDNEY • HAMBURG
STOCKHOLM • ATHENS • TOKYO • MILAN
MADRID • WARSAW • BUDAPEST • AUCKLAND

TYLER

TYLER

American women have always used the art quilt as a means of expressing their views on life and as a commentary on events in the world around them. And in Tyler, quilting has always been a popular communal activity. So what could be a more appropriate theme for our book covers and titles?

BLAZING STAR

This shaded variation of the beloved eight-point Star quilt involves four patches of diamonds with an accent at the end of each point. Some lonely frontier quilter probably thought of this pattern while dreaming on a star or following one home in her best beau's sleigh after dark.

Dear Reader,

Welcome to Harlequin's Tyler, a small Wisconsin town whose citizens we hope you'll soon come to know and love. Like many of the innovative publishing concepts Harlequin has launched over the years, the idea for the Tyler series originated in response to our readers' preferences. Your enthusiasm for sequels and continuing characters within many of the Harlequin lines has prompted us to create a twelve-book series of individual romances whose characters' lives inevitably intertwine.

Tyler faces many challenges typical of small towns, but the fabric of this fictional community will be torn by the revelation of a long-ago murder, the details of which will evolve right through the series.

Renovations are almost complete at the old Timberlake lodge; they're gearing up for the Ingallses' annual Christmas party, which hasn't been held at Timberlake for decades! There's a new owner now, a man with a personal interest in showing Tyler folks his financial clout and with a private objective in reclaiming the love of a town resident he romanced long ago.

Marge is waiting with some home-baked pie at her diner, and policeman Brick Bauer might direct you down Elm Street if it's patriarch Judson Ingalls you're after. Brick calls Kelsey's boardinghouse home, and you're always welcome there. In fact, new police captain Karen Keppler is about to move into the Kelseys' herself. So join us in Tyler, once a month, for the next eight months, for a slice of small-town life that's not as innocent or as quiet as you might expect, and for a sense of community that will capture your mind and your heart.

Marsha Zinberg
Editorial Coordinator, Tyler

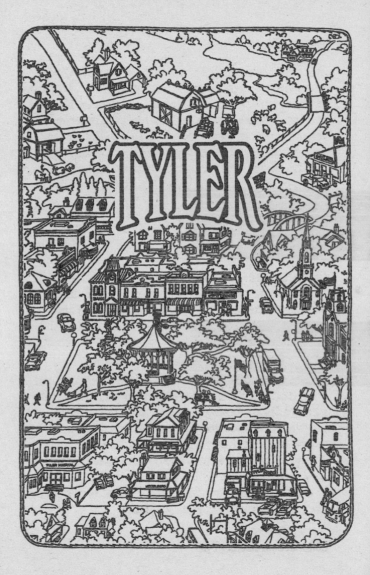

most of the first day figuring out what the boss was
record keeping and dictating memos to Weselindo a

CHAPTER ONE

BRICK BAUER PARKED his old black pickup outside the main gates to the Schmidt farm, then hurried up the long gravel walkway that led through the dark to the house. It was already after eight, and he hoped the chief's retirement party would be in full swing by now—the bigger the crowd, the less conspicuous his token appearance was likely to be. A half hour or so ought to do it, just long enough to say hello to everybody who'd be sure to notice if he lacked the courage to show up here tonight. All week he'd felt like a bug in a specimen jar, and he had no intention of spending the next week the same way.

Since last Monday, Brick's name had been on the lips of every housewife who had her hair done at Tisha Olsen's Hair Affair, every cop who hung out at Marge's Diner and every old codger who was living out his sunset years at Worthington House. Nobody had dared to spread rumors at the Kelsey Boardinghouse, but Brick figured that was because his Aunt Anna had threatened to take a spatula to the backside of any of his fellow boarders who so much as mentioned that he'd been passed over for promotion, let alone that a *woman* from the other end of Sugar Creek County was going to take the helm instead of him.

The worst of it was that Brick still wasn't sure how it had happened. He'd been Chief Paul Schmidt's right-hand man at the Tyler Police Department for the past six years, and back in college he'd been engaged to Paul's daughter, who was supposed to be making one of her rare pilgrimages home for the party tonight. Granted, Brick and Shelley had parted painfully, but nobody could blame him for that. It wasn't his fault that Shelley had decided being a big-city microbiologist suited her better than marriage to a hometown cop. She still hadn't married; she claimed she never would.

Brick was single, too, but it wasn't because he didn't want a family. He just hadn't found his lifetime mate yet. He'd actually grown a bit weary of searching, but his Aunt Anna still spent a good deal of her time trying to find him the perfect wife. Her latest candidate was the new boarder who was moving in tonight.

Aunt Anna and Uncle Johnny had zipped off to Milwaukee at the last minute to put their daughter Kathleen on a plane for Switzerland, conveniently leaving Brick as the resident family member to greet the newcomer anytime after nine. He wasn't holding out any hopes that he'd want to get particularly chummy with the new boarder, but he was pleased that he had such a good excuse to leave the party early.

As he pocketed his key and marched up the gravel walkway, Brick spotted a pair of long, magnificent female legs moving at a good clip in front of him. At once he found himself checking out some impressive curves that not even the stylish wool coat could conceal. Brick knew every woman in the retiring police chief's life—there weren't many—but for a moment he had trouble placing this one. The confidence of that saucy walk made him question his own memory; besides, there was something different about the hair.

Shelley always wore her hair long and loose, the way he liked it. Tonight it was wrapped in a classy chignon but it was still dark and thick and tempting. In fact, in the moonlight, it looked even more silky than Brick remembered it. *Shelley* looked more silky than he remembered her! Womanhood had been good to her. Not only did she move with more compelling grace than she used to, but she'd put on a little weight, too... in all the right places.

As Shelley approached the porch where they'd exchanged fervent kisses so many times, Brick felt an odd sense of déjà vu. Was it possible that he still had deep feelings for her? Was that why he'd never really found another woman to take her place? Was that why she looked so good to him—better than ever—after all this time?

As December's first tiny snowflakes began to fall, Brick remembered how Shelley had looked the first time he'd kissed her snow-sprinkled nose, when she was nineteen. She'd giggled ever after when he'd called her Snowflake. Oh, it was all over and done, but he had special memories of those days. He imagined that Shelley might, too.

Suddenly Brick realized that he didn't want to greet her for the first time in years under the gossip-mongering eyes of every busybody in Tyler. Whatever they had to say to each other should be said alone outside.

He jogged the last few yards between them, reaching Shelley just as she pushed open the chain-link gate at the edge of the porch. Because she seemed to be rushing, Brick reached out with a friendly arm to encircle her waist, about to say, "Hey, Snowflake, you never used to be in such a big hurry to go inside when I took you home."

He got as far as "Hey, Snowflake" when the most amazing thing happened. Shelley grabbed his elbow, jammed her hip into his leg and flipped him straight up and over the gate. Twisting sideways as he struggled to find his feet, Brick came down hard on the protruding edge of the chain link. Raw steel ends clawed his jaw and shoulder, shredded his best suitcoat and bloodied a fair amount of skin before he hit the ground on his side. Gasping for breath, he rolled flat on his back before he caught a good look at his assailant's face.

She wasn't Shelley! In a dizzying rush Brick realized that this classy brunette was a total stranger. She was beautiful; she was curved in all the right places; she was pulling out a .38 Smith & Wesson from underneath the left side of her coat.

"Don't move a millimeter," she threatened in a dry tone that rivaled Dirty Harry's. "Touch me again and you're going to lose a vital portion of your anatomy."

"Lady, I wouldn't touch you with a ten-foot pole!" Brick grumbled, realizing even in his confusion that fear, not malice, was the reason she'd reacted so violently to such a simple touch. This stunning female had clearly been trained in self-defense. She'd also lived with the threat of urban crime or else watched too many cop shows. He wouldn't be surprised if she tried to make a citizen's arrest for...well, for whatever it was she thought he'd tried to do to her.

"I'm a police officer and I thought you were an old friend," Brick explained, too woozy to sort everything out. His voice sounded odd and hollow. "Sorry if I frightened you. Now may I get off the ground?"

To his surprise, the woman did not immediately accept his explanation. She didn't even look embarrassed. In fact, on closer examination, he decided that her beautiful gray eyes looked more fierce than frightened. Sternly she ordered, "Show me your police ID. Slowly."

Brick was too angry to be scared, but he didn't like the way she kept that gun trained on him. "Good God, you could shoot somebody with that thing, lady." He dug out his ID and pushed it a few inches toward her. "Do you have a permit for that piece?" He didn't ask her if she knew how to use it; it was obvious she knew all too well.

She barely glanced at his identification, unreadable in the darkness, before she barked, "What's your badge number?"

Not his name, his badge number. A curiously eerie feeling, worse than the pain now coursing through his back, began to steal over Brick. How many women were so well versed in self-defense, handled a side arm like a pro and instinctively asked a question like that? Now that he was getting a grip on his equilibrium, he realized what all the signs pointed to.

His assailant was a cop.

She was also a rare beauty; she bore no resemblance to the woman who'd gotten his former partner killed. This lady wasn't a tiny thing, but she wasn't a husky bruiser, either. She looked to be five foot nine or ten, sturdy but slender, with high, sculpted cheekbones and infuriatingly well-curved lips. Even in his current situation, Brick found her femininity hard to ignore. He didn't want to think about the effect she'd have on him if she ever traded in that scowl for a dazzling smile.

Brick told her his number, then added darkly, "Lieutenant Donald Bauer, Tyler Police Department. Go ask my chief. He's inside."

"Lieutenant Bauer," the husky voice countered, "Chief Paul Schmidt is now retired and the Tyler Police Department he ran for seventeen years no longer exists. You now represent the Sugar Creek County Sheriff's Department. Archibald Harmon is your regional commander and Captain Karen Keppler is taking charge of the Tyler substation." She sheathed the gun in a shoulder holster he hadn't noticed underneath the thick coat. "Commit that information to memory, Lieutenant. You may be called upon to use it again."

That was when he knew for sure. Brick felt his face flushing a furious red in the darkness, grateful she couldn't see it but certain that she knew his face was hot. He was not a man who easily embarrassed, but he knew that only a miracle would save him from the whole damn town's discovery of his humiliation.

It was bad enough that the brunette was a strikingly beautiful woman who'd gotten the better of him. Under any circumstances, Brick would have hated lying here on the ground, dizzy and wounded, with a looker like that leaning over him. Knowing that *she* was the one who'd hurt him, knowing that *she* was his new boss, knowing that *she* had stolen the job that was rightfully his and would lord it over him—*lady* it over him!—as long as she lasted in Tyler... it was just too damn much.

Incredibly, the brunette had the unmitigated gall to offer a hand to help him up. Brick ignored it. Still steaming, he struggled to stand up on his own, but when his wobbly knees gave out he plopped back down on the ground.

"I'm Captain Keppler, Lieutenant," the beauty informed Brick, still towering over him. "Sorry about the misunderstanding. Are you injured?"

Brick tried to swallow his fury as the front door opened and he heard Paul Schmidt call out, "We thought we heard somebody out here. Glad you found the place all right, Captain." Then, after a sharp breath, "What the devil—"

"Lieutenant Bauer had a little accident," his new captain said bluntly, her husky voice devoid of humor or concern. "He's bleeding."

The next few minutes were a nightmare for Brick. Paul instantly called out, "Somebody get George Phelps out here!" and rushed over to his side. "Brick, what happened? Are you all right?"

Brick had to steady himself on the gate as he tried—and failed again—to stand. His spine felt battered and his scraped jaw stung. Blood dribbled down his chin to the gravel.

By this time half a dozen people had bounded out of the house. Through the din of worried friends and co-workers, he recognized a few voices: Judson Ingalls's, Janice Eber's, and—it was inevitable—Shelley's.

She sounded just the way she used to when he'd gotten hurt playing football. "Brick! Oh, Brick! You're bleeding! Let George take a look at you and—"

"Oh, for Pete's sake!" he burst out, ready to strangle the whole lot of them. He was fully upright now and his head was finally clear. "I'm fine, my suit's a wreck and Aunt Anna wants me to meet some damn boarder at home by nine o'clock. I just dropped by to say hello to Shelley, goodbye to the chief and to meet

Captain Keppler. I guess I've done all three, so if you don't mind—"

"It won't seem right without you here, Brick," protested Zachary Phelps, a former chief of police, a fellow Kelseys' boarder and a member of the town's council. The tone of his voice said more than his words: Zachary was still feeling guilty for having voted to merge the Tyler Police Department with the Sugar Creek County Sheriff's Department, even though he'd explained to Brick in detail why the town's financial situation demanded it. Brick was certain that neither Zachary nor anybody else on the council had ever believed that the regional commander would bring in outside talent to run Tyler's law enforcement in the wake of Paul Schmidt's retirement. As Zachary studied Karen Keppler in the dim porch light, Brick read the same dismay on the old man's face as he was sure Zachary read on his own.

"Brick, I thought we'd have a chance to talk," Shelley said quietly, so quietly that probably no one but the nearby captain could hear. "I haven't seen you in years."

Brick gave his old flame a quick glance, trying to remember why he'd wondered if some seed of love for her still lingered within him. Oh, she was still pretty...though she'd cut her long, black hair. But she was a stranger, a woman who'd chosen the big city and the scientific world over anything Brick could offer, and he knew that his earlier momentary fantasy had had nothing to do with her.

Kindly he said, "I'll call you, Shelley. Maybe we can have lunch sometime before you go."

He saw something different in the eyes of Captain Keppler, who still stood tensely in front of him. Cal-

culation, assessment . . . disapproval that did not bode
well for a police officer under her command.

By this time George Phelps, head of staff at Tyler
General Hospital and Aunt Anna's boss, had pushed
his way through the gathering crowd. "Everybody get
back!" George commanded, like Moses parting the
Red Sea.

They did pull back, but they didn't disperse. Impa-
tiently Brick snapped, "There's nothing wrong with me
a dab of Bactine won't cure, George. If you want to
help, just get all these folks to stop gawking at me,
would you?"

George seemed to get the picture faster than anybody else. Then again, he was a doctor, and he knew
when blood was serious and when it was just as embarrassing as hell.

His eyes were sympathetic as he called out, "Okay,
everybody, Brick's fine. Let's go back inside."

Before Brick could thank him, Captain Keppler
asked in a businesslike tone, "Are you feeling strong
enough to drive, Lieutenant? I can ask one of the other
officers to take you home."

"I can take care of myself, Captain," he snapped. If
she'd been a man, he would have been hard-pressed to
keep from decking her. But he'd been raised to be gentle with women; he'd been raised to obey his boss. Still,
he wasn't used to the raging fury that was strangling
him at the moment. It was something new and terrible, a beast he knew he must learn to subdue. A beast
that drove from his heart the slightest interest in getting reacquainted with Shelley, lauding his old boss or
kissing up to his new one.

Reluctantly Shelley said good-night, then turned
back to the house. Her father shooed a couple of other

men after her. Captain Keppler, rebuttoning her coat, had the nerve to look downright pretty as she brushed past Brick without another word and followed them inside.

While the sounds of laughter from the house drifted out to his still-red ears, Brick limped out to his truck. On the street he ran into two more late arrivals from the substation—Sergeant Steve Fletcher and tubby Orson Clayton—but he ducked into his truck before they could see that he'd been roughed up. Tomorrow would be soon enough for them to start their ribbing.

By the time he turned on the ignition, the scrapes on Brick's jaw were beginning to clot over, but his backbone was hurting worse than ever. He'd broken up barroom brawls with less pain and certainly less humiliation! By morning every damn soul in Tyler would know how Brick Bauer had been bested by the new female captain who'd been hired instead of him. The gouges on his face would heal a lot sooner than the scars on his pride.

KAREN STAYED at the party longer than she'd intended, not because she was enjoying herself—she wasn't—and not because she thought courtesy demanded it. It was Paul Schmidt's moment of honor, which in a town this size meant that most of his fans and foes were likely to make an appearance. Karen wanted to study those people with great care... particularly the ones who'd been an important part of Schmidt's life for the past forty years or so.

At the top of the list was Judson Ingalls. Everybody kowtowed to him as though he owned the town. Ditto for his elegant blond daughter, Alyssa Ingalls Baron. Ingalls also had a niece named Janice Eber, who seemed sweet and unassuming, but Karen wasn't taking anything at face value. The doctor was a Tyler fixture, as was the lady who owned the diner and the flamboyant one who cut everybody's hair.

And then there were the other cops. Lieutenant Bauer—why did they call him Brick?—had only lived here since high school, according to Karen's information, but his relatives had lived here for generations, and that might be highly significant. Both Alyssa and Janice were Bauer's aunt's close friends. The fact that he had some sort of relationship with Schmidt's daughter might also prove important, and not just because it had provided the catalyst for his unfortunate first meeting with Karen.

If only that handsome man had been able to read her mind! If only he'd guessed how terrible she felt about embarrassing him, how frightened she'd been by the way he'd lunged at her, how his virility had unnerved her even after he'd quelled her fear by revealing that he was a cop! She'd done everything in her power to fool him with her tough-as-leather facade, and she hoped she'd succeeded. She would need a full set of armor to run the Tyler substation—not to mention carry out Commander Harmon's secret assignment.

Everything Karen had heard about Brick Bauer— and everything she'd read in his file—caused her to believe that he was a man of powerful convictions, keen loyalties and devoted to his fellow police officers. Under some other circumstances, Karen would have looked forward to working with such a man. Commander Harmon had given her the impression that he truly hoped she wouldn't find any black marks on Bauer's record—he'd even confessed that he still had high hopes for the lieutenant's career. But Harmon was a diligent cop, if a chauvinistic one, and he had a reputation as a man who upheld the letter of the law no matter who got in the way.

Karen had glowed when he told her that she'd earned the same reputation since she'd moved from Milwaukee to Sugar Creek.

Living under the same roof with Bauer would certainly make it easier to ascertain which hometown loyalties bound him, but after their inauspicious meeting, Karen knew that their domestic situation was going to be a strain on both of them. The knowledge did not dishearten her. She'd devoted her life to the badge and she had police work in her blood. From birth her father had urged her, "Make your old man proud," and she'd devoted her life to that goal. His death in the line of duty had only strengthened her determination.

Karen's courage, however, did little to squelch the butterflies in her stomach as she rang the doorbell of Kelsey Boardinghouse, a beacon of cheery light in December's nighttime gloom. The wreath-bedecked door swung open on the first ring, which surprised Karen. The sight of the man who opened it surprised her, too.

He was wearing low-slung jeans, thick socks without shoes and a Green Bay Packers sweatshirt. Droplets of water clung to his freshly washed short black hair; droplets of blood oozed from three deep gouges on his face. His blue eyes sparkled with fun and his square jaw was softened by deep dimples when he smiled. It was the sort of smile that could make a woman forget everything else in the world.

Karen found herself wrestling with her memory.

"Hi, there! I'm Brick Bauer, Anna Kelsey's nephew," he greeted her cheerfully, reaching for the suitcase in her hand. "She asked me to roll out the red carpet and give you the grand tour. Did you have any trouble finding the place?''

Karen stared at him, wondering if Bauer had dual personalities. What a joy to find him so forgiving, so friendly, so...*so damn male.* With a jolt she realized that the man's dimpled smile was triggering an unexpected female response within her, one she ignored a good deal of the time and always suppressed with policemen. Karen had an uneasy hunch that she was safer with this man when he was angry, but it seemed cowardly to go out of her way to make him mad.

As it turned out, such subterfuge was totally unnecessary. The instant she stepped into the lighted hallway, the smile vanished from Brick Bauer's face. A shell-shocked look stilled the magic in his dancing eyes.

"Your aunt's directions were quite clear, Lieutenant," Karen said neutrally, firmly holding the suitcase handle. "I can carry my own things, thank you."

Karen wasn't sure why it hurt her to see Bauer change so drastically before her eyes. She didn't know this man and couldn't afford to like him. But she'd been spellbound by his delightful greeting when he'd assumed she was an utter stranger; now he was smoldering because he realized they'd met before.

"Captain Keppler?" His tightly controlled tone could not conceal the fury that now raged in his eyes. "My aunt didn't mention her new lodger's name. I didn't realize that the new police captain would be—"

"Invading your home?"

His lips tightened at her bluntness. Karen almost regretted the hard words, but she knew that surprise and anger often drove people to reveal things they'd normally keep well hidden. If Bauer had any secrets, she wanted to find them out for Commander Harmon right away. She also wanted to clear the air about their respective positions. Sooner or later, they were likely to have it out over the way she'd been brought in to take the job he'd expected. Better to do it in private than in front of the men. They'd all be on his side. One to one, she had a better chance of victory.

"Captain Keppler, you are free to live wherever you like. I was just . . . startled to realize you were the new boarder. My information was incomplete."

He said the words like a police detective who knew his stuff. Karen wondered how he'd managed to uncover so little in his investigation of the body found at the old Timberlake Lodge, recently purchased by Edward Wocheck.

So did Commander Harmon.

"I don't like to advertise my private life, Lieutenant," Karen told him. She didn't need to add the obvious: she'd deliberately avoided revealing the nature of her job to chatty Anna Kelsey when they'd made arrangements on the phone. "I don't have much off-duty time, but when I do, I want it to be all mine."

"I feel the same way."

"Good," she said stoutly. "Then we have something in common."

Bauer glanced away. He was fuming, she was certain, but trying to show respect. Karen had to admire him for it—even more than she had to admire his massive shoulders. Still, she couldn't afford to let his hidden anger smolder.

"We have something else in common, Lieutenant. We both wanted the job I came here to do."

His harsh gaze swung back on her. "Captain, I'm doing my damnedest to be courteous to you. Why the hell are you baiting me?"

"I don't want you sandbagging me when we're on the job, Lieutenant Bauer," she told him truthfully. "I came here to run the Tyler substation to the best of my ability, and I'll do it—with or without you. But as long as you remain here, we'll have to work closely together. If you've got something to get off your chest, I'd rather deal with it right now."

When he stared at her for a long, bitter moment, Karen had a sense of what it would be like to be a criminal collared by this man. He was a good six feet tall, his body a solid wall of muscle that looked as if he maintained it at a gym. Karen was used to dealing with all kinds of criminals. She was rarely intimidated just by a man's physical strength, but this big guy had her struggling to keep her breathing even. She knew he would not be easy to control, physically or mentally. She'd flipped him over that fence only because he'd been oblivious to danger. She knew she'd never take him off guard again.

With slow, measured anger, he shut the door behind her. "On behalf of my aunt and uncle, welcome to Kelsey Boardinghouse, Captain Keppler," he said as tonelessly as a robot repeating a coded message. Coldly he turned away from the door and began to head toward the back of the house, speaking as she followed. "Breakfast is served at seven o'clock. Dinner is served at six. There's a refrigerator and a microwave you can use yourself as long as you clean up. The living room is for everyone. So is the phone. The den is my aunt and uncle's private space. Only the family goes in there."

He started climbing the back stairs, two at a time, and Karen found it hard to keep up with his long, angry stride while dragging the heavy suitcase she'd refused to let him carry. He took half a dozen steps down the hall, then dug into his pocket. "This is the key to the front door. This is the key to your room." He dropped the keys in her palm, being careful not to touch her skin. Then he opened the door to her room and gestured for her to go inside.

With relief, Karen saw that the room was well-kept and charming. On the old four-poster lay a quilt, hand-pieced in yellows and blues. It matched the curtains. There was a small desk and a tallboy chest of Early American style. A chestnut-and-rust braided rug covered most of the shiny hardwood floor.

Before Karen could comment on the welcoming vase of flowers and the note she spotted on the nightstand, Brick marched over to the far door and pulled it open, revealing an equally quaint bathroom. "This is the bath. You share it with the lodger on the other side." He opened the far door a crack as if to illustrate his point, but Karen couldn't see much of the other bedroom.

When he took a stiff step and grimaced, Karen felt a sharp need to offer another apology. It was obvious that his scrapes and bruises were bothering him. As the secret investigator who might bring about his downfall, she couldn't afford to show much mercy, but as a human being who prided herself on her quiet compassion and tact, Karen found it hard to keep from showing concern.

"Any questions?" he asked brusquely, interrupting her thoughts.

Will you always hate me? Will all the other Tyler cops hate me, too? Will I ever see those incredible dimples again?

Aloud she said, "No, Lieutenant. Thank you. Good night."

"Good night," he said stiffly, his cautious movements revealing his pain as he edged through the far bathroom door.

It took Karen a moment to realize the significance of that simple act. *He's the boarder who lives next to me!* she realized in dismay. *We'll be sharing meals and the same bath.*

As she juggled the memory of his anger with the realization that such proximity would make it easier to uncover Bauer's secrets for Harmon, Karen closed the door between her room and the bath, locked it carefully, then read the note beside her bed. It started personally:

Dear Karen,
I'm so sorry we were called away tonight, but we'll be back in the morning to fix you up with anything you need. In the meantime, you can count on my nephew to make you snug as a bug in a rug.

   Isn't he adorable? He's Tyler's finest police officer and single, too. I'm sure you'll have plenty of time to get acquainted. We're so glad to have you with us. Just make yourself at home!

                                        Anna Kelsey

Karen fought back a lump in her throat. Mrs. Kelsey would never know how much it meant to her to know that one person in Tyler actually welcomed her. The officers she'd met at the Schmidts' had made it clear enough that they'd all been hoping Brick Bauer would be their new captain. And Bauer himself—why the hell did he have to be so handsome, why the hell had he greeted her with that dimpled smile at the door?—was probably already making devious tactical plans to oust her.

Wearily she began unpacking all she'd need for the first few days: her uniforms, a warm robe, jeans, sweatshirts and sturdy barrettes to clip her waist-length braid flat against her head whenever she was on duty. At the bottom of the suitcase Karen found the one sentimental item that followed her everywhere: a framed eight-by-ten glossy of her father in uniform, taken shortly before his death. He was smiling, as he'd so often smiled in life, and she felt his faith in his only child buoy her now.

"I'll do it, Daddy," she vowed softly. "I'm going to make you proud."

She touched his beloved face through the cold glass, then placed the frame on top of the desk, took her gun out of its holster and laid it on the nightstand near the flowers. Quickly she took down her hair, shed her heels and peeled off her panty hose. She was standing in her bare feet, still wearing her slinky black dress and empty shoulder holster, when she heard a knock on the adjoining bathroom door a moment later.

"Yes?" she asked as she opened it uneasily. Karen wasn't used to such domestic proximity with a handsome hostile stranger. *Maybe he's come to clear the air,* she told herself hopefully.

Belatedly Karen realized that she truly didn't want to go to bed in a strange place with her housemate and second in command furious with her, whether he was guilty of a cover-up or not. There was a fifty-fifty chance this man was innocent of any wrongdoing, and besides, a skilled police officer ought to be able to maintain civil relations with another cop without divulging any secrets. Surely she'd displayed enough strength for one night! Now maybe she could set things right.

But the minute she found herself face-to-face with that square, bloody jaw and those blue eyes dark with rage, Karen knew it was way too late for reconciliation.

"Captain Keppler, there's something I think you should understand," Bauer stated baldly, his great size seeming to fill the room. "I'm damn proud to be a Tyler cop, and that's never going to change. If you can't stand to work with me—" his tone grew nearly feral "—*you're* the one who'll have to move on."

CHAPTER TWO

BRICK REACHED the station house early the next morning eager to arrive before Captain Curvaceous started turning his life upside down. Actually, she'd already done that, he mused darkly as he recalled the painful dawn battle between his razor and his half-scabbed face. Fortunately, he hadn't seen hide nor hair of Karen Keppler while he'd limped down to the basement and done a very cautious workout in a futile effort to limber up his battered back. Brick would have preferred to present himself to a new boss feeling his best, but the Keppler woman's acrobatic tricks had already nixed that.

He didn't think she'd last too long, but he knew she'd keep him on his toes until she threw in the towel. Last night's sparring had told him that his nemesis was tougher than he'd expected the new female captain to be. But a woman cop was still a woman cop, which meant she was weak, unpredictable and not to be trusted.

Brick did not consider himself a raging chauvinist. In fact, he generally liked matching wits with women and found them to be as bright and capable as men in most professions. He didn't even mind female dispatchers and file clerks in prisons and police stations. His objection was to women serving on patrol with male partners whose lives depended on them.

Partners whose lives were lost *because of them*.

In Brick's view, putting a female in charge of a group of fighting men—and what was a police squad but a military unit?—bordered on ludicrous. And hiring one from another substation to replace the man who'd been groomed for the position for years was just plain insane.

It was also troubling, because Brick knew that Commander Harmon felt much the same way he did about women in uniform. In fact, a year ago Paul Schmidt had confided that whether Tyler became a county substation or not, Brick was a shoo-in for the captain's job. Last week Brick had asked Paul straight out what had happened, and Paul had looked him in the eye and said he didn't know.

Brick didn't know, either, but now that he'd taken stock of Karen Keppler's physical attributes, he didn't think it was going to take too long to find out. The only question was what bigwig she was cozy with...and whether he'd used blackmail or favors owed to put pressure on the commander or somebody up the line.

When Brick arrived at the station at 7:23, a full half hour before his shift began, he was surprised to find one of Tyler's dispatchers, Cindy Lou, cowering by the police radio. The young blonde looked a bit bedraggled this morning. She could have been sick—this time of year there were a fair number of colds and sore throats going around—but illness wouldn't account for her hangdog expression.

"What's wrong, Cin?" he asked, taken aback by her uncharacteristic sobriety.

"I was over getting a cup of coffee when Clayton and Franklin called in," she told him miserably, not even meeting his eyes. "It was just a doughnut stop, so

I went ahead and put a spoonful of creamer in my cup before I came back over here and called back. By that time *she* had grabbed the mike and barked out a bunch of numbers I didn't understand. *She* told me never to leave my post unless there was somebody else to cover me. Then *she* marched in there and slammed the door.''

Cindy Lou pointed to Paul Schmidt's office, a place that Brick had once considered a source of warmth and strength. Now it was inhabited by a virago.

''I'll talk to her, Cindy,'' he volunteered. Serving as a liaison between the boss and the underlings had always been part of his job, but it hadn't been all that taxing while Paul was in charge. ''She's new here and a bit high-strung. After a while she'll figure out the way we do things in Tyler.''

Cindy Lou, who'd once set her cap for Brick but had recently resigned herself to being a good friend, smiled her gratitude. ''Thanks, Brick. I don't know what we'd do without you here. It's so unfair that you—''

''I know. Let's not talk about it, okay?'' Before she could answer, he asked, ''When did *she* get here?''

''About five. I was so shocked! Paul never came in until after daylight, and even you don't show up that early!''

''Don't ask me to understand the workings of that woman's mind,'' Brick replied darkly. ''I think Captain Curvaceous attended police academy on some other planet.''

When Cindy Lou glanced up at Brick, giggling at the nickname he'd coined, her glance fell on his jaw for the first time. ''Good heavens, Brick! What happened to you? I thought you were off duty last night.''

He was trying to think of a way to avoid confessing the humiliating truth when he heard the captain's office door swing open.

To Brick's dismay, that damned Keppler woman looked every bit as striking in a black uniform as she did dressed for a party. Her braided hair looked more prosaic than it did in a chignon, but somehow the stern image flattered her striking features.

"Bauer, glad you're here," the new boss briskly called out to him from across the room. "We've got a lot to cover this morning before roll call."

"Roll call?" he echoed. With all of six men on each shift, it seemed like a ridiculous formality. "We, uh, don't do roll call here."

Karen Keppler straightened then, looking ominous in her uniform as she took a step toward him.

"I beg your pardon, Lieutenant. I believe I heard you say something like 'we don't do roll call here.'"

Reluctantly Brick nodded, trying to stifle a new wave of resentment. He was uncomfortably aware that the door behind him had just opened and several day-shift guys had just wisecracked their way into the room. "That's what I said, Captain Keppler. Paul always—"

"Lieutenant, I am not interested in the sections of the county code violated by my predecessor unless they are serious enough for prosecution," she cut in, her gray eyes showing all the warmth of a glacier. "I am interested in instituting proper police procedures in accordance with the newly revised manual. I did not devote most of a year of my off-duty time to updating this edition in order to have it ignored by the men under my command. Is that clear?"

During this unexpected speech, Clayton and Franklin had joined the day-shift fellows, gaping wordlessly

as the new boss tongue-lashed the man they all considered their true leader. Brick couldn't say that Paul had
never chewed out a man in public, but he'd only done
it when the man had failed to respond to more subtle
direction.

Not once, not ever, had he done it to Brick.

With all the strength he could muster, he refrained
from cutting Karen Keppler down to size. "I'm sure
that Tyler's officers will follow whatever regulations
are important to you, Captain," he reported stiffly. "I
merely meant to explain that they had not been will-
fully *violating* any county requirements. Paul simply
had a different way—"

"I am not interested in former Chief Schmidt's ways,
nor in his shockingly unprofessional habits," the captain interrupted, ignoring the communal gasp of dismay from the men behind Brick. "From now on you
will refer to him by his proper name, and you will ad-
dress me by my proper rank." Her tone was so sharp it
almost left nicks on Brick's still-bloodied face. "Do we
understand each other, Lieutenant?"

Brick had not expected to like Karen Keppler. He
had not expected to enjoy serving under her command. Last night he'd realized he would have to swallow a great deal of pride to tolerate being her
subordinate, but it was not until this moment that he
realized how seriously this woman was going to color
his world. She'd stolen his promotion; she'd invaded
his home. Brick was sworn by duty to uphold her orders and demand loyalty to her from his men.

But no duty could keep him from wanting to throt-
tle her at this moment. And no badge would keep him
from calling a spade a spade if she ever dressed him
down in public again.

"So how did your first day of work go?" Anna Kelsey cheerfully asked Karen as her new boarder sat down to dinner. She was such a pretty girl, even if she was a bit sparing with her sweet smile. "You should have told me you were going to be the new police captain. I hear you took my favorite nephew by surprise." Actually, she'd heard the story of Brick's real surprise—being flipped on his backside by his new boss—from no fewer than six different people today. Dr. George Phelps, Anna's boss, had told her the tale firsthand.

Karen took her napkin off the table and laid it carefully across her lap. "Well, it's a small town, Mrs. Kelsey—"

"Anna, dear. Only strangers call me Mrs. Kelsey."

Karen's smile was genuine but strained. "Until I have time to buy my own place, Anna, I'm bound to brush elbows with some of my men."

Anna tried to swallow a chuckle as she pondered other possible interpretations of that phrase, but red-haired Tisha Olsen, never one to pull her punches, laughed outright.

"It's a worthy goal for most girls your age, honey," the eccentric hairdresser teased with a good-natured grin. "With all the fine boys on our force, I imagine you'll find yourself a man in no time."

Anna was surprised to see Karen color; she knew Tisha had meant no harm. Still, it wouldn't be easy for any woman of Tisha's generation to understand why the girl wanted to be a police captain. Tisha had certainly never understood why Anna's future daughter-in-law, Pam, wanted to be a football coach. Anna didn't really understand it, either, but if it was what Pam wanted, she wanted it for Pam, and if Karen wanted to take her job seriously, then so should every-body else at Kelsey's. Granted, it was a bit hard for Anna to feel happy about anybody taking the job Brick had wanted for himself, but it wasn't Karen's fault she'd been appointed.

"A pretty girl like Karen could get married anytime she wanted to," Anna pointed out cheerfully. "She's just got more important things to do right now. Isn't that right, Karen?"

Karen flashed Anna a grateful look. "That's about the size of it. My job is my life. I can't imagine that any man would put up with it."

"Brick's the same way," Johnny added laconically. After thirty-five years of marriage, little that her stal-wart husband said took Anna by surprise. Despite his apparent indifference to the conversation, she knew he was trying to bolster the new young boarder in his own quiet way. "There's something about being a cop, he always says. It's not a job, it's a way of life. From the time he was a little boy, it's all Brick ever wanted to be."

"I thought he wanted to be a football player," Tisha countered, reaching for another poppy-seed roll. "Isn't that how he got his nickname?"

Anna watched Karen carefully. Yes, her eyebrows did rise a trifle. She *was* a bit interested in Brick's per-sonal life!

"He was a wonderful guard," Anna explained with renewed enthusiasm after she'd recapped the story of his childhood for Karen. After all, shouldn't the girl know that Brick had lived with his aunt and uncle since his father died when he was fifteen? Shouldn't she know that his mother had died when he was ten? "One night he stopped the Belton team practically all by himself. The sports reporter said they'd have had the same luck trying to score through a brick wall. Our boy, Patrick, started calling him Brick the next day. It caught on, and we've been calling him that ever since."

"Except for your mother," Johnny corrected her. "She's the only one I know who still calls him Donald."

"Well, Martha's a bit long in the tooth to start changing her ways," Tisha replied with a chuckle. She served herself some meat loaf and passed the serving dish to Karen. "I keep hoping she'll match up with some friendly old codger at Worthington House, but she seems content to sit and sew."

"She quilts," explained Anna, who didn't like to think of her darling, bright-eyed mother as growing old. "She belongs to a group of ladies who get together and piece quilts the old-fashioned way. They made a lovely one for Phil when he hurt his hip— Oh, you don't know Phil, do you, Karen?"

Karen was eating carefully now, but her pretty gray eyes reflected interest as she shook her head.

"Phil is another of our lodgers. He's a retired gardener. Used to work for the Ingallses. Have you met Judson Ingalls?"

"Briefly, at Paul Schmidt's party."

Johnny snorted. "You probably met his daughter, Alyssa, too. She never misses an opportunity to make a public appearance."

Anna hoped that Karen hadn't heard the bitterness underlying his neutral tone. Years ago, Alyssa had spurned Johnny's best friend, Eddie Wocheck, and as a result, Eddie had left town. The fact that he'd recently returned to visit, rolling in money and justifiably proud of his accomplishments, had not changed

Johnny's feelings toward the woman who'd broken Eddie's heart. But because Alyssa was one of Anna's best friends, he tried to keep those feelings to himself.

Anna pressed on with her story. "Well, Phil's lived with us for years—was our first boarder—and he's only been at Worthington House—that's our local convalescent home—since he slipped and broke his hip. He'll be back soon, God willing. He's the dearest old man..."

She stopped as Johnny interrupted with a comment of his own. "Honey, I forgot to tell you that Eddie's going to use Phil's room."

"Oh? He's back in town?" To Karen, she said, "Eddie grew up in Tyler but he's been gone a long time. Recently he bought Timberlake Lodge from Judson Ingalls, and he's going to add a wing to create a resort out there. He drops by every now and then—"

"What I meant was, he's coming back to stay. Until things get under way at the lodge, at least. I told him he could stay in Phil's room until Phil's ready to come back."

Tisha smiled, clearly enjoying the Kelseys' attempts to educate their boarder about the town. "Phil is Eddie's daddy, Karen, and Anna and Johnny forgot to tell you that their daughter Kathleen lives here, too, when she's not gallivanting off to Switzerland for the winter. You ought to take notes. You might forget some of this, and you cops need to keep track of local gossip to solve your cases, don't you? Would you like to wiretap my shop?"

Karen smiled warily, so warily that Anna wondered if she'd already figured out that Tisha deliberately tossed off outrageous comments to help maintain her flamboyant image. Karen had chosen a tough career, so she must be a pretty tough person. But Anna suspected that she'd had a hard first day at work, and tonight she needed warmth and support from her fellow boarders. Tisha often showed her affection for people by teasing, but Anna didn't think Karen was in the mood to be teased. "You were about to tell us how things went today," she tried again.

Karen met her eyes gratefully. "Well, it was... exciting, Mrs. Kel—Anna. Demanding. Different from... just being a regular cop."

"Honey, are you telling us it isn't exciting to be a regular cop? Why, I can't tell you the number of nights we've sat here and listened to Brick tell us how satisfying it is to—" Tisha broke off and turned to Anna. "Where is Brick, anyway? He loves meat loaf. Didn't I hear him ask the cook to make it tonight?"

Now Anna flushed. This morning Brick had asked for meat loaf, but he'd called an hour ago and told her he'd be coming home late because he was helping Patrick fix Pam's carburetor after work. But Anna wasn't fooled for an instant. It was far too cold to fuss with a car outside after dark at this time of year. It bothered Anna that she'd heard a tension in Brick's voice that hadn't been there since Shelley Schmidt had dumped him.

As she glanced at Karen, she realized there was only one recent change in Brick's life: Karen Keppler. Despite the incident at Paul Schmidt's party, she still had hopes for the two of them. After all, what woman could understand her nephew's commitment to law enforcement better than another cop? Besides, Brick was such a sweet boy, so kind and loving, so much fun! He didn't blow up often, and when he did, he was always quick to apologize. He wasn't one to hold a grudge.

Anna wondered if the same was true of Karen.

"Brick's busy tonight," she explained. "I'll save him some leftovers. And Zachary's having dinner with Judson."

Anna caught a glimpse of interest in Karen's eyes as she listened to the news, and she hoped that Brick would come back before Karen finished eating. When she saw the two of them together she'd have a lot better sense of how they were really getting along.

Johnny asked another polite question about police work, and Karen was quick to answer it. Overall, she seemed happy to talk about her new job—in general, upbeat terms—but there was a tension in her that revealed to Anna that things were not going as well as she'd hoped. Karen praised Anna's cooking and did her best to listen courteously to Tisha's exuberant suggestions for styling her long black hair, but Anna had the feeling that this bright and cheery dinner was the highlight of Karen's first day on the job. Loneliness would be her only ally once she retreated to her room.

Anna dragged out the dinner conversation as long as she could, urging Karen to have seconds of the chocolate cheesecake she'd made that afternoon. The girl had just finished the last crumb, insisting that she'd had enough, when the door to the kitchen swung open and Brick burst into the house.

"Where's that meat loaf, Aunt Anna?" he called out cheerfully as he pulled off his jacket. "I've had one hell of a rotten day and I'm starving."

Brick strode into the dining room, then spotted Karen. His smile vanished. As Karen rose to her feet with dignity, nobody in the room could fail to feel the electric charge that zapped between them. But to Anna's dismay, it wasn't a charge of passion or hope or pleasure. Karen's face radiated uncertainty and distrust. Brick's eyes darkened with rage.

For a long, tense moment they stared at each other. Nobody spoke. Not even Tisha could come up with a joke to break the tension.

Then Karen said stiffly, "You missed a fine dinner, Lieutenant, but I believe your aunt saved some for you."

Bitterly he answered, "Did you instruct her on the proper procedure for labeling and marking the provisions, Captain Keppler? Did you provide her with the proper forms to account for culinary consumption by late-night nibblers? Did you dictate a memo regarding how many ounces each boarder should be served?"

That was when Anna knew that her dear nephew was in terrible trouble. In all the years Brick had lived with her, she had never heard him be rude to a guest.

And this one was his boss!

Karen ignored his needling tone—ignored him, in fact, altogether—and said to Anna, "Thank you so much for the wonderful dinner. If you'll excuse me now, I have some work to do in my room."

She gave the rest of them a quick good-night, then turned and marched up the stairs. Her steps were firm and she held her head high, but Anna wasn't fooled.

She was a woman and she knew a woman's heart. And she knew that her young boarder would shed some private tears tonight.

DESPITE HER EXHAUSTING first day at work, Karen had a hard time going to sleep. It hadn't been easy holding her own with Brick Bauer, let alone weeping silently into her pillow so he couldn't hear her as he settled into bed next door. It was after two when she finally dozed off, and long after six when she woke from a frightening dream in which Bauer was towering over her with a steak knife, threatening to kill her if she didn't surrender her job.

Trying to ignore the nightmare, Karen quickly tugged off her nightgown, slipped into a robe and headed for the shower. To her dismay, the door to the bathroom was locked. She could hear Bauer singing "On Wisconsin" in the shower.

She was surprised that he knew how to sing, let alone that he had the heart for it. Apparently he felt better this morning. After all, last night he'd let off a little steam. So far he'd addressed her with stiff courtesy at the station house, regardless of his poorly concealed irritation, but apparently it was too much to ask him to keep his gloves off in his own home.

Karen couldn't really blame him. She'd been tough yesterday, tougher than she would have been if she'd taken over a job supervising women. But women would have accepted her authority once she proved she knew what she was doing. That wouldn't be enough for the men.

Worse yet, Paul Schmidt had left the place in a bureaucratic shambles. Oh, Karen imagined things had lumped along all right as long as there was some good ol' boy to say, "Oh, sure, I remember that night five years ago. Don't you remember that break-in, Steve? The kid had brown hair..."

It wasn't good enough for a complex county system, and it wasn't good enough for Karen. She'd spent most of the first day figuring out what had passed for record keeping and dictating memos to reestablish a professional code of conduct and an efficient game plan for day-to-day organization. Today she was going to do what she would have done the first day if things hadn't been in such a mess. She was going to get acquainted with Tyler from a cop's-eye view. And that meant she had to go cruise the town with the help of her right-hand man.

Assuming he ever got out of the shower.

After ten minutes, she banged on the door. "Lieutenant! Would you hurry up in there?"

There was no reply. She banged again, several times, but nothing happened. Finally she gave up, until she heard the buzz of an electric razor.

When Bauer opened the door at last and glared at her, Karen was struck at once by the realization that he was wearing nothing but a towel, casually knotted around his waist. His massive chest and biceps looked even more daunting naked than they did clothed. His legs were well muscled and hairy and compellingly male.

"Is there some emergency that won't wait?" he grumped, not bothering to say good-morning. One of the gouges on his face had started bleeding again, but he'd done nothing to stanch the flow. "Is there some reason I can't get dressed in peace?"

Karen felt a bit guilty for disturbing him, but she had her own agenda for the day. Besides, it was obvious that Brick was going to hate her no matter what she did. Why bend over backward to make him happy?

"I have to get ready for work, Lieutenant," she explained briskly. "I can't twiddle my thumbs while you sing in the shower for fifteen minutes. Didn't you hear me knocking?"

"As a matter of fact, Captain, I did." His blue eyes glittered with rage. "But since the house didn't seem to be burning down, I couldn't think of a good reason why I should cut short my shower just so you could assert your feminist authority in my bathroom."

"It's *our* bathroom, Lieutenant, and I assure you, my motives were quite mundane. I can't even braid my hair until I wash it this morning, let alone get dressed until I shower. I have to be at work before the day shift arrives and—"

"And I don't?"

"Well, of course you do. I made it clear yesterday that punctuali—"

"But you're the captain. That makes your shower more important than mine?"

"I didn't say that, Bauer."

"I don't recall what you had to say on the subject of showers, Captain. Aren't they listed in Keppler's revised police manual? I don't recall receiving a memo instructing me on how many gallons of water I might use at exactly what temperature for precisely how many minutes. Silly me, I thought I'd just keep showering my old-fashioned way. But that wouldn't work, would it? That would be one small portion of my life that you couldn't regulate!"

Karen was so stung by the depth of his anger that she didn't know what to say. Maybe she *had* come on a little strong at the station house, but . . . it had been necessary. Hadn't it?

Unable to meet his furious glare, her gaze dropped, inadvertently focusing once more on the towel wrapped around his waist. Determined not to think about what lay beneath it, she concentrated on what she saw—that broad, virile chest, still sprinkled with drops of water from the shower. She was at war with this man. Why the hell did he have to have a physique that was so damned impressive? Thank God he was too angry to smile at her! She still remembered that radiant smile she'd only seen once—tempting, playful, unbearably appealing.

For a moment Karen was so engrossed with the sight of Brick's magnificent body that she almost forgot they were having a fight. But she remembered as soon as she met his glowering eyes again.

Uncomfortably she told him, "Just let me know when you're through, Lieutenant. Maybe tomorrow we can divvy up the time. I can get ready, say, from six to six-thirty, and then it'll be all yours."

"You work up a plan and send me a memo," he answered sarcastically. "And be sure to specify how many minutes I should spend shaving as opposed to brushing my teeth."

This time his razored tone really did hurt, but Karen wasn't about to let him know it. "You decide what's best for you and let me know," she acquiesced, surprised when her voice came out pinched and low. She hadn't yet put her armor on for the day, and it was hard to sound tough and haughty when she felt so alone.

"Ah, a compromise." His eyes narrowed; suspicion laced his deep tone. "Coming from you, more likely a trap."

"It's a straightforward offer!" Karen burst out. "Damn you, Bauer, are you paranoid? Or just searching for more reasons to hate me? Don't you have enough of them already?"

"I'm not the one who rode into town with my pistols cocked, Captain! I'm not the one who's determined to gun everybody down!"

"Lieutenant, I'm just doing my job," she insisted, torn between sounding tough as iron and begging him to give her a fair trial. "I'm trying to clean up an administrative mess. If there are a few emotional casualties—"

"A few? Open your eyes, Captain! There's not one person at our substation whom you failed to offend yesterday! How can you believe that's a requirement of your position? How can you be proud of that?"

Karen wasn't proud of it; she wished she could have handled things more diplomatically. She especially regretted the way she'd shredded chubby Orson Clayton and tongue-lashed Cindy Lou. But she didn't dare admit that to Bruiser Bauer.

"Lieutenant, it is not easy for a woman in my position to earn the personal regard or loyalty of her men," she confessed reluctantly, forcing herself to meet his steely gaze. "It may never happen here. But I can and will demand a display of respect for my position. You know perfectly well that if I don't crush any hint of rebellion in these first crucial days, I'll never be able to do this job."

Brick looked puzzled by something she'd said . . . or maybe by the fact that she was still talking to him at all. He reached down to tighten his blue-and-gold towel— it was starting to slip—as he said slowly, "Captain, I think you can consider the staff sufficiently crushed. One or two of them may be pulverized."

Karen wanted to ask, *How about you?* but before she could speak, he turned away. She drew in a sharp breath as she gazed at his broad, bare back, purpled with bruises from his encounter with the gate. *God, that must hurt!* she realized painfully. *And I barely even apologized.*

Suddenly Karen knew she couldn't let their discussion end like this. They had to smoke a peace pipe, or neither one of them would last another day.

"Lieutenant?"

He stopped, but he did not turn around. His towel was hanging dangerously low again.

"I'm sorry things have started out so badly between us," Karen said sincerely. "I really wish it didn't have to be this way."

Now he did turn to face her, one hand lazily gripping the intersection of the terry-cloth tails. "What would you do over, Captain? Our spectacular greeting, when you embarrassed me in front of the whole damn town? Or yesterday morning, when you could hardly wait for me to step foot in the station house before you dressed me down in front of the men?" When he took a rough step toward her, Karen had to steel herself to keep from retreating. "Or would you like to replay this charming scene, when you barged into my shower and started giving me orders about my personal grooming?"

Karen swallowed hard, but she stood her ground. "I won't deny that I've been rough on you, Lieutenant, but let's be fair. We share the responsibility for this impasse. You know damn well that if I'd ridden into town as sweet as sunshine, you'd still be gunning for me."

His square jaw jutted out. "You stole my job, *damn you.*" His voice was hard and low.

Karen straightened. This was the heart of the problem. She knew she had to meet his accusation head-on. The best defence was the truth—at least as much of it as she was at liberty to share with him. "I got this job fair and square, Lieutenant. I didn't even know there was a Tyler man who expected to get this position until after I'd accepted it. I felt a twinge of regret for your misfortune, but not enough to toss away my own career." She met his eyes boldly. "In my position, what would you have done?"

Brick did not look away, but his voice was stripped of most of his earlier anger when he finally answered, "I would have come to Tyler."

Karen nodded, then pressed on to her next point. "When I tossed you over that fence, Lieutenant, I was acting on pure instinct. It was dark, I was alone, and I'd been listening to a large man's footsteps moving faster and faster. He seemed to be chasing me. I didn't know a soul in town, so I knew he couldn't be a friend. When he grabbed me before I could reach the house, I defended myself the way I've been trained." She shivered as an old memory stabbed her. "That maneuver once saved my life, Bauer. I wouldn't be surprised if someday it saves my life again."

He grabbed a tissue from the sink and patted the blood on his chin, but his eyes were still on Karen.

"I'm sorry it had to be you. I'm sorry everybody had to be there to see it. But I couldn't undo it, and I couldn't risk looking weak by fussing over you. Even a simple apology was risky. Considering your response to the situation, you wouldn't have listened if I'd gotten down on my knees. You were far too concerned with your own reputation to give a plugged nickel for mine."

Brick tossed the bloody tissue into the wastebasket and readjusted his towel one more time. It was a big towel, but it seemed to be causing him a great deal of trouble. It didn't seem to cover quite as much of him as it had before.

"As to our first encounter in the squad room, you openly defied me within my first hour on the job. If you'd expressed your opinions privately, I could have heard you out, even if I disagreed. I might even have been able to compromise. But under the circumstances, the need to establish my authority outweighed my concern for your personal feelings." This issue went beyond her pride and position. The safety of her men was on the line. "Someday we're going to have a police crisis on our hands, Bauer. I'll have to bark out orders. If the men waffle—if they ignore me and look to you—it could be a disaster. It could cost lives."

She took a step forward then, so close that she could almost touch his powerful chest. Suddenly Karen realized that she wasn't wearing a thing beneath her bright pink bathrobe, and every female inch of her was aware of it. "Lieutenant, I don't doubt that you could do my job admirably. Nobody in Tyler doubts it, either. But at this moment in space and time, I have authority over you. That's not good or bad, fair or rotten. It's just the way it is. Cops have to accept bad luck all the time."

"Cops don't have to accept orders from women."

She stared at him for a full minute, then said coldly, "The cops in *Tyler* do."

Brick swore under his breath. His gaze swiveled to the wall.

"It would help us all if you could just think of me as a fellow officer instead of a woman. On the job, we all have to be sexless."

His head jerked up. "Do we have to be sexless in our private bathroom, too?"

To Karen's surprise, a slow blush flamed along her neck. She felt her cheeks go hot.

She could have admitted that she was acutely aware that he was a man—a naked man—and she was a naked woman in her bathrobe. But somehow it didn't fit into their conversation. Her purpose had been to break the ice as fellow officers, not to open up new vistas of trouble.

"I didn't mean to invade your privacy, Lieutenant," she managed to utter.

"Well, you did! I don't generally shave or shower with a woman unless I've specifically invited her to spend the night."

Karen's cheeks grew hotter as she fought a sudden vision of this powerful hunk of manhood with a woman in his arms...a woman with her face. Desperately she wished she'd started this conversation when they were both in uniform. She was accustomed to dealing with half-dressed men, but they never affected her the way this one did.

A terrible voice within her warned, *Face it, Karen, this man alerts your female instincts even when he's fully dressed.* She was reasonably safe when he was angry. She knew that trouble lay ahead now that he'd calmed down.

"Obviously your sexual habits do not apply to our unique domestic arrangement, Lieutenant," she declared crisply, sorely regretting the fact that they never would. "I am far more concerned with our situation at the station house. Have we cleared up any... misunderstandings?"

Brick eyed her carefully; she had the feeling it was a struggle for him to keep his gaze on her face. Did he realize that she was also bare beneath her robe?

Suddenly Karen felt hot and foolish. Utterly unarmed. To her astonishment, her nipples peaked, and she prayed that the thick pink fabric would conceal the hint of surrender from his view.

"Captain, I'm not sure if we've straightened anything out," Brick said carefully, "but I have to admit that I'm not as mad as I was before. I thought you had it in for me. I didn't realize that you were simply...scared."

"Scared?" The word came out in a squeak. Surely he didn't sense that he'd unwittingly aroused her!

"You're scared to death you can't do this job. You're afraid the men will never obey you."

The truth hurt more than Karen had ever expected it to. Worse yet was her terror that if Brick Bauer knew the truth, the rest of the men might know it, too.

"Bauer, I'd have to be run over by a locomotive to step down from this job," she told him fiercely. It was the naked truth.

Slowly, he nodded. Karen thought she saw a glimmer of respect in his eyes.

"I didn't say you were a quitter, Captain. I just said you were scared to death to be swimming upstream."

"I'll do what I came here to do, Bauer. With or without you." *And I won't yield to these sexual feelings, not now, not ever.*

This time he shrugged. "Maybe. Maybe not. But I'll tell you this, Captain. If you need me to shore you up, you're not fit to command."

"I don't need you for anything, Bauer," she insisted, desperately hoping that it was true.

And then he smiled, that lazy dimpled smile that had touched her so profoundly once before. "That remains to be seen, Captain. But I'll make you a promise. I'm going to do my job the way I would if any other outsider was brought in here to run my station. I won't go out of my way to keep you afloat, but I won't stab you in the back, either.''

"Thank you, Lieutenant. I can't expect any more than that.''

"You can't expect any less, either,'' he answered resolutely. "I'm not doing it for you, Captain. I owe it to the badge.''

There didn't seem to be anything left to say after that. But as Brick took a step toward the door, Karen heard him chuckle.

"Lieutenant,'' she demanded tartly, certain he was laughing at her expense, "you want to let me in on the joke?''

He laughed out loud, really beside himself now. "Do you do jokes, Captain? I wouldn't think there was a place for them in the manual.''

"Dammit, Bauer!'' she burst out. "Can't you just—''

"Lighten up?'' Again he laughed.

For no good reason, Karen started to chuckle, too. It was a brief moment of good feeling, but a shared one.

"Tell me,'' she pressed. "God knows, after yesterday, I need a good laugh.''

"Forgive me, Captain,'' he apologized, still smothering a fetching grin. "I was just trying to imagine if you'd be any good in a towel fight. It's one of our favorite activities in the locker room. And then I had a sudden vision of your face if I whipped off this towel...'' He stopped as a sudden flush darkened his neck.

Karen sobered, acutely aware of his gender. The look in his eyes warned her that he was acutely aware of the difference in their genders, too. "I, uh, have seen a naked man before, Lieutenant."

"Yeah, I bet you have," Bauer drawled in a tone so richly laced with innuendo that it would have required a reprimand if he hadn't taken that moment to march through the door to his room.

Karen drew a deep breath of relief and ordered her sizzling body to cool down. But before she could lock the bathroom door behind him, Brick opened it a crack and tossed her his towel.

"Hang it up, would you, bunkie?" he asked with a fresh chuckle in his voice. Once more he dazzled her with his dimpled smile.

Suddenly Karen saw the rest of him—every manly inch—in her female imagination. It didn't seem to make much difference that his body was completely hidden by the door.

CHAPTER THREE

BRICK MANAGED to beat Karen to the station house, but Sergeant Steve Fletcher poked his head out of the locker room and motioned him inside the moment he arrived. About Brick's age and one of his closest friends on the force, Steve had been divorced for years and had two children. At the moment he was living with a pretty young woman in nearby Belton and trying to decide if he was ready to take the plunge again.

Steve was not alone in the locker room. Every man on the day shift was waiting for Brick, plus two guys from the night shift about to go home.

Some of them looked angry. Some of them looked shell-shocked. Orson Clayton, who was overweight and had trouble keeping his uniform buttoned, wore a pathetic frown. Brick remembered only too well Karen's scathing comments the day before about Clayton's appearance—delivered in front of the other men.

"You've gotta do something about Captain Curvaceous, Brick," was Steve's blunt greeting. "We've been talking it over, and we're just not going to last. It'd be bad enough to take this kind of abuse from a man, even if we deserved it. But from a looker like that..."

"If I didn't have another baby on the way, I'd quit right now," vowed Clayton. "I'm a damn good cop, Brick. You know I've never shirked my duty, never run from a fight, never protested when you or Paul asked me to put in overtime. But I'll be damned if I'll take fashion lessons from a female!''

Each one of the men had a specific complaint to air. Some of them objected to writing meticulous reports; some objected to being told to shine their shoes. All of them objected to having to put the word *Captain* in front of a woman's name. And all of them looked to Brick to make Karen vanish so everything would be the way it used to be.

Brick himself was torn. Up until this morning, he'd been quite certain that Karen Keppler was the enemy, a vicious-hearted woman who had no redeeming human features despite her tantalizing beauty. But during their latest sparring session, he'd glimpsed something in Karen he hadn't seen before. A *reason* for her toughness ... and a powerful longing for respect.

She wasn't at all the cold fish he'd first expected. There was a genuine person inside that protective shell...an intelligent woman with hopes and fears and maybe even a sense of humor. Karen was determined to do her duty, but that didn't mean she enjoyed being disliked. Brick was quite certain that his own resentment had truly wounded her.

After promising not to stab her in the back, he now felt a curious obligation to defend her from this communal onslaught. "Look, guys," he said carefully, "we've got a difficult situation here. At the moment, this woman is the boss. Paul can't help us anymore. I think our best bet is to try to play the game her way, at least until we get the lay of the land.''

"Why doesn't somebody lay her instead?" one of the men joked.

"Well, hell, Brick's got the best shot at it. He's sleeping right next door to her.''

Brick battled with a sudden memory of the morning's tango in the bathroom...Karen in her robe, he in his towel. He was rarely uneasy with women, but this morning he'd felt positively disconnected...and, to his absolute fury, he'd also felt aroused. He didn't know what she'd been wearing underneath her robe and that magnificent black mane, but he knew it wasn't a uniform. And he also knew, though he hated like hell to admit it, that he'd spent entirely too much time imagining what she looked like in the altogether.

His imagination was speaking to him now.

"I don't know if ol' Brick could stand sleeping with that porcupine. Talk about whips and chains! Can you imagine—"

"My point," Brick said firmly, uncomfortable with the tone the men's jokes were taking, "is that the oath I swore when I became a police officer means I have to obey her...at least when I'm on duty."

Steve shook his head. "You can't mean you're just going to roll over and play dead, Brick! You can't mean you're just giving up."

Brick's lips tightened as he thought about the job that was rightfully his. But Karen's rank required his public respect, and to his surprise, her honesty this morning commanded his personal respect as well.

Swallowing his own apprehensions, he insisted, "As long as she's the captain, she's the captain. No matter how bitter this pill is to swallow, in the line of duty we've got to give her the same allegiance we'd give any other cop."

Orson Clayton said, "Hell, Brick, I'd like to strangle that broad, but that doesn't mean I'd ever forget she's a fellow cop when the chips are down."

"Neither would I," agreed Steve. "Neither would any of us. But I can't see her rushing to an officer-in-need-of-assistance call if she'd scheduled the afternoon to dictate some damned memo."

A day-shift guy said, "It's just not fair."

Another growled, "Dammit, we can't count on her out there! I don't want to get shot just because she does something stupid."

Brick wondered, as the men shuffled out of the room grumbling, if Karen's worst-case scenario might someday come to pass. What if she gave an order in a crisis and they all looked to Brick instead? Professional prudence would dictate that he relay his captain's commands no matter what his own judgment told him. But his career wouldn't be worth a damn to him if he ignored his own conscience and one of these fellows ended up dead.

BRICK LOOKED uncomfortable, but not surprised, when Karen asked him to give her a tour of the town later in the morning. Their odd encounter in the bathroom seemed to have cleared the air. She decided to ignore his whimsical farewell—bunkie, indeed!—and he seemed willing to give the illusion of respect during their encounters at the station house. There was a difference in the other men this morning also. They didn't look quite so sullen and shocked as they had the day before.

Karen usually drove the first time she got in a car with a man, just to set him thinking of her in an equal light. This time, however, she decided that she needed to listen and observe. It was Brick's town and Brick's beat. She sat on the passenger side of the cruiser as he effortlessly took the wheel and filled her in on all the subtle things that a police officer needs to know about a new town. She couldn't remember everything, but she made mental notes and a few written ones, too... especially on everything that pertained to Judson Ingalls.

As he drove, Brick recounted the highlights of Tyler's history: tall tales of a Winnebago burial ground, stories of the original German and Swedish settlers, the beginnings of the now-fading tradition of dairy farming. When he told her a funny story about a local man who'd lost his favorite cow and found her in the middle of the town-square fountain, Karen was inspired to regale him with the highlights of her own disastrous first day as a rookie. They shared a hearty laugh together, and a little more ice was broken.

"This is the poorer side of town," Brick informed her as they cruised to the south after riding for half an hour. "Not that any part of Tyler is really slummy. We're not rich, we're not poor. We're just heartland."

Karen took the opportunity Brick had unwittingly given her to probe into the subject of her secret investigation. "Does that go for the Ingallses, too?"

He raised an eyebrow. "What do you know about the Ingalls clan?"

"Not a whole lot," she replied vaguely. "Your aunt and uncle were talking about them last night at dinner. Tisha was bringing me up to speed about a lot of things."

"Tisha!" He laughed. "You'd be surprised how many tips we get from her. Not that anybody confesses to her, you understand, but she's a shrewd observer with some experience in these things."

"What kind of experience?"

Brick shrugged. "The story's a bit cloudy, but I understand she used to be a gangster's moll."

"You're kidding! And she lives under our roof?"

"Captain, give her a break. It was a long time ago. Besides, Tisha's a good person at heart. She's just...distinctive. I'd rather have a woman like that than one who's colorless."

Karen wondered if he was talking about her. She did her best to appear colorless on the job—she didn't dare come across as sexy, especially with men under her command—but that didn't mean she wanted a hunk like Brick Bauer to think of her as a dishrag. Her potent response to him this morning didn't change the fact that their professional situation precluded even the most subtle of flirtations.

Before Brick could divine her thoughts, Karen asked, "So when Tisha comes across some evidence, does she report it to the station?"

He rolled his eyes. "Of course not. This is Tyler. She deliberately drops some seemingly innocent remark over dinner that no one can ever trace to her. I put two and two together and go check things out. Sometimes it doesn't add up to anything, but sometimes I make an arrest based on her tips."

Karen watched him closely. "Is that the way you carried out investigations under Paul Schmidt?"

Now his eyes narrowed suspiciously. "That's only one part of the picture, Captain. I use every tool. There's doing it by the book, and there's doing it by the seat of your pants. Sometimes you need both approaches."

Karen took a deep breath before she asked carefully, "Which one is helping you find out the identity of that woman they found out by Timberlake Lodge?"

Brick turned a corner and waved to a toddler digging a hole in the front yard before he nonchalantly observed, "That's not really an active case, Captain. We figure she was either Margaret Ingalls or one of Margaret's out-of-town guests. Nobody local was reported missing around that time, and we'd have no way of knowing who all was invited to those wild bashes."

"The Judson Ingalls I met at the Schmidts didn't seem like the partying type." Tall, gray-haired, still robust, he hadn't seemed like a candidate for Worthington House, but he'd given Karen the impression that he'd just as soon spend his Saturday nights at home.

"He's not. That's one reason Margaret left him. But before she did, she often brought her Chicago crowd back to Tyler."

"You'd think Margaret would have noticed if one of her friends had disappeared," Karen observed, certain that some names could be unearthed with sufficient legwork. "Judson doesn't remember her mentioning anybody?"

"No," Brick replied unhappily. "He doesn't like to talk about Margaret. His daughter is one of Aunt Anna's best friends, and she says she's almost never heard him mention Margaret since she walked out on the two of them."

The words struck Karen hard. A father and daughter, left alone by a high-flying mother: this she could understand.

Ashamed of the tightness of her voice, she asked, "How old was Alyssa when that happened? Was she grown?"

"Oh, no. She was a little kid. It was a long, long time ago."

"About the time that woman they found near the lodge probably died?"

Brick did not answer at once. When he did, his tone seemed more guarded than before. "Yes, it was, and yes, we checked to see if anybody had ever seen Margaret again. The answer is no. But we can't find her dental records, to check them with what's left of the body."

Karen wanted to ask how hard he'd looked, but she knew that question would take careful handling. Brick must never suspect she was secretly investigating him— Commander Harmon's directions had been most specific in that respect. "When we get back to the station, Lieutenant, I'd like to go over the file with you," she suggested, deciding that the best course of action would be to covertly track down the dental records, then assign the task to Brick to see if he tried to dodge taking the same steps. "Sometimes a new pair of eyes can spot something that you miss when you go over and over the same thing." Before he could take umbrage, Karen added, "It's happened to me lots of times."

Brick nodded without comment, then pointed to a cozy-looking diner near the town square. "This place belongs to Marge Peterson. It's where Tyler cops eat on their breaks and hang out when they're off duty."

"In that case, it would probably be a good place to stop for lunch," said Karen, who was getting hungry. She also wanted to see her men in a different atmosphere than the station house. She knew it wouldn't be possible for her to be accepted as "one of the guys," but she still might gain some valuable insights about her officers and their town.

"Is that an order, Captain?" Brick didn't sound angry this time, just unsure.

"It's an invitation, Lieutenant. My treat. Good heavens, I never had to explain it when I said the same thing to my partner."

She'd intended the words as a cheerful pleasantry, but for some reason Brick's tone was jarringly cool as he muttered, "I guess now's as good a time as any," and parked the car.

Karen was sorry to see that he was glowering again, just when she'd hoped they were making genuine progress. It was an old story, but sometimes it really wore her down. How many times in her career had she run up against professional hostility from men? How many times had they opposed her openly or sabotaged her career behind her back? Her file was bulging with undocumented petty complaints by misogynist fellow cops. She didn't know why she'd ever hoped she could expect better from Brick Bauer.

"Sometimes I think you forget that I'm a police officer, too, Bauer," she said bitterly. "I'm really not so different from the rest of you."

"Captain, you convinced me you were a real cop the first night we met," Brick snapped. "You didn't even have to show me your badge. You just dumped me on my head." He studied her gravely. "Has it ever occurred to you that you might be working overtime trying to prove yourself?"

"Wouldn't you?" Karen asked defensively. "I've taken over a substation where not one man likes me or trusts me. Every damn one of them would like to see my backside hightailing it out of town so you could take my place. I have nightmares about waking up with you standing over my bed with a knife!" She hadn't meant to confess that, not to Brick, not to anyone. But the words were out, and now all she could say was,

"I'm in an armed camp, alone against the enemy. In my position, don't you think you'd be guarding your flanks, too?"

His square jaw jutted out as he faced her. "Permission to speak freely, Captain?"

Warily Karen answered, "Of course."

"You're right that the men don't trust you. They think you're mean as hell. But you're missing the whole picture of the Tyler substation if you think you're surrounded by the enemy. You haven't yet managed to destroy the camaraderie that makes being a cop in Tyler something special, and at bedrock, you're still an officer, still part of us. We're sworn to protect the public, and by God, we're sworn to protect each other, too. The men may joke about you in the locker room and curse each time they hold one of your stupid memos in their hands, but if you ever have to draw your weapon in the line of duty, Captain, there's not a man on the force who wouldn't lay down his life for you." Before she could respond, he finished, "What hurts us all is that we don't think you'd do the same for any one of us."

Karen wasn't sure how to answer that. She was touched and wounded, honored and crushed. Clumsily she said, "I'm good with a gun, Bauer. If I thought I could save a fellow officer's life, I'd use it without reservation."

"That's what Sara Ralston claimed," he hissed. "Brave as a man! Every bit as smart. She was teamed up with Mark McVey when I made sergeant. She froze during a robbery, and some bastard shot him right through the heart!"

Brick made no effort to cloak his grief, and Karen knew he couldn't have done so, anyway. She knew what it meant to lose a partner. Rob Laney had once come perilously close to death. The bullet scar on her left shoulder was a permanent reminder of how she'd saved his life.

"Oh, Bauer, I know how that hurts," Karen sympathetically confessed. "When my partner was shot, I—"

"You froze on him, too?"

Karen pulled back, angry and hurt all over again. "Isn't it remotely possible that I did my part? My God, officers go down all the time when they're teamed with men! Nobody jumps at the chance to cast blame in those cases!"

"Maybe you did your part and maybe you didn't," Brick growled. "Maybe your partner was too busy worrying about you to cover his own back. All I know is that Mark McVey was my partner, dammit, and I *know* that if I'd been beside him, he'd still be alive!"

"Then blame yourself for leaving him behind when you got promoted, Bauer! Don't blame me and don't blame every female cop!"

He jerked back as though she'd hit him. "You don't think I feel guilty for moving on and leaving him? You don't think I feel the weight of it bearing down on me at night like a tombstone on my chest?"

The anguish that filled his eyes made Karen ashamed she'd added to his pain. In hindsight she realized that Bauer wasn't trying to attack her. He was only wrestling with his own despair.

"Bauer, I'm sorry." Instinctively she gripped his arm. "I had no right to say that. This is a terrible business. People die in any war. Your partner's death was tragic, but it's *not* your fault."

Through his regulation jacket, Karen could feel the masculine strength of his corded biceps. His tense breathing seemed to match her own, heightening her keen awareness of his powerful warmth. She didn't want to be touched by his humanity, his maleness, the vulnerable corners of his heart. It was so much easier to see him as the enemy. So much easier to keep a hostile distance.

Brick turned away from her sharply, breaking her hold on his arm. While Karen swallowed her hurt, he stared out the window for a long, quiet moment, then confessed, "Captain, I've got a lot of reasons to resent you. Deep in my heart, I know that most of them don't have a lot to do with you as a person. I'm sorry I've been so damn hard to work with."

To her surprise, Karen said, "I'm sorry, too."

He managed a thin smile. His dimples barely winked. "When I said most of them didn't have a lot to do with you, I didn't mean I like the way you're running the station. You can be a bear. I just meant that...if I'm going to hate you, I ought to hate you for the right reasons. All this other baggage—my promotion, Mark's death—well, that's not playing fair."

Karen had to admire Brick's ethics. Even when he was angry, he seemed like a man she could trust. He'd come a long way in the past two days, and she didn't want to push him. Still, she had to ask, "I don't suppose you could consider not hating me at all? The men will take their cue from you. I'd rather not spend the next few years on the outside looking in."

Brick studied her for a long, thoughtful moment. "You've spent most of your career that way, haven't you, Captain?" he perceptively observed. "On the outside looking in."

Reluctantly she nodded. It was too obvious to deny. "I'm a woman doing a man's job in a man's world, Bauer. I'm always staring at somebody's back." She paused a moment, then went on to say, "I am who I am, Lieutenant. I can't be anybody else."

"No," he quietly agreed, his blue eyes finally showing a glimmer of warmth. "I guess you can't. And frankly...I don't think you should have to be. I'm sorry if I made you feel that...well, that the real Karen Keppler wasn't welcome here."

Karen had no idea how to reply to that, but fortunately, she didn't have to say anything. Brick abruptly ended their heart-to-heart talk by opening his door and hopping out of the car. He didn't open Karen's door for her—some policemen actually had tried to—but he did keep the diner door from slamming in her face as she followed him inside.

Blocked by his impressive height and broad shoulders, Karen couldn't see around Brick to get a good look at the place, but she could certainly smell the pepperoni and hear the cheery repartee. The instant he set foot inside, half a dozen people raised a hand or called out, "Hey, Brick!" while Brick himself gave the group one of those dazzling grins that felled Karen every time it was cast in her direction.

One grizzled old farmer called out, "I hear that new she-bear is blistering your backside, boy! How can we help you get rid of her?"

The fellow next to him joshed, "Oh, Brick don't need no help. Just you wait. He'll have that filly on the run in no time. Everybody knows that captain's chair is Brick's rightful place."

"Ain't it the truth," said a woman behind the counter in a pink uniform, an old-fashioned beehive and nurse's shoes. The name tag said Marge, and the tone of her voice announced quite clearly that she was proud to own the place. She snapped a dish towel at Brick, smacking him sharply on his badge as she grinned at him.

Brick stepped aside so Karen could see everybody in the restaurant better, and so everybody could see *her*. Marge swallowed a small gasp as she read the name on Karen's badge, and gave an embarrassed grin.

"Marge, this is Captain Karen Keppler," Brick declared with more dignity than Karen thought she could have managed in the same situation. And then, as the room went from jovially cheerful to starkly silent, he said, "I imagine if you serve the captain one of your corned beef sandwiches, you'll have a friend for life."

Under the circumstances, it was a gift...far more than Karen had expected from Brick Bauer. "Nice to meet you, Marge," she said cordially.

"Nice to meet you, uh, Captain."

Karen was about to feign an enthusiastic comment about corned beef—even though she hated it—when Brick started ushering her toward a booth in the back. As he sat down, her eyes met his with open gratitude, and he looked back with a curious blend of pleasure and discomfort.

Suddenly she felt ashamed of how crusty she'd been with him ever since she'd arrived in Tyler. He *was* a man, and her promotion had certainly stripped him of his pride before his friends. How many men would have treated her with warmth under the circumstances?

Yet abruptly, to Karen's astonishment, Brick smiled. It didn't seem like an accident this time; it didn't seem artificial or strained. He looked like a man who was happy to stop for lunch with a friend or a colleague. Who was maybe even proud to be seen with a beautiful woman. Who might be pleased to know that the woman in question secretly thought he was the sexiest man she'd ever seen.

Unable to stop herself, Karen found herself grinning back, thrilled to see those blue eyes sparkle, thrilled to share even the briefest moment of camaraderie with Brick. Her happiness grew as she heard him say to Marge with deceptive nonchalance, "The captain says it's her treat today, so you better start running her a tab."

Karen swallowed hard as she realized that Brick had just handed Marge Peterson—and everybody else within earshot—his personal letter of recommendation. He could have let this crowd assume that he was stuck with her today because he couldn't refuse to eat lunch with his captain. Instead he'd found a way to say, "I'll vouch for Karen Keppler."

It was nickels and dimes, but it was a start.

CHAPTER FOUR

BY THE END of Karen's first week on the job, Brick had resigned himself to accepting her captaincy. They were certainly on much better terms than they'd been the first time she'd rousted him from the shower, but most of the time she still remained pretty formal, especially at work. At home or alone in her office she sometimes said something downright friendly, and if Brick really worked at it, he could get her to laugh. But in front of the men she was still all business, and in their presence Brick made sure to treat her with the utmost respect. They were still wary around her, but they kept their anger in check. Steve still didn't trust her, and said so on a regular basis. Cindy Lou cowered every time Karen entered the room. Orson Clayton had bought a larger shirt and had gone on a diet. Everybody knew but Karen.

Everybody also knew that there was no point in worrying about a woman who'd been dead for forty years, but Karen insisted on pursuing that investigation, too. She'd even set up an appointment to talk privately with Zachary Phelps, who'd been chief of police back then. Naturally Zachary had notified Brick at once and had confidentially reported the gist of the conversation. Karen didn't know that, either.

She also didn't know that although Judson had divorced Margaret on grounds of desertion years ago, he'd never gotten over her. Proof of her death, even now, would rock him. It would devastate Alyssa. Brick dreaded having to break such grim news, but it was not a job that he'd entrust to anybody else. The Ingallses were practically family.

When Joe Santori had discovered the body some months ago, Brick had gone through the motions of a preliminary investigation. When he'd found out that Margaret Ingalls's dentist was dead, Paul had told him that the time-consuming task of tracking down her dental records would have to wait until after he finished the legwork on a current case or two. Paul had kept him busy with something else ever since.

But Captain Curvaceous had insisted that Brick hit the trail of the dental records again, and to his surprise, he'd turned up some new leads at once. A few quick calls to the dental association in Chicago had netted him the necessary records. The overworked county coroner had promised to cross-check them with the deceased's teeth as soon as possible and get back to him sometime in the next week or two.

In the meantime, he had an investigation of his own to pursue, one he kept quite diligently from Karen. A few discreet calls here and there had sent out the hounds, and the first to report came to Brick by mid-December from Bill Riley, an old pal from the police academy. Nowadays Bill was a lieutenant at the Belton substation, with his eye on the captain's chair.

"Sorry I'm late," Bill apologized as he joined Brick for lunch at a coffee shop on the highway one Friday afternoon. It was about halfway between Belton and Tyler, a natural place to get together to catch up on old times, which they did every month or so. "We just got hit for the second time by two punks in a blue van. I had to check out an anonymous tip on my way here, but it didn't pan out."

"That's okay. Sorry you couldn't nail the guys," commiserated Brick, who was enjoying spending his day off in a sweatsuit instead of a uniform. "Things have been pretty quiet out our way."

"Well, that may be about to change," warned Bill. "These two guys were working Casner for a few weeks before they moved on to us. Just when the Casner substation gathered enough information to lay a trap, they vanished into thin air."

"And showed up ten miles down the road."

"You got it. And since you're another ten miles or so away from Belton, I figured they'll head on to Tyler when they feel us nipping at their heels. Why don't I have a copy of the file sent over to you? It might help you get the jump on them."

They broke off long enough to order, then Bill asked, "I imagine you're eager to know what I found out about your captain."

"Well, now that you mention it..." Brick's eyes met his friend's. Two weeks ago he'd been reasonably certain that Bill, or one of the other guys he'd put on Karen's trail, would turn up some dirt. Now, curiously, he suspected that her record was as clean as his own. Odder yet, he really hoped that nobody would uncover evidence that he'd be honor-bound to turn over to Commander Harmon for the protection of his men.

Brick couldn't describe his relationship with Karen; he wasn't even sure he could call it that. But he knew that he felt something for her that made him feel edgy about gathering information behind her back. If he'd been the only one involved, he would have called off his cronies by now. But Mark's ghost still followed him some days at the station house, and he could not shake his obligation to the other men.

"The Keppler woman has an interesting history. Three partners within the first two years in the county. The first two both asked to be reassigned."

Brick wasn't surprised. What man in his right mind would want to be Karen Keppler's riding partner? Even if a guy could learn to trust a female cop, Karen's penchant for bureaucratic details would wear him down. Besides, you wanted to feel close to your partner going into a fight. Karen kept everybody at a distance.

Still, Brick was secretly glad that she kept to herself. A man could get into a lot of trouble getting close to Karen Keppler. She was one of the prettiest women he'd ever met, especially when that long black hair fell over her shoulders and licked at her cleavage...a sight he'd been allowed to savor only once or twice, when he'd encountered her in her bathrobe. When she was playing supercop, she wasn't too hard to ignore. But during those rare sweet moments when she'd let him see past her captain's shell, he'd glimpsed a caring, vulnerable woman who could be a powerful temptation.

Fortunately, those glimpses had been few and far between. And the temptation had been...well, Brick was doing his damnedest not to dwell on the temptation. He had his hands full just dealing with reality.

As he pondered the possible reasons a cop generally asked for a new partner, he realized that Karen's prior partners' motives mattered a great deal to him. Personality clashes or prejudice against women cops were one thing; safety snafus were something else. Warily he asked, "Do you know why they asked for a change, Bill?"

"Not yet, but I've got their names and I'll get more feedback pretty soon. As to the third guy, he didn't ask for another partner, but that's probably because he was in the hospital when Keppler was promoted to sergeant six years ago."

"Hospital?" Brick repeated the word like an epithet, recalling Karen's defensiveness when he'd accused her of letting her partner down. "What happened, exactly? Was he shot in the line of duty?" He knew Karen was right when she said it wasn't fair of him to assume she was responsible for whatever had happened, but Mark's death was a raw wound that had not yet healed, and he found it hard to believe that in a shoot-out a woman cop could be anything but a liability.

"She was riding with him in that crummy downtown area of Sugar Creek when he got shot," Bill replied. "That's all I've got so far. You told me it was more important to be subtle than speedy, so I've sort of had to wait until I just run into these guys, you know?"

"I know, Bill. You're doing it right. If she finds out I'm having her checked out, I'll be crucified. But there are twenty-five men at this substation, Bill. I can't..." He paused a moment, then said guardedly, "They count on me. I have to know."

"I don't blame you, buddy," Bill said almost gently. "I'll get back to you with an update as soon as I can scratch up any more details."

"Thanks, Bill. I owe you one."

After that the conversation drifted off to Bill's wife and kids—a new baby had arrived just last month—and Brick did his best to show some interest. Normally he was glad to hear that Bill was doing well, but for some reason, he didn't want to hear about another man's happy family life today. He was tired of being alone, tired of being single...and tired of fantasizing about Karen's supple form each time he heard her turn on the shower.

"MY FATHER DECIDED that, under the circumstances, we should invite Eddie to our annual Christmas Eve party and ask his permission to hold it out at the lodge even though it's not ours anymore," Alyssa Baron confided to Anna. The two sat side by side at the Hair Affair waiting for their weekly appointments. "He thinks that since Eddie's going to be a force to be reckoned with in Tyler, we should—and I quote—'capitalize on our family ties.'"

The irony of that statement wasn't lost on Anna. Years ago Judson had maintained that his gardener's son wasn't good enough for his only daughter. The sole reason he was on speaking terms with him now was that Eddie had come home rich as Croesus and had purchased Timberlake Lodge when Judson was desperate for cash.

"I hope we can get Janice to let Tisha do her hair for the party," Alyssa continued nervously, as though she were skittish about talking too much about her former fiancé. "She's been wearing it the same way since high school."

"I think Janice's hair suits her," Anna said loyally, though privately she thought that a change of pace would do her friend good. If the past was anything to go on, dear Janice would probably end up attending the party alone, because her husband was out of town on business so much of the time. "I just hope she'll be well enough to go in two weeks. She's been down with that awful strep throat that's been making the rounds. George says it's a particularly nasty strain this winter."

Alyssa clucked sympathetically. "Amanda had it last week and I've been keeping my fingers crossed that I won't get it, too. Has it hit the boardinghouse?"

Anna shook her head. "Not yet. But Brick said poor Cindy Lou has been out with it for three days already. I just hope he doesn't get it. He has so much to do right now."

"You mean showing the ropes to that awful woman who stole his job?"

Anna wasn't sure how to answer that. The part of her that was Brick's aunt agreed with this harsh assessment of the new captain, but the part of her that was becoming fond of Karen forced her to rise to the girl's defense.

"It's not her fault she was assigned to Tyler. She didn't deliberately set out to unseat Brick."

"It's still not fair. Everybody in town knows that Brick should have been made captain," Alyssa maintained staunchly, her blue eyes wide with distress. "I just don't understand what happened."

"Maybe he rubbed somebody's fur the wrong way," Tisha suggested as she sailed toward the nearby manicure table, clucking at Alyssa to join her. "That's pretty easy to do in his line of work."

"I don't think so," Anna answered. "Brick's not the hot-tempered type. I know he's had a lot of trouble swallowing his pride with Karen, but I can't think of anybody else he's had much trouble with."

"No," agreed Alyssa, "he never was the rebellious type, even when he was a teenager."

From there the conversation moved on to more general things. After a few minutes, Tisha said, "Your dad told me last week he was going to invite Eddie over to lunch to work out some business details. Is that really all he has in mind?"

Anna gave her a sharp, warning glance, but Tisha shook her head and said gently, "Anna, it's better to talk about these things out in the open. We all know that Alyssa's been thinking about Eddie ever since he came back to town. Why should we pretend we don't know? Don't you think she'll feel better if she talks—"

"Tisha, if she wants to talk about him, she will! If she doesn't, I think we should leave well enough alone!"

Alyssa said nothing, just sank a little lower in her chair.

Tisha glared at Anna, but said almost softly to Alyssa, "I didn't mean to rub salt in your wounds, Alyssa. I only meant that... if there's ever been a time when Judson might be willing to reconsider his attitude about your old beau, this is it."

Alyssa looked at her bleakly and shook her head. "I know you mean well, Tisha, but it's really... well, it's just too late. It was over long ago."

Before Tisha could answer, Nouci, her raucous parrot, started to screech something in French. Anna took advantage of the interruption to change the subject.

It wasn't until the two women, freshly coiffed and manicured, made their way out of the beauty salon that Alyssa confided, "I haven't talked to him yet, Anna. Not once in all his visits to town. I've seen his Mercedes two or three times, and I caught the back of his head in a crowd. But we haven't . . . well, spoken. Met eye to eye."

Anna said kindly, "Maybe that's for the best, Alyssa. As you said, it was all so long ago. You're both different people now."

Alyssa nodded. "I know. And I—I wouldn't want to try to get to know him again. It would be too hard. But I just feel . . ." She stopped again and struggled for words. "It wasn't right, you know, the way we parted. The way I married Ron. Eddie loved me and I let him down. I let Dad talk me into something I knew wasn't right." After a brooding moment, she added, "And not for the first time."

Anna wasn't sure what to say. She was worried about her friend, and not just because of Eddie. Ever since they'd found that body out at the lake, Alyssa had been looking a little wan. Everybody knew that the skeleton was probably her mother's, but no one had proved it yet. Anna still remembered the look on Alyssa's face the first time she'd announced that her mother had disappeared. With tears streaming down her seven-year-old face, she had whispered, "Annie, my mommy's gone."

She had also confided that her father didn't want her to talk about her mom; the mere mention of her upset him. Anna knew how hard his attitude was on his daughter, but she understood his strong feelings. If she ever lost Johnny—God forbid!—she wasn't sure she'd ever be able to speak of him again. Some pain ran just too deep for words.

It was not pain but crisp December sunshine that greeted them as they headed across the town square. Alyssa had picked Anna up at work today, but it was so beautiful that Anna decided to walk back to

George's office at the hospital. She still had to finish some filing for George before she and Johnny took off for Milwaukee to spend the weekend with friends.

But before she could mention her decision to Alyssa, Anna spotted Eddie's black Mercedes heading their way.

She remembered the first time he'd driven up to the boardinghouse in his sleek new car a few months back, surprising her not only by his unexpected plans to invest in Tyler real estate, but by the fact that he looked so much like his father had at his age. Of course, old Phil had never been flashy, and Eddie did have...well, a certain manliness that was hard to ignore.

As the car slowed down and pulled up beside her, Anna remembered the old days, thirty years ago, when she and Alyssa had walked down this very street after school and this same boy had so often pulled up beside them in his beat-up Chevy. Back then, Eddie would say howdy to Anna as though she were his sister, then his gaze would inevitably fall on her friend.

Alyssa would glow and Eddie would grin. A sparkling rainbow of sensual magic would arc between them, and Anna would wonder if either one of them would notice if the sun simply disappeared.

It happened again today. Eddie greeted Anna warmly, then let his gaze drift to Alyssa's face for the first time in thirty years.

"Alyssa," he said softly.

"Eddie," she murmured back, an unmistakable wash of pain and loss and remembered joy darkening her blue eyes. "Hello."

After a heartbeat, he answered awkwardly, "You look...different, but the same."

Alyssa blinked uncertainly. "So do you."

She smiled.

Eddie smiled back.

Then Anna tried to join in the conversation, but neither of them seemed to know she was there. For the next ten minutes Alyssa and Eddie chatted about Tyler business and the upcoming Christmas party instead of high school classes and football games, but otherwise it seemed to Anna that nothing much had changed.

The same old sparkling sensual rainbow arced between them.

ON HIS WAY BACK from lunch with Bill Riley, Brick dropped by the high school and played a little one-on-one with Patrick at the gym. He was hot and sweaty and ready to head for the shower when he came home around suppertime, but the phone was ringing as he walked in the door. Nobody else seemed to be around, so he hurried into the kitchen and caught it on the seventh ring.

It was Steve Fletcher, who said with evident relief, "Brick, I've been trying to reach you all afternoon. The coroner called and confirmed that Margaret Ingalls's dental records matched the teeth of the body Joe Santori found out at the lake. Captain Curvaceous wants to go tell the Ingallses right away, but she asked me if there was somebody on the force who knew them well. I told her how it is with your aunt and Alyssa, and she decided it would be better if the news came from you."

Brick was surprised—and curiously pleased—that Karen was sensitive enough to recognize the delicacy of the situation. "Tell her I'll go right over there, Steve. Thanks for tracking me down."

"Wait a minute. She doesn't want you to go by yourself. She wants to go along."

Brick pondered that a minute. "Why?"

"Ask her. I'm just the messenger boy. And, Brick?"

"Hmm?"

"Tell Judson I'm really sorry."

"Will do."

Brick barely had time to shower and change before Karen picked him up at the curb in her cruiser. He wasn't sure if her casual, almost indifferent greeting was a good sign or not. It could mean either that they were growing comfortable enough with each other to dispense with formalities, or that she was pulling back from him again.

"May I ask a question, Captain?" he asked after he gave her directions to Judson's house. "Why didn't you want me to deliver this news by myself?"

She shrugged. "I'm not sure that I'm under any obligation to justify my decisions to you, Lieutenant," she answered evasively. "But I will tell you I've had some personal experiences...experiences that help me understand what such news may mean to this family. I know it's been forty years or so, and it can't be too much of a surprise, but still..."

Brick didn't trust the sudden softness in her tone. He never knew what to do with Karen Keppler when her shell cracked and he caught a glimpse into her heart, and he had a hunch he was catching a glimpse of it now.

He waited for her to continue. When she didn't, he prodded. "What personal experiences?"

Soberly, Karen's eyes met his. For a moment Brick didn't think she was going to speak. Then she said softly, "All her life Alyssa Ingalls has believed that her

mother abandoned her when she was a little girl. I..."
She stopped and swallowed hard, as though she wasn't
at all sure she wanted to continue.

As though she might be swallowing tears.

Brick had a sudden eerie feeling that he wasn't seeing a compassionate mirage of a kindly Karen; *this was
the real thing*. It was the hard-nosed cop that was the
mirage.

The notion shook him, rocked him back on his heels.
If the real Karen Keppler was a sensitive woman, with
old lingering wounds and fresh hopes and fears, then
he'd treated her abysmally! His feeble efforts at superficial friendliness meant nothing.

Guardedly he studied her as she pulled up for a yellow light, then lingered until it had been green for half
a minute before driving on again. It was the first time
Brick had ever seen her do anything slowly. She was
always on the run, cracking orders, hustling here and
there.

But not today. There was no snap in Captain Keppler this afternoon. No whip crack. No fire.

"Captain," Brick said carefully as she pulled up in
front of the house, "I'm open to any insight you can
offer. They'll know I'm as sorry as hell, but I'd welcome any help I can get."

Karen seemed to shrink before his eyes. She didn't
look at him, and she was so quiet while they walked up
to the front door that Brick thought she was going to
refuse to answer him. If she'd acted angry, he wouldn't
have minded; it was her complete absence of resistance that worried him.

It was not until she'd rung the doorbell that Karen
said softly, "I knew a man whose woman abandoned
him and their newborn daughter. It was a crushing

blow from which he never really recovered. He used to say it would have been easier to bear if she'd died outright. Knowing she was alive somewhere without him made it impossible to bury her.''

Again she swallowed hard, then met his eyes. There was a sadness in those gray depths Brick had never seen before, and he knew that the man in question wasn't a casual stranger.

''If Alyssa and Judson could think about Margaret's death as proof that she didn't just run off and leave them, they might be able to... to salve some of those old wounds.'' Her voice dropped to an impassioned whisper. ''It's terrible for a little girl to learn that her mother is dead, but it can't be any worse than believing that she never loved her at all.''

With sudden piercing clarity, Brick realized that Karen wasn't talking about Alyssa. She was talking about herself! He couldn't believe how deeply the realization wounded him. No wonder Karen was so hellbent on independence, so afraid to show weakness or to risk depending on anybody else! No wonder this contradictory, compelling woman was as hard as iron and soft as eiderdown!

She'd been abandoned by her mother as a little girl.

CHAPTER FIVE

KAREN HADN'T MEANT to reveal so much of herself to Brick, but she was operating on only half her cylinders and was no match for him tonight. All day she'd been fighting a fever and swollen tonsils; now she was certain she'd caught strep throat from Cindy Lou. If she hadn't been feeling so weak and vulnerable, she would never have told him about her mother. She most certainly wouldn't be standing on the Ingallses' front porch fighting back tears.

She was surprised to feel a warm male arm settle around her shoulders. It was an intimate, tender gesture that Brick would never have risked in the past. "Captain," he said gently, "I'm sorry that—"

He broke off as the door to the house flew open to reveal a gorgeous, leggy blonde in her late twenties. Despite the cold, she was wearing a skimpy red dress and stiletto heels that looked totally out of place in Tyler.

"Brick Wall!" she greeted Brick enthusiastically. "How come you always show up just in time for dinner? Come on in. Everybody's here." Winking at Karen, the blonde gave Brick a sisterly hug. He bussed her on the cheek, then asked her a personal question about her recent marriage. She gave him a saucy answer, but when she mentioned her husband's name, she positively glowed.

"Hi! I'm Liza. You must be Brick's new boss," she said with a mischievous grin. "He just *loves* working with women cops. Ask anyone."

Brick gave his friend a mock glare, but his tone was cheerfully indulgent as he chided her. "Liza, this is Captain Karen Keppler. Zip it up while I've still got a job, okay?"

Liza laughed. "Don't let him buffalo you, Karen," she said. "Brick talks tough but he's really a pussycat. I imagine you've figured that out by now."

Karen wasn't sure what to say. She wanted to respond with a joke of her own, but she was feeling increasingly weak and dizzy, and humor was the last thing on her mind. Besides, Brick did have his gentle moments, but if she'd been comparing him to a feline, she would have chosen a tiger or a mountain lion.

"He's a splendid officer," Karen finally sputtered, trying not to meet Brick's eyes when he quickly glanced her way.

Slipping her arm through Brick's, Liza smiled again. "He's not too bad as a friend, either."

Brick grinned back, but not for long. Karen suspected that he was having trouble bringing himself to spoil Liza's good mood. Sharing bad news with this family wasn't going to be easy for him.

For all her giddiness, Liza seemed to sense that their call wasn't as casual as it looked. More seriously she asked, "Is something wrong, Brickie, or did you and Captain Keppler just stop by to say hello?"

Brick squeezed her hand as though she were a child. "A little of both, Liza."

Her eyes grew big. The sauciness began to fade. Karen noticed that Liza swallowed hard, looking curiously guilty as much as afraid. She wondered what the cocky blonde was hiding.

"Tell me, Brick," she whispered. "It's my grandmother, isn't it?"

Slowly, he nodded. "I'm sorry, hon."

His gentleness touched something deep inside of Karen. Worse yet, it reminded her of her dad. On the surface, he'd always seemed crusty, teasing, superficially cheerful and almost shallow. But underneath, when the chips were down, he'd been there for the people who loved him. He'd been there for the people he served.

"I guess I sort of knew right from the start. I just didn't want to believe it was really her."

"I know."

"I've always thought of her ... off somewhere, living a life of glamour, a free spirit. Sort of like me." Her eyes suddenly pooled, and Karen realized why Brick had been worried about this family. If the news could reduce this spunky granddaughter to tears, she could imagine how it would strike the rest of them. "It's going to kill Granddad, Brick. It's going to tear Mom apart."

Suddenly Karen understood the tears; the tone in Liza's voice said it all. It wasn't Margaret she was grieving for. It was her mother.

Brick put his arms around Liza, then said softly, "Oh, I don't know, Liza. Think of it this way. Alyssa's always believed her mother didn't give a damn about her or your grandpa. At last she's going to know that Margaret didn't abandon her. I bet she loved her with all her heart."

Liza looked mystified, but somehow soothed as she stepped back. "Do you really think so, Brick?"

He squeezed her arm once more. "I think it'll help a little. I think it might help cushion the blow for your grandfather, too."

Karen didn't think it would make any difference to Judson; she was more than half-sure he'd killed his flighty wife. But she was certain that Brick's kind words would be relayed to Alyssa and would give her some small measure of comfort.

The fact that he'd trusted Karen's judgment enough to share her insight gave her comfort, too. She had an odd feeling that it would be very nice to be hugged by this kind man, so nice, when she was feeling so low, to shed a few tears in his arms. Karen shook herself as she realized that even if she weren't feeling tearful, it would be all too pleasant to spend some time in Brick's arms. It was a fantasy she couldn't indulge for even a second. Some things weren't even safe to dream.

Karen followed Brick inside, where he gently shared the news with the rest of the family—Alyssa, Judson and another young man and woman about Liza's age whom Brick introduced as her doctor brother, Jeff, and her lawyer sister, Amanda. Liza's husband, Cliff, got up and moved quietly to stand beside her, his mere presence a mute buffer between Liza and the world.

One glance around the room convinced Karen that Judson Ingalls could afford to buy the law in Tyler. The massive Victorian house was beautifully restored, and the Picasso on the wall looked like an original oil. After Karen's preliminary discussion of Margaret's disappearance with Zachary Phelps, she was fairly certain that the old chief knew—or at least suspected—more than he was telling. She feared the same might be true of Brick.

Zachary claimed that forty years ago Judson had reported his wife missing and filed for divorce on the grounds of desertion. End of story. The retired chief claimed to have no recollection of any personal problems the couple might have been having, any extramarital affairs, any previous displays of temper, any weapons kept at the lodge, any evidence of foul play. In fact, he showed not even the most rudimentary interest in what had actually transpired—odd for any cop.

But Karen's interest in the truth was keen, and despite how she was feeling, she watched Judson closely as the whole family waited stiffly for Brick to explain why they'd come. Karen suspected every one of them was sure what he was going to say before he said it. Still, when Judson actually heard the words, "I'm sorry, Judson, but Margaret's dental records match the coroner's report on the woman Joe Santori found by the lodge," he slumped as though somebody had punched him in the stomach. He didn't seem to notice when Brick laid a kind hand on his shoulder.

Alyssa responded to Brick's announcement with a tiny cry. She covered her mouth and stood perfectly still, her eyes dry but haunted. At first none of the children moved. Then all three of them took quick steps toward their mother.

Why, Karen wondered, did none of them rush to comfort Judson? Was it because Brick was already offering unspoken support? Or was there some other reason?

Karen and Brick stayed about fifteen minutes, until the shock had subsided and it became obvious that the family needed time alone. Karen said little, letting Brick handle everything. It was obvious that this wasn't the time to grill Judson Ingalls. Besides, by then Karen knew she was in no condition to do any grilling.

After Brick had shaken hands with all the men and hugged all the women, he walked in silence to Karen's cruiser, keeping remarkably close to her side. As she slipped into the passenger seat—afraid she was too weak to drive—he took the wheel and said softly, "Captain, I have a confession to make."

Not now, she wanted to tell him. *Whatever you've done to betray me, it'll have to wait until I'm well.*

But he continued, "I suspected that you were hoping to catch Judson off guard tonight. I thought you might take advantage of the situation to interrogate him."

There was a long, slow silence. Damn, he was sharp. Karen didn't want to lie to him, but she didn't want to betray her mission, either. She was fairly confident—or merely hopeful?—that Brick wasn't involved in a cover-up, but she wasn't entirely certain yet. All she knew for sure was that she was too woozy to make intelligent decisions tonight.

Guardedly, she admitted, "To be honest with you, Lieutenant, you were half-right. It bothers me that nobody pushed harder to identify Margaret's body before I came to Tyler. Obviously it wasn't that difficult to do. I think someone would just as soon leave the questions surrounding her death unanswered. The only question is who."

Brick studied her quietly. "You think it's Judson."

"He's the most obvious suspect. I have no trouble imagining that a man might fly into a rage when he finds out his wife is about to leave him. But there are lots of other people who've lived here long enough to have killed Margaret, or long enough to want to protect whoever was involved in her death." When Brick didn't answer, Karen reminded him, "I think somebody murdered that poor woman, Bauer! I don't care how many years have passed. I want the killer to pay for that."

For a long moment Brick studied her face, as though he were trying to hear something she hadn't said. At last he assured her, "Captain, that's what I want, too."

His eyes held a curious look that Karen was too weary to ponder, but she knew that the quiet smile slowly stealing over his virile face made her feel terribly happy... and afraid. She needed Brick's friendship... longed for it almost too much. Karen told herself that wanting the cheerful companionship of one's peers was a sensible, healthy thing, but as much as she'd cared for her former partner, she knew that her heart had never flip-flopped when he'd warmed her with a grin.

Her heart was flip-flopping now.

Dutifully Karen reviewed her litany of reasons why she could never consider getting involved with Brick, but tonight they seemed to ring a bit hollow. She'd never particularly wanted to break her own golden rule about not dating subordinates, had never given any thought to risking her career. She wasn't giving it serious thought now, either... but it bothered her that she couldn't just shut Brick out of her mind as easily as she did most inappropriate men. Her father had taught her early never to lean on anybody, never to let emotion cloud her judgment. She never had, and in order to keep the hard edge that was vital to her success as a woman cop, she'd vowed she never would. But it wasn't easy to keep a hard edge when she was fighting a fever.

Of any kind.

Brick drove silently for a mile or two, then asked, "You haven't had dinner yet, have you, Captain?"

"No, but—"

"You want to swing by Marge's and pick up something?"

It was the most casual of invitations, an exact match in tone to Karen's offer to take Brick to lunch the first day they'd ridden together. It was the first time anybody in Tyler had asked her to do anything social. It was the sort of offer she had longed for.

The sort of offer she couldn't possibly accept tonight.

"Lieutenant, that's sounds like a great idea, but I'll...I'll have to take a rain check."

He shot her a wounded glance. "Hot date tonight, huh, Captain?"

"No, it's nothing like that. It's just—"

"You don't need to explain, Captain. I was just trying to be civil. No disrespect intended. Don't get your back up."

His tone was caustic, more caustic, it seemed to Karen, than she deserved. She was sick, dammit! Couldn't he see that? Oh, she'd gone out of her way not to tell him. Professionally, it had seemed quite wise. Personally, she was beginning to regret it.

Awkwardly she hedged, "I really would like a rain check, Lieutenant. The truth is, I've had a very long day and all I want to do right now is go home and crawl into bed."

Brick pulled up to the curb, turned off the engine and tossed Karen the keys. "Your call, Captain." He quickly hopped from her cruiser and headed for his truck. He was already halfway there by the time he said goodbye.

Karen echoed him bleakly. She was tempted to stop him, to gush out all the feelings that had been building up inside her since her first week on the job. She wanted to tell him that she enjoyed his company greatly, that she was flattered and touched he wanted to spend even a moment of his spare time with her, let alone risk a ribbing from the guys by taking her to their hangout on a Friday night. She wanted to tell him how very ill she was. She wanted to confess that she was tired of her solitary battle with job frustration, loneliness and holiday grief.

But Karen knew that opening up to Brick when she was at such a low ebb might well be fatal. There were too many secrets she might inadvertently divulge. She should have gone to bed hours ago when she'd first become aware of her symptoms; by now the virus had leveled her completely. She was feeling so faint and tearful that she'd be lucky to make it up the stairs by herself.

It took all Karen's strength to drag herself out of the car and up the sidewalk. Her greatest fear was that she might collapse in front of Brick and he'd have to carry her to her room. If that happened, she knew he'd never let her live it down.

BRICK SPENT the next day cleaning out the basement as a favor to Uncle Johnny, who always worked too hard. It would take some digging to find the Christmas tree ornaments Aunt Anna would want any day, so it was a good time to sort through the rest of the family junk and throw some of it away.

By late afternoon Brick had spent hours going through boxes of his childhood mementos and his parents' things. He still kept several pieces of their favorite furniture—and a Blazing Star quilt his grandmother had made for his parents' wedding—in hopes of recapturing a sense of their home when he furnished his own someday. Until recently, he'd been happy enough living with the Kelseys, but a loving aunt and uncle didn't take the place of a wife.

When Brick found an old black-and-white TV—a relic of his childhood—he decided to haul it upstairs and see if he could get it working. The Packers were having such a great season that he didn't want to miss a single game—a difficult task when he had to share TV time with Tisha. A few new wires and a replacement tube would give him a backup set for his room in no time.

He was rummaging for parts when he heard the phone ring in the kitchen. As soon as he answered it, Brick recognized the voice of Hedda Rakes, one of the police dispatchers. Hedda was a crusty old gal, a lot tougher than Cindy Lou, so Karen didn't intimidate her much.

"I've got a message for Captain Curvaceous," Hedda declared sarcastically, "if Her Highness will deign to come to the phone."

"The captain isn't here, Hedda. I haven't seen her all day," Brick replied. "I figured she was working. That's all she does when she's awake. The woman is absolutely indefatigable." Last night she'd been singing a different tune, he remembered sourly, but that had only been a courteous way to reject his invitation. What had he been thinking of, asking her out like that? At the time it had seemed like a natural thing for two cops to do at dinnertime, but Karen's stilted response had made Brick reconsider his motivation. It was scary to think that he might have been asking Captain Keppler for a date.

"Well, she's not here either," said Hedda, "and she left word last night that she could be reached at home in case of an emergency."

Brick stiffened, his professional instincts moving into high gear. "Give me the scoop, Hedda. I can be there in five—"

"No, you don't need to come in, Brick. In fact, if Paul were still in charge, I'd just take a message and wait till Monday. But you know how *she* is . . ." Hedda sighed dramatically. "Orson Clayton hurt himself when he fell off a ladder putting up his Christmas tree. Got dizzy from that diet he's been on to get the captain off his back. Wrenched his neck. Jeff Baron checked him over, says he'll be all right, but that he shouldn't work for a few weeks. *She* might want to juggle schedules or something. And she'll probably come up with eight new forms to fill out to cover any and all contingencies."

Brick wanted to tell Hedda that she was exaggerating—she was—but he understood her frustration. The new paperwork was excessive, and even if Karen did insist it was required by the county, the fact remained that she approved of the system.

Aloud, he said, "Look, Hedda, I'll just leave her a note. She stuck a little bulletin board on her door so we won't lose her messages. She's even got memo forms at home!" After he hung up, Brick did the one thing he figured Karen would never do: he called Orson Clayton's wife to see if he needed anything.

Once assured that his friend was okay, he wrote a careful note for Karen—with three times the details he would have left for Paul—then glanced out the front window before clumping up the stairs to leave the message.

It was odd that Karen hadn't checked in with Hedda if she'd been gone all day...and odder yet that her cruiser had been out front since he'd parked it there last night. Karen's Toyota still sat in the driveway. Surely she hadn't gone off for the weekend with somebody else—some man? Had her phony excuse about feeling tired last night been a deliberate ruse to help her slip away without arousing his suspicions?

Brick felt a sudden, tense fury that he knew had no place in their relationship, a fury that seemed suspiciously close to jealousy. He didn't like the idea of Karen turning him down, but he couldn't *stand* the idea of her lying to him so she could slink off with some other man!

He shook himself as he realized that Karen couldn't leave town without telling him: he was second in command. Granted, they weren't on intimate terms, but they were at least trying to work together, and she was a stickler for playing by the rules.

Besides, he wondered, what man in his right mind would *want* to spend a weekend with Karen Keppler?

Brick's neck suddenly flamed as he realized the answer he'd been dodging now for days: *he would.* It was crazy. He wasn't sure just how he felt about Karen; he knew he didn't quite trust her. But there was something about her that kept drawing him closer, something that went beyond her beautiful eyes and magnificent legs. Maybe it was the paradox he sensed in her—she acted so tough and invulnerable, doing her

damnedest not to let anybody know that inside she was
a sweetie. Maybe it was the paradox she brought out in
him. Brick kept finding himself cheering Karen on, but
deep inside, he knew he still expected her to fall flat on
her face.

Vigorously he pushed away everything he'd learned
to feel for Karen—sexual need, deepening empathy, a
healthy dose of respect—and forced himself to leave
Hedda's message on her door and get on with fixing the
TV. But as he tacked the note on the bulletin board
with one bop of his fist, he was startled by the sound
of a small voice calling from inside her room.

"What is it?"

At least, that was what he thought the voice said.
Karen must have thought he was knocking. But how
could she be home? Brick had been home for twenty-
four hours and hadn't seen hide nor hair of her!

"Captain?" he called out cautiously. "Are you in
there?"

She muttered something unintelligible, so he tried
again.

"Captain, you just got a call from Hedda. Orson
Clayton has been injured. He—"

He heard her bare feet hit the floor before he could
finish. "Injured? Is he alive?" she cried out, rushing
to the door.

The panic in her voice shamed Brick. If Karen had
been anybody else on the force, he would have been
careful to word the message to avoid causing a moment's fear that another cop might have been shot. It
simply hadn't occurred to him that Karen would worry
so intensely, especially about a man she'd publicly
shredded. He'd misjudged her again.

"Captain, he's fine. He just fell off a ladder. I'm sorry if I..."

She pulled open the door, and Brick was too startled by her appearance to continue. Karen didn't look like the severe, orderly police captain he knew. She was wearing a ruffled blue-plaid flannel nightgown that almost touched the floor, one that made her look like a little girl instead of a superior officer. More amazing was her black hair, long and flowing, wildly askew. Her lips were colorless and her cheeks were flushed. Her heavy eyelids made her look all but comatose. It took no doctor to diagnose that she was very ill.

For just a moment Brick saw a glimmer of relief pass over her fragile features. "Not shot? Not dead?" she whispered, leaning dizzily against the open door.

"No, Captain." He was shaken by the depth of concern that gripped him. Karen was certainly in worse shape than Clayton, yet at the first hint that one of her officers was injured, she'd leaped from her sickbed in alarm. "He won't be able to work for a while, but—"

After the first word or two, Karen stopped listening. She turned around and started stumbling back toward the bed.

She didn't make it. Her legs seemed to crumple beneath her, and she pitched headlong to the floor.

"Karen! For God's sake!" Brick called, too stunned to remember the rigid rules of conduct she'd laid out for him. He rushed into the room and knelt beside her, feeling her neck for a pulse. He got one, strong and steady, but he also could feel the raging heat of a fever. He wasn't a doctor, but he'd felt enough neck pulses to know that Karen's glands were badly swollen.

Worse yet, she'd passed out cold.

Brick didn't want to leave her there on the braided rug, but he didn't want to move her, either, until she came around. If all that was wrong with her was light-headedness from getting out of bed too fast when she was ill, she'd come to in a minute. He told himself that she'd be fine, but the claw of worry in his chest made him fear otherwise.

"Karen!" he said urgently. "Karen, come back to me. Just flutter your eyelashes, sweetheart. Come on."

He took a deep breath as she groaned and rolled toward him. Instinctively he cradled her head in his arms.

"Karen, you just passed out. You're in your room. I think you're sick as a dog and shouldn't have rushed out of bed." His stomach tightened as he waited for her to answer. *Say something, anything,* he silently begged her. *Let me know you're all right.* "Is there anything else wrong? Do you hurt anywhere?"

She murmured something Brick couldn't make out, so he lowered his ear to her lips. "Tell me again. Do I need to take you to the hospital? Are you in pain? Are you sick?"

"Strip," she mumbled.

The word took him by surprise. He blinked, thrusting away the sudden vision of wild-haired Karen without this heavy nightgown. She was burning up with fever, yes, but—

"Strep throat. Got it from Cindy Lou."

Brick steadied himself. Strep throat. He could cope with that. No clothes off. Deep breath. Nothing life-threatening. Nothing a few days in bed and a call to George Phelps or Jeff Baron couldn't cure.

So why did he still feel so odd, so upset, so protective? And so damn guilty because he'd thought she was lying to him last night?

"Karen, listen to me," he said softly, ashamed of the tenderness in his voice. "I want you to put your arms around my neck. I'm going to pick you up and put you back in bed."

"Neck," she murmured. "Don't make me move."

"Come on, honey. I can't leave you here on the floor."

He squatted, to protect his back, then gathered her close. Karen was a tall woman and a sturdy one, but when he stood up with her in his arms, she seemed surprisingly frail and fragile. She didn't feel like a hard-nosed captain while she lay limply against him.

Brick laid her on the bed, carefully stretching out her exquisitely shaped legs—so smooth and silky!—before he tugged her nightgown into place. Gingerly he started to pull the blankets up.

"No," she protested. "So hot."

He stopped, once more feeling powerless.

"Water. Wanted water since last night. Should have got it before I went to bed."

Brick could not account for the terrible pang that shook him then. For twenty-four hours this woman had lain here, hot and hurting, unable to call out for him? Unable to get past their differences to reach out to a stranger...or a friend?

He was angry with himself for failing to realize that she was in trouble, and he was angry with Karen for not trusting him. Had she figured on lying here feebly until this disease ran its course? She needed more than water. She needed medication. She needed nursing. She needed to know that somebody cared whether she was alive or dead.

"I'm going to get you some water, Karen, and a wet washcloth. Then I'm going to call a doctor."

"Can't go see a doctor." She whimpered. "Can't drive. Can't stand up."

Can't trust Brick Bauer enough to ask him for help, he could have finished for her.

"I can get one to come here, Karen. I've got a couple who are old friends." Brick hurried from the room, dashed into his room to grab an empty soda can, then rinsed it out in the bathroom. When he came back with water and the washcloth, Karen hadn't moved a millimeter.

As he sat down on the mattress beside her, she whispered, "Don't leave me, Brick," so softly he had to strain to hear. "I feel so weak. So helpless." Her voice cracked tearfully. "Nobody to call. Nobody to care. Nobody to turn to if I get worse and need help."

Brick didn't tell her that she already was in need of help and too sick to know it. He couldn't believe how deeply her vulnerability touched him; he couldn't believe how much it made him ache. Last night he'd had some half-formed fantasy about Karen lying in this very bed, naked and—he could finally admit it—reaching for him.

Now all he wanted was to know that she was well.

"I won't leave you, Karen," he promised, embarrassed by the urgency of his tone. "I'll be right here as long as you need me, and I'll sleep with the doors open between us tonight."

With infinite patience, Brick cradled her neck and shoulders, lifting her up with one strong arm while he trickled the water onto her parched lips. Karen opened her mouth and licked it with her tongue. During the slow, painful process, he saw that her face was awash with silent tears, tears he could have sworn Captain Curvaceous did not know how to shed. Even when he laid her back down and cooled her face and hands with the dripping washcloth, the tears didn't stop.

"Baby, don't cry," he whispered. "I can't bear to see you cry."

But Karen must have misunderstood his aching plea. As Brick pulled her tenderly against his solid chest, she put her arms around him and started crying harder.

CHAPTER SIX

On Sunday afternoon, Anna came home from her weekend in Milwaukee to some genuine surprises. Brick was watching football, as usual, but not at Pam and Patrick's and not downstairs in the living room. She found him slouched over the foot of Karen's bed, watching an old black-and-white set he'd repaired and installed in her room. Karen herself was under the covers, looking pale but grateful for the company.

Brick seemed quite relaxed, but Karen was quick to explain the saga of her illness and Brick's role as her nurse in great detail...far more detail than the situation merited. Anna didn't care what had happened, or even where it might lead. What mattered was that her nephew was no longer wearing that tense frown and dreading coming home. She was sorry Karen was sick, but she had a hunch that the outcome had made her suffering worthwhile.

By Thursday, when Johnny brought home a six-foot Scotch pine, Karen was back at work. She came home late that evening just as Anna started stringing lights on the tree.

"Karen! I'm sorry you missed dinner, dear, but I'm glad you got here in time to help us decorate the tree. We have so many ornaments we can't use them all, so we just put up whatever is special to whoever's living here each year. Each lodger adds his or her own favorites. If you want to unpack your ornaments, we can—"

"I don't . . . I don't have any ornaments, Anna. You just . . . go ahead."

Anna stood up and stared at the girl. She noticed that Brick, who'd been helping rather cheerfully, was watching her also. A curious sadness stole over his face.

"No ornaments?" Anna protested. "Are they still packed somewhere with your other things? Does your family—"

"No." Karen licked her lower lip. "I don't have time for Christmas. It's nice that you...do what you do. But I don't generally put up a tree or...whatever."

"Everybody should have time for Christmas," Anna insisted, deeply concerned. "Now go eat your dinner, Karen, then come back here. We always sing carols in the evening and—"

"Aunt Anna, I need to go over some things with Karen tonight," Brick interrupted, moving over to stand by Karen in an almost protective gesture. "Police business. If we finish early, we'll come back downstairs and help you."

He gave her a smile as he followed Karen to the kitchen, so Anna pretended his excuse was genuine. But it was obvious that Brick was covering for Karen, protecting her from—from what? Anna's determination to help make the girl happy? She worked too hard. She never played. Imagine ignoring Christmas!

At least she wasn't ignoring Brick anymore. Anna didn't know how Karen treated him at the station, but it seemed to her that they were starting to spend a lot of time together at home.

And now the tension that zapped between them was an entirely different kind.

"So WHAT'S THIS vital police business that won't wait till morning?" Karen asked Brick as she put the plate Anna had set aside for her into the microwave. "I thought we'd agreed not to talk shop at home unless it was absolutely necessary."

It was one of the many agreements, tacit and explicit, that they'd come to during the strangely intimate days of Karen's illness. By the time she'd gotten a grip on herself, it had been entirely too late to go back to calling Brick "Lieutenant" and treating him with formal disdain. She'd wept in his arms like a child while he'd cuddled her. She'd confessed that she hadn't told him she was sick because she was afraid he'd take advantage of the situation to try to stage some sort of station-house coup. She'd told him the truth about how her mother, at eighteen, had gotten pregnant but refused to marry her twenty-year-old father, and left him alone to raise their baby. Brick had shared the details of his own parents' loss and had told Karen he still kept all their furniture in the basement—even their Blazing Star wedding quilt—so he could honor their memory in his own home someday.

Since then he'd done nothing to indicate that he viewed their growing friendship as anything but platonic, but Karen's instincts told her it wouldn't take much for that to change. She was sorely tempted by this big, gentle man, and her instincts told her that he wanted her. Brick risked nothing by becoming involved with Karen except getting ribbed by the guys, but Karen's career would be destroyed if they ever forgot the rules that bound them. She knew she'd have to do all the work to maintain the status quo.

It wasn't easy to remember why keeping Brick at a distance was vital to her self-respect when he was sitting across from her, straddling a chair, grinning his most adorable dimpled grin. It wasn't easy to remember that she couldn't possibly stay tough enough to rule a bunch of chauvinistic men if she got soft and mushy over this one.

"Karen, we have an important situation coming up that requires some serious undercover work," Brick informed her with a straight face once she started eating. "There's a party out at Timberlake Lodge on the twenty-third. It's the scene of the crime and all the living principals will be there. We're bound to dig up some evidence relating to the death of Margaret Ingalls."

He sounded so enthusiastic that Karen had to smile, but inside, she felt a little shaky. The night Brick had asked her to join him at Marge's for a bite to eat, she'd passed it off as casual camaraderie. This was a transparent invitation for a date.

Stalwartly she told him, "Brick, I usually work on evenings close to Christmas in place of some married man who has a family. Besides, I'm really not a party person."

"Oh? So how is it that we met at a party on your very first night in town?"

Karen couldn't meet his eyes. She'd collected enough data to convince herself that he wasn't involved in a cover-up of the investigation of Margaret Ingalls's death, but until she got the green light from Commander Harmon, she couldn't share her secret assignment with Brick. The fact that she longed so much to violate her orders and tell him the truth—so nothing stood between them—was one of the many warning signs that told Karen she needed to start putting back up some of the barriers her illness had knocked down.

No man had ever made her question the wisdom of adhering to the rules before.

"I just thought I should meet a few of the townsfolk, Brick. To sort of break the ice."

"You nearly broke my head!"

Karen laughed with him, delighted that what had started as a major fiasco had become a shared joke.

"I can't guarantee I wouldn't do it again if we went to another party, Brick. Besides, with that rash of break-ins we've had this week, I've been thinking of riding patrol on Friday and Saturday nights. Or else assigning you to the task."

He groaned. "Have a heart, Karen. Wait until after the party, okay?"

She held her ground. "That depends on how things turn out this weekend." The trouble with the two burglars in the blue van had started while Karen was sick. Several Tyler stores had been hit; so had Timberlake Lodge. Brick had done a follow-up investigation at all the places involved and had gotten an itemized list of missing items. While most of them were easy to sell—VCRs, stereos, silver—nobody could explain why a beat-up old suitcase had been stolen from the Timberlake potting shed. The only reason Cliff Forrester had even noticed it was missing was that he'd been using the decrepit thing, long abandoned in the shed, to add some height to his worktable. Ironically, he'd found some of his best tools scattered on the ground following the burglary. While it was possible that all the recent publicity about Margaret's death and Judson's wealth made anything at Timberlake, new or old, appear to have resale value, Karen felt that the matter merited further scrutiny.

"Well, the burglars in the van may move on soon, Karen," Brick declared nonchalantly. "They hit Casner for two weeks before they moved on to Belton, and they were only there ten days before they moved on to us."

Karen blinked. "We've got a previous record on these guys at two other substations? Why didn't you let me know?"

"I gave the information to the guys riding patrol." He stood abruptly and marched over to the refrigerator. "I found out the day you got sick, Karen, when I had lunch with a guy from Belton, and I've been more or less running things since then."

"You were filling in for a few days, Brick," she reminded him coolly, uncomfortable with his evasive tone. "I'm well now and back at the helm."

His eyes met hers with a hint of anger. "I only meant—"

"I know what you meant. I just don't want you to be sloppy about something so important when you talk to the public or the other men."

Brick grabbed a cold chicken drumstick and started chewing it as he straddled his chair once more. He devoted himself to eating in silence, but Karen was sure he was using the time to simmer down.

She used the time to assure herself that she'd made the right decision to delegate authority for Tyler's law enforcement to Brick for the duration of her illness. Although his style with the men was different from her own, she'd found no fault with the way he'd handled things in her absence, a fact she was going to relay to Commander Harmon tomorrow when she turned in her report on the delay in the Margaret Ingalls investigation.

But that didn't mean she wouldn't need to keep reminding Brick that she was still in charge.

After an awkward silence, he returned to the subject of the party. "This Christmas bash has been an annual event since Margaret Ingalls first moved to town, Karen. Anybody who's anybody in Tyler shows up. If you refuse to go, you'll *really* be on the outside looking in."

Karen didn't appreciate the fact that he'd deliberately pushed one of her buttons in order to manipulate her into going out with him. Rather stiffly she replied, "Brick, as it happens, I haven't received an invitation from the Ingallses. I'm not sure it would be appropriate for me to attend."

Brick rolled his eyes. "Karen, be sensible. If Alyssa hasn't invited you personally, it's only because you live with us and she knows that we'll bring you along. How many times do I have to tell you we're practically family?"

Karen pushed away her plate and boldly met his eyes. "And how many times do I have to tell you how difficult it is for a woman police captain to keep the respect of her staff?"

He tossed the bare chicken bone onto her empty plate. "Karen, do you doubt that you've earned my respect?" He looked very serious now. "Do you doubt that you're earning the respect of the other officers?"

She pondered the question for some time, struggling to frame a safe but honest answer. At last she said, "Brick, I think that you and I have come to understand each other. I hope you won't take offense when I tell you that I don't want to go to this party with you because it might undercut my position. Not everyone in Tyler would view it as a pleasant duty for a

public official. Some people might see it as a date."
Including you and me, she added mutely. That was the
real problem, the far larger one that she didn't dare reveal. Karen's I-don't-date-subordinates excuse was a
legitimate one that had always worked for her before.
Why risk probing beneath the surface, where her
deepest vulnerabilities as a woman lay?

Brick's jaw tightened, but he still tried to respond
with a clumsy joke as he carried Karen's plate to the
sink to rinse before standing it in the dishwasher. "You
know, Karen, I've had a lot of women turn me down
over the years, but I think you're the first one who ever
said that being seen in public with a cop would be bad
for her business."

"I'm not kidding, Brick," Karen told him gravely.

He stuck the plate in the dish rack, then turned and
met her eyes. "Neither am I. I play football with my
old teammates in the town square. I've been known to
take a dispatcher to the movies. Every now and then I
take my grandmother to church. None of those people
seems to think that associating with me has hurt their
reputation."

"None of those people find herself depicted in lewd
cartoons in the station-house locker room," Karen retorted. "None of them hears her staff refer to her as
Captain Curvaceous when they think she's out of earshot. And none of those people has Tyler cops taking
bets on which one of them will be the first to take her
to bed." She stood up and faced him squarely. "I understand you're the odds-on favorite to win."

Brick flushed. The red started at his neck and quickly
flooded his whole face. Karen didn't think she'd ever
seen a man look more embarrassed. She hadn't delib-

erately sought to humiliate him, but she was glad that she felt back in control.

Only now, from her newfound security, could she afford to admit to herself how often she teetered on the edge where Brick was concerned. She was used to dealing with fleeting desire for an unsuitable fellow; she simply turned away. But she couldn't turn away from Brick, even though she knew that he posed an increasingly dangerous threat to her career. The mere thought of such a drastic rearrangement of her priorities was frightening. It was a damn good thing Captain Keppler was back in control.

"Karen, if you think that's why I asked you to this party—"

"If I did, I wouldn't be wasting my breath explaining this to you." Despite her quick denial, Karen realized she did have a niggling doubt about that at the back of her mind. "But surely you can see that making a public appearance that looks like a date might be misinterpreted by police officers who still find it easier to view me as a sex object than as a commanding officer."

Brick leaned back against the tile counter, his hands stuffed into his pockets. "Karen, I want you to know that I had nothing to do with that office pool," he vowed. "They started taking bets the first week, when you were still being such a hardnose. That's when all the cartoons were drawn, too. As to the nickname—"

"For which I have you to thank..."

He winced. "It came to me on the spur of the moment when you and I were still at war. My face was still bleeding and my spine was black and blue."

Karen hated to think about the way she'd injured him that first night. She was happy the cuts on his face had finally healed.

"When you think about it, Karen, that nickname is a compliment."

"Considering the spirit in which it's used, I can't say I'm particularly flattered," she replied. Karen knew she should sound more angry and indignant, but tonight she was having difficulty acting stern with him. "A complimentary nickname conveys respect, even in an offbeat way. I once knew a cop named Toothless because he'd knocked out five teeth in one blow from the mouth of a man twice his size, one who attacked him during an arrest. I know another called Baldy because he's so proud of his thick hair. And there's another guy—" Karen gave him the ghost of a grin "—they call Brick. I've been told it's because he was solid as a brick wall during a football game, but I think maybe it's because he's what my father used to call a brick when he meant a man among men."

Brick's eyes flashed. Karen knew she'd surprised him, and she wasn't sure why she'd risked giving him such praise. Maybe it was to make up for all the wear and tear on his pride during her first weeks in town. Maybe it was because she was going to turn down his offer to take her to the party and she'd already embarrassed him once tonight. Maybe it was because it was so damned hard to be with him day after day without ever admitting how honored she felt that he'd chosen to be her friend.

"I like you, Brick," she guardedly confessed. "I'm glad that we get along. But I can't allow myself to be seen in public with you in a potentially compromising situation."

"Karen, you're a good-looking single woman. People could imagine you're in a compromising situation *anytime* you're with a man! Are you going to let the mere possibility of gossip ruin your social life?"

She sidestepped his question. "On duty, I'm a police captain, Brick. Not a man, not a woman, just the head cop."

"You can't live your whole life on duty, Karen."

"I'll live it however I please!"

He took a step toward her then, filling the small kitchen with his immense size and strength. There was nothing platonic about Karen's response to his proximity.

"Perhaps it's slipped your mind that you're not the only person on this planet, Karen. You're not the only one involved here." He took his hands out of his pockets and stepped closer yet. "I could have asked anybody to go to the party with me. I asked you because I thought it would be fun."

Karen tried to face him squarely, wishing he wouldn't stand so close. She could smell a faint hint of after-shave; she could feel that dangerous essence of pure man.

"I think it'd be fun, too, Brick. It's not—"

"I love being a cop, Karen, but there are moments now and then when I take off my gun and badge." He took another step closer. Only a few inches separated their bodies now. "In or out of uniform, I'm still a person, Karen. I'm a man."

Karen swallowed hard and dropped her gaze to the linoleum. "Brick," she admitted unsteadily, "believe me, I know you're a man."

For a moment the room grew deathly silent. She hadn't meant to put it that way; she'd only meant to accept and acknowledge his emotions. But Karen knew that he'd taken her words as a confession of womanly feelings for him . . . feelings she didn't dare possess.

She also knew she was standing on the edge of a precipice. She battled a sudden wave of vertigo. Ever since Brick had picked her up off the floor and she'd entrusted him with her tears, she'd realized that it wouldn't take much for him to seize control of her heart.

Fiercely she reminded herself that her career would collapse if that ever happened.

"Brick, what I mean is—"

"I know what you mean, bunkie." His private nickname for her sounded as sweet as honey on his tongue.

Helplessly Karen's eyes flitted up to meet his. She struggled to keep her distance, but Brick moved closer yet. In what might have been a platonic spirit, he took her hand, kneading it as he promised, "Nobody thinks of this party as a dating situation, anyway. It's like going to a church potluck or spending Saturday afternoon skating on the lake. A bunch of us always drive over together—Aunt Anna, Uncle Johnny, Tisha . . . whoever else is living here. You'll fit right in."

Karen couldn't argue with this fresh piece of logic, but she wasn't sure whether that was because it made sense or whether it was something she very much wanted to hear. How was she supposed to think clearly when he was toying with her hand?

What a thrill it would be to spend a whole evening with Brick, looking like a beautiful woman instead of a soldier! What a thrill it would be to spend a whole night dancing with him! Surely she'd be safe going to the party with a group of people from the boardinghouse. She and Brick could mingle freely. They'd never be alone.

"Well . . . that sheds a different light on the subject, Brick," she told him, wavering. "I'll give it some thought."

Both dimples deepened. "You do that, Karen. I think a dignified public appearance could only help your public image. Your reputation won't be the least bit endangered."

As Karen watched his victorious eyes devour her like a cougar stalking prey, she knew she couldn't say the same for her heart.

IT WAS JUST ABOUT SEVEN when Brick caught up with his grandmother at Worthington House, a charming old Victorian inn where she lived with seventy or eighty other oldsters. Accompanied by Tillie Phelps—and by Eddie Wocheck, who'd come to see his father, Phil—Martha Bauer was finishing her dessert in the dining room as Brick strolled through the door.

"Why, Donald! What a delightful surprise," his grandmother greeted him cheerfully. "You don't get over here very much anymore."

He kissed her on the cheek and accepted her loving rebuke. It had been a week, ten days tops, since he'd last dropped by. When things weren't busy at the station, he sometimes visited her every day or two.

"Sorry, Grandma. We've got a new captain at the station house and I've been showing her the ropes."

"She needs a lot of attention," said Eddie, who'd moved back to the boardinghouse a few days before and had been involved in some lively dinner conversations. He gave Brick a man-to-man wink as he teased,

"If cops had looked like that when I was a kid, I might have gone into law enforcement myself."

It was the sort of comment that any halfway normal man might make after a glimpse of Karen's beauty, but for some reason Eddie's observation made Brick uneasy. Tonight she'd made him see that the common male vision of her—as a knockout, not as a capable human being—was what made her job so difficult. He'd never given much thought to the men's ribald locker humor before, but now he saw that their behavior stripped Karen of her dignity, and he made a mental note to speak to them about it.

Partly to atone for naming her Captain Curvaceous, Brick told Eddie, "Believe it or not, she's a damn fine cop. A stickler for details, true, but she takes care of business. The men are learning to respect her." Eager to change the subject, he then asked, "How are things going at the lodge, Eddie? Will it be in shape for the party?"

Eddie shrugged expressively. "I think so. The architectural designs for the expansion are nearly ready, too. We're going to unveil them at the Christmas party, when we announce the spring date for ground breaking. Showing off the lodge is one of the reasons I agreed to let the Ingalls throw their party out there this year. In the past it's been at the house on Elm Street." He cast a warm glance at his father. "Dad's been giving me some pointers on the landscaping. In fact, we're going to drive out there tonight and talk it over. Nobody knows better what grows well at Timberlake, that's for sure."

When Phil grinned proudly, Brick thought Eddie was merely trying to make his old man feel useful. But then he recalled that Phil's experience gardening at

Timberlake Lodge had made him an expert in his narrow field. More than once he'd heard Alyssa say that nobody could make flowers bloom like Phil Wocheck.

"I'm glad we've got our families to help us out, Eddie," Brick declared, his eyes on his grandmother now. "Just so happens I've got a special problem that needs Grandma's magic hands."

Martha Bauer beamed dramatically. "I always said he was a fine boy."

Tillie laughed as she stood and ruffled his hair. "We all did." She said good-night and left the dining room, with Phil, in his wheelchair, and Eddie right behind her.

"What did you want to see me about, dear?" asked Martha after her friends had gone. "Somehow I have the feeling this isn't just a casual visit."

Brick pulled up the chair Tillie had vacated, smoothing his hair back into place. He loved his hometown, but sometimes he got tired of having the old folks treat him like a child. "Grandma, I need you to make a Christmas tree ornament."

"A what?"

He flushed. "Something cute. Sweet. Feminine. But right for a—"

"Police officer?" his grandmother said shrewdly.

His eyes met hers, imploring her to secrecy. "Aunt Anna invited her to help us decorate our tree with her own ornaments—you know how she encourages all the boarders to be part of the family like that?—and Karen said she didn't have a single one. Not even hidden away." He wanted his grandmother to get the picture, but he wasn't about to share anything Karen had told him in confidence. His aunt was likely to report her own conversation with Karen, anyway.

"Karen, you say? Not that vile, evil Captain Curvaceous I heard about the first day?"

Brick took a deep breath. Did the whole damn town know what he'd once called her? "At work it's Captain Keppler, Grandma. And this ornament is strictly on the qt."

His grandmother patted his hand. "Why, Donald, darling, why should a gift from Anna Kelsey to a boarder be a secret? It was kind of you to deliver your aunt's message to me."

He grinned as he recognized her clever subterfuge, then leaned forward to buss her soft cheek. His grandmother's eyes were still twinkling when he left her, buttoning up his jacket against the cold, clear night.

On the way out of Worthington House, Brick was surprised to run into Alyssa and her cousin, Janice Eber. They were both carrying tinfoil-covered trays that held something that smelled delicious.

"Hi, Alyssa. How's it going, Janice?" he greeted them warmly. "What brings you out here tonight?"

"Christmas cookies, Brick," said Alyssa, who was often busy with civic affairs or charity work. "We make some for Worthington House ever year."

"Well, it's nice to know I'll have something to look forward to when I'm old or otherwise incapacitated."

Janice pulled back a piece of tinfoil. "You can have one now, Brick, and I won't tell."

With a grin he snatched a ginger cookie shaped like a Christmas tree. "You're too good to me, Janice."

Alyssa chuckled, then held her own tray toward him. "Norwegian balls. Your favorite."

He sighed happily, then took two.

"Better not tell your boss, Brick. She might accuse you of accepting a bribe."

Brick inwardly stiffened. Did people have to talk about Karen wherever he went? No wonder she was paranoid.

Loyally he said to Alyssa, "Captain Keppler is very serious about her work. I think she'll do just fine here."

Alyssa didn't look appeased. "I hope so, Brick, but all the same I wish she hadn't come along when you broke the news of Mother's death to Dad. It was hard enough to cope with."

He felt the blaze of tension again—loyalty to the hometown, loyalty to Karen. He'd seen an old Bret Maverick show once where a whole town had conspired together against an outsider, and he had a feeling Tyler was doing it now. But Karen wasn't the enemy. She was only trying to find out the truth about Margaret Ingalls's death. It shouldn't bother people unless they had something to hide.

Liza did have something to hide, he was convinced of that. She'd been skittish when he'd showed up at the house, even before he'd introduced Karen. Liza was a free spirit, that was for sure, and she'd certainly done some things in the past that would make any cop wince. But there had to be something more immediate worrying her. She'd looked scared the minute she'd seen Karen's uniform.

He felt guilty that he hadn't shared his suspicions about Liza with Karen, but he owed the Ingallses loyalty, too. If he wasn't so close to them, he wouldn't have realized that Liza hadn't been quite herself that night. In Karen's eyes, she probably appeared downright raucous. Anybody who knew the real Liza Baron Forrester would have realized that she'd actually been a bit subdued.

Brick was about to pose a gently probing question to Alyssa when Eddie showed up on the porch behind him, pushing Phil's wheelchair. Phil was wearing a heavy down jacket and a very proud smile. Eddie, too, looked quite pleased with himself, until he glanced down the steps and saw whom Brick was talking to.

He barely looked at Janice. It was the sight of Alyssa that seemed to make him freeze.

Brick didn't know Eddie all that well, but he'd known Alyssa Baron all his life. He'd never seen her unable to handle a social situation, let alone unable to speak. Now she stared at the dashing gray-haired man as though he'd commanded her to utter stillness. Guilt and hurt and the tiniest wash of hope colored her delicate features.

On Eddie Wocheck's face there was a curiously bewildered look that Brick had never seen him wear before.

"Good evening," he said tensely.

"Good evening, Eddie." Alyssa smiled at Phil, then her gaze drifted back to Eddie's as she said, "I don't think you've met my cousin, Janice."

Janice took a step forward. "Well, no, we've never met, but I've certainly heard of you."

When Alyssa winced at the words, Janice hurriedly said, "All I meant was—"

"It's nice to meet you, Janice," said Eddie. "I've heard of you, too."

It was a good save, but it didn't do much to dispel the tension that radiated between Alyssa and Eddie throughout the next few minutes of conversation. They were making Brick nervous, too.

He was glad when Phil spotted the cookies and burst out happily, "Oh, it's that time of year again! Did you bring the *springerle?*"

Slowly, Alyssa nodded, struggling to draw her gaze away from Eddie's. "Of course, Phil. They've always been your favorites. I still use the recipe Mother's old cook always used."

The old man grinned from ear to ear. "You are so good to me, *maluska.*"

To Brick's shock, Alyssa's jaw went slack. Her eyes took on a frightened glaze. She looked at Phil, then back to Eddie, but not the way she'd looked at him before. It was as though she weren't quite sure which man had spoken.

The moment passed, and then she straightened and mentioned that it was cold outside. After a cheerful farewell word or two, she proudly marched into Worthington House in true Ingalls style, with Janice at her heels.

But Brick knew her too well. Despite the regal set of her head, Alyssa was sorely troubled, and not just by the identification of her mother's body and the reappearance of her old boyfriend.

It was the word *maluska* that rattled her. Polish, maybe? But Phil almost never used Polish anymore, and he'd used the name as though it had some special meaning for the two of them. The cop in Brick itched to find out what it meant, and why Phil's kindly use of the word had shaken her so badly.

Liza wasn't the only one of Judson's womenfolk who was hiding something that might be related to Margaret Ingalls's death. The possibility that Alyssa could also be wrestling with a secret was one Brick could not ignore.

CHAPTER SEVEN

KAREN CAME HOME around seven on Monday night, dragging her feet like lead weights as she picked up her mail, greeted Anna and Johnny, and headed up the stairs. She'd had a long day and her physical energy wasn't quite back up to par, but she knew that wasn't what was weighing her down. It was a long time since she'd come down with love—a far more virulent disease than strep throat—but not so long that she'd forgotten the symptoms. A curious buoyancy combined with an equally curious tendency to despair. A certain tenderness that made her too sensitive to the joys and pains of life, even when it wasn't so close to Christmas. Quiet surges of joy whenever the man in question came into the room; not-so-quiet surges of need whenever he accidentally touched her.

Karen hadn't fallen flat on her face yet, but as she flipped through the day's incoming Christmas cards, she had to admit that she was leaning that way as fast as her heart could carry her. Even now, dreading their impending confrontation, she couldn't deny that her pulse was picking up speed as she heard the TV blaring and realized that Brick was waiting for her in her room. He'd set up his old black-and-white set for her during her illness and hadn't moved it yet. Several times they'd stayed up late and watched old movies, munching popcorn and giggling like kids. Karen had loved sharing those times with Brick, oblivious to the fact that he'd betrayed her.

Now she sorely regretted the trust she'd placed in him. Rob Laney's call this afternoon had been a real eye-opener, one that made her see Brick's recent friendliness in a whole different light.

In hindsight, Karen marveled that he'd beguiled her into agreeing to go to that Christmas party with him—it was too late to get out of it now—and she marveled that she'd almost convinced herself that it didn't really count as a date.

It was not a mistake she could afford to make again.

"Hi, Kare," Brick greeted her cheerfully as she marched into the room. Shoeless, he was lying on her bed—not slouched over the end, but propped up with a pair of pillows on top of the quilt as though he belonged there. He wore what he usually did at home—a pair of jeans, his Packers sweatshirt and a sexy five o'clock shadow. Karen knew his habits so well by now that she could tell just by looking at his face how many hours had passed since he'd last shaved.

She stared at him for a long, sad moment before she coolly declared, "I need to talk to you before you leave my room."

Brick sat up at once. "Trouble downtown?"

She did not try to smile. "You might say that."

"You look a little peaked, Kare. Why don't you sit down?"

"I would be happy to if you'd be so kind as to get off my bed."

Brick's lips tightened at her unsubtle rebuke, but he didn't speak as he rose and turned off the set. Slowly he walked to the bathroom door—the route he always took to his room—and waited for her to continue, his posture a fair imitation of parade rest.

Karen took the spot he'd vacated on her bed—it was still warm with the feel of him—but she sat tensely on the edge of the mattress. "I got a call from Rob Laney today," she announced bluntly.

"Rob Laney?"

To Karen's surprise, Brick didn't look chastened or ashamed. He sounded tense and—surely not!—almost jealous.

"This is . . . an old friend?" The word *friend* was laced with innuendo.

"My dearest friend," Karen clarified. "My former partner. The one whose life I once saved." Instinctively she rubbed the scar on her left shoulder that was proof of her courage under fire. "I'm surprised the name doesn't ring a bell with you, Brick. Surely you've encountered it a dozen times during your background check of Karen Keppler."

That was when the color drained from his face. His gaze dropped to the floor. For a long, tense moment he said nothing. Any hope she might have had that Rob's information had been inaccurate died right then and there.

"I don't suppose it ever occurred to you that I might have a single loyal friend in the whole Sugar Creek County Sheriff's Department, did it, Brick? Imagine a cop being loyal to *me* instead of your good-ol'-boy fraternity!" Her anger was starting to push aside the pain. "Surprise, Lieutenant Bauer. Did you really think word wouldn't get back to me?"

At last Brick's eyes met Karen's. He looked embarrassed but not ashamed. "I took a chance, Karen. I was as discreet as possible, but it's inevitable in this sort of background check that sooner or later the subject gets wind of it. If you'd just let me explain—"

"Explain? Why, Lieutenant, I may be slow but I'm not stupid. You never made any bones about the fact that you wanted my job. First you tried to intimidate me, and when that didn't work you bamboozled me with your good looks and your pseudokindness. You took care of me when I was sick. You pretended to be my friend." Karen stood up and took a grim step in his direction. "What a pity you couldn't find any dirt to help you overthrow me while I was off balance. Are you planning to manufacture some?"

"Dammit, Karen, if I'd wanted to overthrow you, I didn't need to make anything up!" His square jaw jutted out as he swore his innocence. "The men were ready to hang you in effigy the first week you got here, but I quelled every hint of revolt. Ask any one of them! Recently I've been more friendly—" now those blue eyes begged her to believe him "—because I thought we truly had become friends."

Karen refused to be seduced by his fake sincerity. "I have no need of friends who stab me in the back, Lieutenant."

"I didn't stab you in the back, Karen! I just tried to gather some background information! I wanted to know what kind of woman we were dealing with. I needed to know if you were someone we could trust."

"Well, now you know. You're dealing with a woman who holds her own under fire. You're dealing with a woman who rarely makes the same mistake twice. You're dealing with a woman who never forgets when she's been crossed."

"I'm dealing with a woman who's letting her own pride blind her to the truth!" he growled. "If you ever cool off long enough to listen to the real reason I had you checked out, Karen, I'll be more than happy to tell you. In the meantime, I'm going downstairs to catch the rest of the game."

"Lieutenant!" she called out before he could march through the bathroom door. "Don't you want to know the results of *my* secret investigation?" As he stopped, turned around and faced her gravely, she thrust the knife home. "Don't you want to know what I found out about *you?*"

Brick had looked grim before, but he looked positively devastated now. Karen had hoped to take him by surprise, but suddenly her victory seemed small and petty. He'd said there was a reason he'd betrayed her, implied it was one she could forgive. In spite of everything, Karen found herself longing to believe him.

"I have no other secrets, Karen," Brick said wearily, looking as depressed as she felt. He ran a hand through his thick black hair. "I do have some curiosity, though, as to why you were paranoid enough to feel a background check on me was necessary."

Karen hated the feeling of distance between them, but she didn't dare move any closer. "I'm not the one who ordered the investigation on you, Brick," she told him truthfully, holding her ground in the center of the room. "Commander Harmon ordered me to gather information pertinent to a possible police cover-up."

He stared at her blankly. "A cover-up of what?"

"Of the truth about the body found at Timberlake Lodge."

Brick's mouth fell open. He looked shell-shocked.

"Harmon felt that Schmidt was dragging his feet," Karen explained a bit more gently, "and you were his right-hand man. You'd almost become his son-in-law.

Harmon hoped you were just following orders without knowing what might be at stake, but he didn't dare put you at the helm if there was any chance you were willingly conspiring to sidestep your official duties."

Brick visibly reeled. "Oh, my God."

"He couldn't pick anybody else who was eligible because they were all men with some connection to Tyler cops or citizens. I, on the other hand, have had to do battle everywhere I've been assigned. Over the years you've collected friends while I've collected enemies."

Brick was leaning against the doorway now, as if for support. "I thought you got the job because you were kissing up to somebody at the top," he raggedly confessed. "In the beginning, I mean. Once I got to know you, I knew there had to be some other reason, but I couldn't figure out what it could be."

"Join the club, Lieutenant," Karen retorted. "I've been accused of sleeping with somebody each and every time I've been promoted. The truth of the matter is that I've never so much as kissed another cop."

"Karen, I know you'd never—"

"You're right that I wouldn't have been chosen over Tyler's native son under normal circumstances," she plowed on, "but I worked damn hard for my captaincy and I'm not stepping aside for you now that I've got it, Brick. Make no mistake about that."

For a moment Brick seemed to be having trouble breathing. His pain and shock were difficult for Karen to bear.

"I can't believe it." His tone was numb. "I lost my promotion because Paul is getting old and soft?"

"I don't think Paul's age had anything to do with it. He goes back a long way with Judson Ingalls, and I think he dragged his feet a bit. Not enough to be convicted of obstructing justice, just enough to keep Judson's old scars from being paraded around in the light of day."

Brick shook his head. He closed his eyes. When he opened them, he pleaded, "Don't muddy Paul's name over this, Karen. I beg you. All he's guilty of is having different priorities than yours. If he'd ever found any evidence to implicate Judson in his wife's death, I swear to you, he would have brought him in."

"I don't know that for sure, Brick. Neither do you. But I can't prove that he tampered with any evidence, and frankly, I think he just hoped that if he kept his people busy with other tasks, the pressure to identify a long-dead body would eventually fade. I put all my facts and suspicions in my report. The rest is up to Commander Harmon." Belatedly it struck Karen that Brick seemed a lot more concerned about his former chief than about his own fate. "Don't you want to know what I said about you?"

He straightened then, and tensely met her eye to eye. "I know what you said about me, Karen. If you hadn't cleared me to your satisfaction, you wouldn't be divulging all of this. You'd be finding ways to torpedo our friendship. You'd be pushing me away."

"I *am* pushing you away!" she snapped. "You betrayed me, Brick. You pretended to be my friend. If you think—"

Suddenly his virile face was an inch away from hers. One large male hand was gripping her arm. It was a warm and compelling hand, forgiving and strong. The male body that pressed in close simmered with anger and regret…and made Karen simmer with feelings she knew she had to forget. Why, out of all the men in the world, did she have to respond so potently to this one? Why did he wound her with his fury and gentle her with his pain? Why did she make resolution after resolution where he was concerned, only to find herself magnetized by his touch again?

Suddenly Karen couldn't remember why she was mad at Brick. She couldn't even remember why she had to stay away from him.

"I never faked my feelings for you, Kare," he vowed in a voice that was dark and low. "When I hated you, I let you know it. When I started to like you, I let you know that, too. I had my reasons for checking you out—honorable reasons—and if I had it to do over, I'd do it all again. Hate me if you want, but I'm telling you the truth." His grip tightened, kneading Karen's skin in a way that called all of her female senses to full alert. "With Brick Bauer, what you see is what you get."

On that note he dropped her arm and stomped out through the bathroom. Karen listened tensely for him to pound down the stairs to catch the rest of the football game, but she didn't hear him leave his room. She wondered if he was waiting for her to rush through the bathroom doors and apologize. She wondered if it might be the right thing to do.

Karen glanced down at her uniform and remembered vaguely that nothing meant more to her than being a cop. She turned back to her father's picture by the bed and waited for his memory to tell her she'd made her old man proud. But tonight Brick's accusations were so loud that they drowned out her father's compliments. It was hard to recall the lessons he'd taught her when Brick was in the room.

For the past week or so they'd practically lived like roommates sharing an apartment, leaving their ad-

joining doors open as they passed back and forth freely
during the course of the day. With Brick on Karen's
bed watching television, the Kelseys' boardinghouse
had felt like home.

Now it was just a place to pass the night. A lonely
rented room.

Karen was trying to deal with her latest broken
dream when she spotted the small red-and-green box on
top of the TV. Taped to the bottom of it was a tag in
the shape of a snowman that said, "Merry Christmas
from Brick to Bunkie—Open Now!"

Sick with the memory of how they'd parted, Karen
remembered his last words: *With Brick Bauer, what
you see is what you get.* Her captain's mind was still
suspicious, but her woman's heart knew he was telling
the truth. The real Brick Bauer had brought her something for Christmas. The real Brick Bauer had lovingly nursed her when she was sick. The real Brick
Bauer had a legitimate reason for starting an inquiry on
her background.

Quickly she tore open the package, surprised at what
she found inside. It was a handmade ornament for the
Christmas tree, exquisitely fashioned out of fabric
scraps and felt. The figure was a darling little girl with
long black hair and a black uniform complete with a
holly-shaped badge that said Keppler. Lovingly shaped
wings sprouted from her back and a tiny hanger for the
tree hung from her miniature halo.

It was the first Christmas present Karen had received this year...the first ornament she'd owned since
her father's death. She knew it wasn't a last-minute gift
or a deliberate bribe. Brick had been looking straight
into her heart when he'd asked somebody to make this
angel cop.

A moment later Karen found herself darting through the two bathroom doors into Brick's room, not bothering to knock. When she found him staring glumly out the window, she flew across the room, threw both arms around his neck and kissed him on the cheek.

Her kiss was so quick, so spontaneous, that Karen didn't just surprise Brick, she surprised herself. When his arms came around her, she tried to step back, but it was too late to escape from his powerful embrace. After keeping herself so sternly at a distance from this man who always aroused her most sensual feelings, she realized that she'd inadvertently placed herself in danger.

"Thank you, Brick," Karen whispered, hoping he'd believe her apologetic display of affection was purely sisterly. "She's adorable."

For a moment Brick simply stared at Karen. Then one of his hands slipped up to cradle her head. "So are you," he answered, his voice still low but not at all angry now. "I wanted you to have some new memories of Christmas, Karen. That's one of the reasons I invited you to the party."

But that's not the only one, the voice of prudence warned Karen. She knew she had to break away from him right now. Right now, their embrace was still platonic, but they were both leaning in another direction and the tiniest breeze of attraction would be enough to blow them over. Karen struggled to escape—all she had to do was step away—but her whole body seemed to be trapped in Brick's undertow.

His compelling eyes were commanding her to kiss him, and not on the cheek this time. Karen tried to remember why she could not take the risk, but no reasons came to mind. It felt so natural, so beautifully right, to melt into his arms at this moment. After the past few dark hours, she suddenly felt secure and happy and deliciously warm. She could not imagine a more natural and wonderful sensation than the feel of Brick's lips against hers. She could not remember why she believed that later, when she could think again, she would be desperately sorry if she let it happen.

But her safety as an officer often depended on sheer instinct. A cop frequently had to make survival choices in the blink of an eye. If Karen had walked into a shoot-out, she would have ducked when the bullets started flying. Instinctively, she tried to duck Brick now.

"I'm sorry I had to keep my investigation secret, Brick," she blurted out, hoping that such a dark topic would defuse the increasingly erotic mood between them. "I was just doing my job. I was being a good cop."

Undeterred, Brick's hands slipped up and down her back in what might have been a fraternal massage. But there was nothing sisterly about Karen's response, especially when she imagined those fingers a little lower than the base of her spine. "I know you were, Karen. I don't hold it against you. If anything, it makes me respect you more."

Karen knew she had to get away. Brick was talking like a friend but his hands inflamed her like a lover's. If she didn't escape from him this instant, she knew it would be too late.

"Tell me why you sicced your cronies on me, Brick," she challenged him in desperation. "Tell me why you tried to ruin my life."

"I didn't try to ruin you, Karen!"

To Karen's relief—and unaccountable sorrow—Brick suddenly dropped his hands and turned away.

"If I'd been the only one involved, I would have covered my own back and taken my chances. But I owed it to the other men to be sure of you!" There was no hint of seduction now as he whispered, "Dammit, Kare, don't you see? I owed it to Mark."

Reeling from the abrupt mood shift, Karen told herself that she was glad Brick hadn't really betrayed her, glad he clung to such loyalty to his late partner, glad that she'd escaped from his mesmerizing hands.

But her body still quivered with yearning...where he had touched her and where he had not.

BRICK WAS GLAD to find Karen waiting in the car when he joined his aunt and uncle for a trip to Tyler's frozen lake on Saturday afternoon. Anna had been working on her all week, insisting that she needed some time off, and Brick had seconded his aunt's motion. He'd privately told Karen that he'd think she was still mad at him if she didn't come along, and though he was quite sure she saw through his blatant manipulation, she'd finally agreed to come, anyway.

He really did want some playtime with Karen. He missed watching TV with her in the evening or sharing a midnight snack. On the surface they had mended their fences, but ever since the day she'd gotten that call from Rob Laney, she'd seemed skittish about having Brick in her room.

She hadn't tried to back out of their date to the party, though, even though he was sure she wanted to. Karen always referred to it as "attending the Christmas get-together with the Kelseys," and acted as though Brick were just tagging along as Anna's nephew. The little angel cop never made it down to the Christmas tree, but he'd noticed that it was hanging from her father's picture in her room.

Brick had planned to play hockey with his old gang this afternoon, but after a half hour or so he asked Patrick to fill in for him as goalie, and he joined Karen on the other side of the ice. She had warned him she couldn't skate worth beans, and by now he knew she'd been telling the truth. Ice skating seemed to be the one thing Karen Keppler couldn't do.

Brick slid toward her effortlessly, bringing himself up short while she wobbled in surprise, then grabbed his arm to steady herself. "Whoa, gal. What would you say to some remedial tutoring?"

She grimaced. "That obvious, huh?"

"Plain as day, bunkie. Weren't you ever a kid?"

Apologetically she answered, "Well, I did learn how to ride a bike. It was the fastest way to run my dad's dinner down to the station house."

Whenever she mentioned her father, there was an ache in Karen's voice that wounded Brick. He knew from personal experience that her memories were getting harder to handle the closer she got to Christmas.

"I bet he was damn proud of you," he said gently.

To his surprise, she blinked rapidly, almost as though she were fighting tears. "Well, he was certainly proud the day I graduated from the police academy. He wasn't around to see much after that."

Brick waited for the rest. He'd asked questions about her dad before, but she'd never given him many details. Now he sensed she was ready to share more of her past with him.

"His partner was a good man, but it didn't make any difference. They went down together. A pimp on speed."

There had been a time when her terse expression would have fooled Brick into thinking that she had no feelings. But he knew better now. That tight mask of control she often wore at work did not come to her naturally. The colder she sounded, the more she was probably hurting.

"I'm sorry, Kare," he said, trying to console her. "I won't pretend to know exactly how you feel, but...I've been there. The hurt doesn't go away, but you sort of learn to live with it in time."

She licked her lips. "You know how you kept everything of your parents? Furniture and Christmas ornaments and everything?"

Brick nodded.

"I did just the opposite. I couldn't bear to sit in Dad's favorite chair or see Christmas ornaments that had hung on his tree. I sold what I could and gave the rest away. Ever since then I've just rented furnished places." She looked almost sheepish. "I've got a healthy savings account, but I don't own a single piece of furniture."

"But you do have a Christmas ornament," he reminded her gently, rejoicing that his instincts had been keen enough to realize how much she'd needed it. "Maybe it's time to start some new memories, Karen. Time to come out of mourning."

She nodded, but she didn't look very certain. "Well, I am planning to buy a house once I get settled in better at the station. You were right, you know, when you said I couldn't live my whole life on duty. I think maybe that's what I've been trying to do. It's time I had a place worth coming home to." At last she smiled. "I want a calico cat in the kitchen and a huge philodendron in every room."

Brick grinned. "Hey, you don't have to wait until you buy a house to start making your room a bit more homey." *You only have to wait a few more days,* he added silently as he started planning some more Christmas surprises for her. "I'm not sure how Aunt Anna would feel about a cat, but you could at least get a nice plant right away."

Karen's broadening smile warmed him inside and out. Suddenly Brick was acutely aware that she was still clinging to his arm, even though she had long since stabilized her position. He had an odd, gratifying feeling that she was leaning on him for more than physical support.

As he remembered what she'd told him about her mother, Brick realized that Karen's life had always been pretty austere. She'd never lived in a normal family with a loving man and woman who shared babies or anything else. Her father had been everything to her, and her father had been married to the badge. Was it any wonder she'd made the same choice?

Was it any wonder nobody had ever taught her how to skate? How to laugh? How to love?

I'm going to teach her everything, a voice within him vowed. With Karen fighting their growing intimacy, it wasn't going to be easy, but Brick was a determined man.

His hopes rose when Karen pressed closer, ostensibly to get a better grip on his arm. As she brushed against his thigh, he thought about the last time she'd been so close...when she'd kissed his cheek and, for one exquisite moment, had let him hold her in his arms.

Suddenly he felt off center, uneasy, too big for the front of his jeans. This was no time to be aroused! He didn't dare risk embarrassing Karen publicly. When the time was finally right to let her know how much he cared for her, he'd be damn certain that she was in the right mood.

"I think it would help if you'd shift your weight from one leg to the other, really glide," he told her quickly, determined to end their tête-à-tête before he got into trouble. "Then the motion is smoother, and you can get up some speed."

"Speed?" She laughed, a truly beautiful sound that rang through the crisp, piny air and seemed to add sparkle to the sunlight on the ice. "Brick, I can hardly stay upright holding still!"

"Oh, come on. Where's your spirit of adventure? Give me your hand and I'll be your rudder till you get the hang of it."

For a moment her face grew quite still, and he waited, expecting her to tell him she couldn't possibly hold his hand in public, even for such a prosaic reason. But when she glanced at the other townsfolk— some doing figures, some whooping it up in the hockey game—she was apparently reassured by what she saw.

"If you think you can stand working with such a slow student, Brick, God knows I could use the help."

"I won't argue with you there."

He took her hand—or rather, his glove found her mitten—as they began to skate in slow, careful stretches. Karen trudged along clumsily, courageously, making him feel curiously protective of her. He wanted to teach her how to have fun with a family or play with a friend. He wanted to make up for her father's death and her mother's abandonment.

He wanted to sleep in her room tonight.

Brick nipped that fantasy in the bud, but not soon enough to keep his jeans from getting even tighter.

He put one arm around Karen as she nestled against his side, wobbling and lurching on her skates.

"There must be a trick to this I'm missing," Karen confessed after she'd accidentally nicked his ankle with a sharp blade. "I'm normally not this clumsy. I won some awards for track in school and I was always good in gymnastics."

"You have to relax, Kare. Just let go."

"If I let go, I'll fall over!"

"I didn't mean letting go of me," Brick said with a laugh. "I mean let go of the tension, the need to control. Let me get you rolling here. Just loosen up and put yourself in my hands."

It was the wrong thing to say. He felt tension rocket through her body...a flash of arousal echoing his own? So far he'd been holding her in a perfectly platonic fashion, but he couldn't seem to conceal the fact that his fantasies were moving along more sensual lines.

Apparently Karen's thoughts were moving in the same direction. Her eyes met his with an unspoken reprimand as she replied unsteadily, "I'm not so sure this was a good idea, Brick. I tend to do better on my own."

While Brick mutely cursed himself, Karen pulled her hand loose and started to skate away from him. Her rough, jerky takeoff barely got her launched before she started to career, lurching back toward Brick for help. At once he reached out to catch her, but he was too late.

Karen fell toward him at an odd angle that made it hard for him to break her fall. She crashed through his arms, but caught one knee going down, pulling his leg out from under him.

A moment later they were both laid out flat on the ice.

As Brick slammed onto the frozen pond, inwardly cursing, he recalled the last time Karen had toppled him on his back with an audience. At least this time she'd gone down, too. And this time, she was on top of him.

Acutely aware of the warmth of her female body—aware of each delicate, womanly curve—he held his breath and tried not to move until she could roll off him. The force of her impact had inflamed his already heightened senses, and her nearness was now loudly reminding him of the warnings he'd ignored before.

While Brick did his damnedest to still his throbbing passion, he suddenly felt a frozen female hand touch his throat. Somehow Karen had pulled off her mitten. She was taking his pulse.

"Brick?" she begged him, her voice hoarse and low. She sounded frightened, the way she had when she'd first heard that Orson Clayton was injured. But there was something else in her tone that he knew he hadn't heard before. She said his name almost like a prayer. "Brick, tell me you're all right!"

He opened his eyes at once, stunned and touched by her concern. "Karen, I'm fine," he whispered, so eager to soothe her that he almost forgot the need for caution. "I probably broke my shoulder, and my reputation as an athlete is shot to hell, but other than that—"

He stopped abruptly as he saw the look on Karen's face. Her beautifully curved mouth was only a few inches away from his own, and her eyes were full of fear that was changing, as he watched, to unmitigated joy.

"Thank God!" she whispered.

Instinctively, unknowingly, Brick cradled her face with his good hand. Her skin was soft and smooth. She smelled like soap and sunshine. "I'm tough as a rhino, bunkie. It would take a lot more than the world's clumsiest skater to leave me at death's door."

"I'm sorry," she said, smiling openly in relief. She still lay on top of him, her body so close to his that her sweet breath warmed his face and her thighs pressed against his own.

It took all of Brick's strength of will not to move erotically against her. He had an eerie feeling that Karen was fighting some powerful instincts, too.

"You're so incredibly strong, Brick. It never occurred to me that I could knock you down."

"You've done it before," he reminded her.

Karen shook her head, causing a chunk of thick black hair to spill loose from its lacy band. A few silky strands feathered his face and tugged at his heart. "That was on purpose. This was a mistake."

The moment the words were out, Brick realized that falling down wasn't the only mistake Karen had made. She still hadn't moved. Their bodies were lodged ever so intimately together, and his hand was still caressing her face.

He wanted her. He wanted her with a heat that all but left him speechless, a heat that he could no longer deny. And though Brick knew she would die before she admitted it, he was certain that Karen wanted him, too.

The sight of him "wounded," even the fear of it, had rocked her to the core. Even now, assured of his well-being, she couldn't seem to hurry to her feet, didn't even seem to realize that he was ready to kiss her as she straddled him atop the ice.

"Bunkie?" Brick queried softly, unable to hide his own urgency. His fingers splayed across her cheek; his thumb erotically stroked her fine jaw. When she licked her lower lip and met his eyes with unbanked need, he dipped his fingers deep into her hair and pulled her closer, breathing her name in a wordless moan.

But Brick's lips did not find Karen's. At the last second, she closed her eyes and turned her face away.

While he reeled from the rejection, Brick tensed for her rebuke. How could he have forgotten they were surrounded by people, even for a second? Karen would never forgive him for such a bald faux pas.

But when Karen tugged his hand away from her hair, there was nothing angry or arrogant about the gesture. She was silent as her small fingers closed around his palm, kneading his skin for a tense, hungry moment. Brick could have sworn she was caressing him.

For a long, heart-stopping moment, the strong woman who'd rejected Brick's kiss clung to his hand, her legs all but intwined with his. By the time she shakily found her feet, Karen's silence had already told Brick everything she could not say.

CHAPTER EIGHT

NEVER, in the thirty years Anna had been coming to the Ingallses' Christmas parties, had she arrived at one in a car that bristled with so much tension. Eddie, dressed to kill in a superbly tailored black suit, had been edgy all day. Karen looked like a princess; no stranger would ever have guessed she was a cop. Brick always looked good to Anna, but she had to admit that he'd outdone himself tonight. To replace the suit Karen had ruined, he'd bought a dark navy one that brought out the blue in his eyes.

Wedged thigh to thigh with Karen in the confines of the back seat, Brick couldn't seem to take his eyes off her...and she couldn't seem to look at him. Eddie, on Karen's other side, seemed oblivious to her presence. Tonight he seemed oblivious to all of them.

Anna, preoccupied with the news of Rose Atkins' death, was silent. But, of course, Johnny was his typical loving self as he drove the group to Timberlake Lodge. He even joined Tisha, perched in the front seat next to Anna, in a few loud bars of "Deck the Hall."

Timberlake Lodge was a cheery sight this evening, rising like a beacon from the snowbanks that lined the road. Streams of people were pressing toward it, happily gossiping about Margaret's last party at the lodge, and what had really happened to her. Everybody seemed to think that Liza had done a terrific job remodeling the lodge, and several people openly praised Alyssa's extensive efforts to decorate it tonight.

The main lobby was bedecked with pine boughs and holly. In the very center stood a twenty-foot tree glittering with lights and decorations. In one corner a live nine-piece band was playing Christmas carols and old dance tunes; in another a huge table sported an architectural model of the projected expansion of Timberlake Lodge. A beautiful Oriental rug—an artful design of wines and blues and golds—graced the reception area where drinks and hors d'oeuvres were being served. As always, Orson Clayton ho-ho-hoed as Santa, but the red suit seemed a bit loose on him this year.

Judson and Alyssa were greeting George Phelps and Marge Peterson as Johnny ushered Anna toward the doorway. Marge looked positively radiant, and Anna was happy for her. George was finally separated from his wife, ending an ice-cold marriage that had plagued him for years.

Alyssa's separation from Eddie, on the other hand, had taken place a long time ago. Now Anna watched as her friend's gaze fell on her teenage flame, one man among dozens in the cheerful Christmas crowd, and the old need and the new hurt washed over her pale face. Eddie, taking in Alyssa's stylish V-necked black satin sheath, seemed to catch his breath.

He had just reached Alyssa and was about to say hello when Marge called out in a loud, teasing voice, "Well, Eddie, looks like you finally caught that girl under the mistletoe!"

In unison, Alyssa and Eddie glanced up at the doorway, where a lovely sprig of red-ribboned mistletoe had been hung. Alyssa's cheeks reddened. Eddie looked tense and pale.

Anna was furious with Marge. Just because she could finally make her own secret love public didn't mean that everybody else could! Eddie and Alyssa were barely getting acquainted again, and things were still uncomfortable and tense between them. Surely Marge knew how awkward it would be for them to share a public kiss after thirty years since their last private one! But she had left them with little choice. To avoid the kiss now would draw a great deal of attention to both of them.

"Hurry up, Eddie. We've got another carload behind us," Marge pointed out, grinning happily and hugging George's arm. "It's Christmas. Everybody gets a kiss under the mistletoe."

Eddie's eyes met Alyssa's almost apologetically. Despite his eight-hundred-dollar suit, there was a bit of the teenage Eddie left in his face . . . the misunderstood rebel with a heart. He took a tentative step forward. Alyssa, looking terribly tense, leaned slightly toward him. She could have offered him her cheek, but she met his lips uncertainly with hers instead.

It was a brief kiss, a Christmas kiss, a kiss that any man could have given any woman in the midst of the holiday season. But when Eddie pulled back, his eyes didn't leave Alyssa's. And Alyssa's hands were shaking.

FROM THE FIRST INSTANT Karen had seen Brick's face in the car, she knew she'd made a terrible mistake.

It was bad enough that she'd let Tisha do her hair in dramatic curls and sexy waves that billowed half-tamed around her head. Worse yet was her decision to follow

Anna's advice to buy this magnificent emerald satin gown, cut low in the back and lower yet in the front, where an enticing glimpse of cleavage drew Brick's eye away from her pearls. The dress had sleeves just long enough to cover the bullet scar on her left shoulder.

No fabric could have concealed the turmoil in Karen's heart.

She had told herself that propriety forced her to look her best for the evening. The truth was—she had to face it now—she'd wanted to feel radiant and ultrafeminine for Brick. She'd wanted to feel beautiful the way a woman feels when she sees her own beauty reflected in the eyes of the man she loves.

Just once. Just tonight. She wanted a harmless fantasy to remember.

But the tension on Brick's square-jawed face told Karen that her fantasy was anything but harmless. Her memory of his hand on her face last Saturday on the ice was all too keen. She could still feel the force of his hard body against her legs. There was no way she could pretend that he had not wanted her. Karen was grasping at straws when she tried to believe that he didn't know by now how desperately she wanted him.

She'd been assailed by unbearably erotic dreams the night before. Brick had slipped into her room wearing nothing but a towel, snapping it at her before Karen was awake enough to stop him. Then he'd leaned over and claimed her breasts, bringing her fiercely to consciousness and full arousal as her dream self had flipped him onto the floor.

Karen knew she'd have to keep Brick at arm's length. And by the look in his eyes, he had no intention of staying at arm's length tonight.

He hadn't left her side once since they'd arrived at the party, introducing her politely to everyone in sight. He couldn't seem to say Karen's name without laying a hand on her arm, nor anyone else's without touching her own. If he'd been anyone but Brick, Karen would have been oblivious to his courteous, platonic touch. But she was anything but oblivious to this man who had reached her so deeply, who made her sizzle with no more than a heated glance. By the time he stepped away to fetch her some punch, she knew it would take all of her strength of will to get through this evening without doing something she would sorely regret.

"Thank you for the punch, Brick," Karen murmured when he returned with her glass.

"Careful there, Captain. You almost sounded friendly," he teased her playfully. "God forbid you should act as though you're enjoying my company this evening."

"I always enjoy your company," she replied with feigned nonchalance. "It's a nice party, isn't it?"

"I hadn't noticed." His voice was husky. "I thought we were here all alone."

Karen swallowed a breath of panic. There were many times when Brick had come too close, times when he'd said things it was hard to ignore. But he'd always given her room to dodge his innuendos. He didn't seem to be giving her room to back off now.

"I agreed to attend this event with you because you assured me it was . . . dateless."

"Dateless?" he echoed with a dimpled grin. "Do you want me to pretend that you took hours to look drop-dead gorgeous tonight for the general public?"

Karen gulped back a protest, but she had less luck with a blush. "This is a formal event, Brick. Your aunt told me it would be rude to show up looking shabby."

"You're a long way from shabby, bunkie. You look good enough to eat."

"I thought I made my position clear, Brick. My professional reputa—"

"Karen," he cut her off, his voice commandingly low and sexy, "stop fighting me. This is a party. It's Christmastime. Everybody's in a loving mood. Nobody's going to think we're having a raging affair just because you're nice to me tonight."

At that moment somebody bumped into Karen, forcing her to step closer to Brick. When her breasts grazed his chest, she lost a grip on the punch glass in her hand. Karen winced as the bright liquid seeped quickly into the beautiful Oriental rug. *I'll have to pay to have this rug cleaned; it's the least I can do,* she told herself as she leaned down to pick up the glass, which at least hadn't broken. But Brick leaned down at the same moment, taking the glass with one hand as he brushed her arm with the other.

She waited for him to step away, but instead he moved still closer.

Karen couldn't meet his smoldering blue eyes, afraid they might ignite something inextinguishable within her. "You've made me feel welcome," she admitted shakily. Then, in a fair imitation of her captain's voice, she suggested, "Now maybe it would be best if you welcomed some other guests."

For a long moment Brick didn't answer, didn't protest, didn't step away. Then he ordered softly, "Dance with me, Kare."

Karen shook her head. She struggled for breath. The mere idea of touching him made parts of her body tingle. He was already way too close.

"I don't think that's a good idea." She tried to sound strong and haughty, but her voice came out as a squeak.

"I think you're wrong." His voice was husky now.

She tried to walk away—run away—but she could not. The band was starting up a sentimental Christmas tune that had a curiously melting effect on her resolutions. She wanted to put her arms around Brick's neck. She wanted to kiss him. She wanted to press her breasts against his broad chest and pull him close.

Then, to her astonishment, Brick confessed, "I'm not going to make it another five minutes without putting my arms around you, Karen. Don't you think it'd be less obvious if I did it on the dance floor?"

A wild swirl of need erupted somewhere within Karen. Against all common sense, she was thrilled by his words. God, how she wanted him to hold her! How she wanted the kiss she'd turned away on the ice!

Suddenly she could not protest. She could not speak. Worse yet, she couldn't look away. She knew it was folly not to run or fight; she knew Brick would take anything less as a sign of surrender.

And then he smiled. It was that blue-eyed dimpled smile that had melted Karen the first time she'd ever seen it. It was twice as devastating now. It was a lover's smile, a smile of need and promise, a smile that begged her to give in.

Through the low-cut satin, Karen felt a broad, warm male hand guide her toward the dance floor. She could feel hot fingerprints on her spine as Brick stopped to introduce her to an old friend on the way. She didn't catch the man's name. She wasn't even sure if she responded to his greeting. All she knew was that her senses were on overload.

The room was stuffy, but she knew that wasn't why she could hardly breathe. The heat from Brick's hand was spreading up and down her legs. Her nipples were tingling, surging upright. Karen felt too shaky to stand, let alone to dance in a roomful of people.

By the time they reached the dance floor, the band had started playing an old love song in waltz time.

"I don't know how to waltz," Karen said, surprised to hear the quavering in her own voice.

"Neither do I," Brick answered. He took her in his arms, anyway.

Karen knew there was some vital reason why she shouldn't feel so light-headed, so flagrantly aroused by his touch. It had to do with her career, which meant her life. It had to do with some vision of herself that she'd left at home when she'd slipped into this emerald dress . . . and forgotten to don her armor.

Mercifully, Karen and Brick weren't the only couple on the dance floor mixing the dance styles of generations; besides, the corner of the room was so dim and crowded that nobody seemed to be paying any attention to them. Karen told herself she would be courteous and stay for just one dance before she tore herself away from him. Surely she could last a few minutes without plastering herself against Brick and begging for a kiss!

The music was a sad, aching melody with lyrics that revealed how the singer had reached the edge of his endurance.

How long can I pretend not to love you?
How cruel, baby, can you really be?
How long can I live without you?
How long can you live without me?

Karen did her best to ignore the lyrics, even though
Brick started caressing her bare back when the chorus
started. She felt herself moving closer, struggling to
keep from pressing her forehead against his shoulder,
struggling to keep from pressing her lower half against
his thighs. Even when she felt the top of her hair brush
his chin, she couldn't seem to pull back from him.

The hand that had claimed her fingers began to tug
her closer; the hand on her back nudged her closer, too.
Karen was drowning now...fighting wild eddies of
longing...certain she had to escape him...utterly
unable to.

By this time she was trembling. Worse yet, Brick was
trembling, too. When Karen foolishly glanced up at
him, she saw naked hunger flame in his eyes. Urgently
he pulled her nearer. Every line of his face confessed
the potency of his desire.

Karen didn't need a road map to see where Brick was
heading. He was a virile man who'd run out of patience. If they'd been alone, Karen knew he would have
been tearing off her clothes by now. She also knew she
couldn't count on her own self-control tonight. Her
only protection was the crowd of people in this room.

The second time the chorus started, Brick began
humming. It was too subtle a message for anyone
nearby to understand, but to Karen, it was as though
he were singing the aching words right along with the
anguished lover in thc song.

How long can I pretend not to love you?
How cruel, baby, can you really be?
How long can I live without you?
How long can you live without me?

By the time the song mercifully ended, Karen was shaking. She knew she was out of control. Her panic was like that of a wild bird trapped inside a room; she was ready to throw herself against a window.

"Brick, I want to go get something to eat. Alone," she declared desperately, struggling to free herself from the firm, erotic hold he now had on her waist. "I'll talk to you later—"

"Come to me, Karen. Come tonight to my room."

Her eyes flashed up in naked terror. Was she really so transparent to him? Could he feel the rush of desire he triggered just by that suggestion? Did he know what he was doing to her?

His blue eyes were blazing with the same desire he surely read in hers. His frustration was palpable, his need a living thing she could almost see and hold.

"Brick, I can't," she begged in panic. "I've told you and told you—"

"Then I'll come to yours."

BRICK WASN'T SORRY he'd pushed Karen so hard. For a while there—for most of the past week—he'd wondered if he'd imagined that she shared his feelings for her. But most of his questions had been answered on the ice; the rest had been answered tonight. The last of Karen's resistance had cracked during that dance. If they'd been alone, he'd have claimed her by now.

He was damned well going to claim her by morning.

He decided to mingle while he gave her a little time to collect herself, but he didn't get very far before he was buttonholed by Liza.

The dress she wore was pure Liza—neon purple, strapless, with a wild shooting-star display of rhinestones across the miniskirt and almost nonexistent bodice. It gave new meaning to the word *risqué*. After confirming that Susannah Atkins had decided to wait till after Christmas to hold her grandmother's funeral, Liza started right in.

"Where's your roomie tonight, Brick?" she asked with a cocky grin.

Brick played along with her, knowing that in Liza's case it was high spirits, not insight, that caused her to tease him about Karen.

"Lost her to some other man. We were dancing and then—whoops! Some tall, dark and handsome stranger cut in."

Liza giggled, then dropped her voice. "She's a real hardnose, Brickie. Came out to see me Friday. About the burglary last week, you know?"

The news surprised Brick. Karen hadn't mentioned her follow-up visit to Liza. Of course, they hadn't been talking shop tonight. Police work was the last thing on his mind.

"So, what happened?"

"She wanted to know about some old suitcase that got stolen from the potting shed. I didn't even know about it. Cliff just remembered it because last summer he used it to prop up his worktable."

"And?"

She didn't meet his eyes. One ankle dipped, as though she were resting a sore foot. "Brickie, she wanted to know all about the suitcase, how long it had been there, what was in it . . . stuff like that."

He waited.

"Then she asked about how I'd decided to remodel my grandmother's old room. She wanted to know all sorts of things that nobody ever asked before. After she left I got to thinking. . . ." Her eyes flashed up at his with an expression he'd never seen on Liza's face before, a look that bore a strong resemblance to fear. "Brick, drop by when you can, okay? I don't think we should go into this here."

Before he could reply, Janice Eber joined him as Liza slipped away. Poor Janice, dressed like a fifties sorority queen, had come to the party alone because Kurt was out of town again on business. Anna had expressed some concern that he might not make it home for Christmas Day, either, and she'd invited Janice and the kids for Christmas dinner just in case.

The Kelseys had a full house at the holidays. Friends and relatives were always welcome. This year, Brick's widowed cousin, Britt Hansen, would also join them for Christmas dinner. Brick hoped that nothing that happened tonight would keep Karen from joining them, too.

"Anna asked me to relay a message to you from your captain," Janice said soberly. "Apparently there's been another robbery that she felt needed her immediate attention. She told Hedda to send a cruiser to pick her up, but she wants you to stay here and represent the station, so to speak. She'll get her own ride home."

Brick wasn't sure how to answer. Since when did a police captain have to leave a party just because there was a robbery? Only one or two reasons would justify sending out a cruiser. . . . Suddenly afraid for his men, he asked, "Was there an officer-in-need-of-assistance call?"

Quickly Janice shook her head. "Oh, no, Brick. Nothing like that. I would remember. Actually, I think Anna did say something about reassuring you that nobody was injured." Before he had time to relax, she added, "She also said something about a van, but I don't think she understood quite what Karen meant by that."

Clearly the van had no significance for Janice or Anna, but it mean a lot to Brick. It meant that those two punks were leaving a hell of a lot of egg on the faces of Tyler's finest. Worse yet, it meant that Karen was grasping at straws in a desperate, last-ditch attempt to run away from him.

But she'd never run fast enough. Not in the mood he was in tonight.

KAREN KNEW that she was behaving like a coward. She'd escaped from the party on the flimsiest of excuses, and sooner or later she'd have to go home and face Brick.

But she couldn't live at the boardinghouse. Not anymore. Not after tonight. She'd never intended to stay there very long; she'd always planned to buy a little house. But she hadn't intended to run out and buy any old place just to get away from the only man who'd ever made her wonder whether her career was worth the price she'd always paid for it. She had to escape from the man who had the power to soften her hard edge, ruin her reputation and destroy her life.

In the private cocoon of her office, Karen tried to think clearly. Before she saw Brick again, she simply had to have a plan. It wasn't cheating to put him on the four-to-twelve shift until they nailed the two punks in the van. Even Hedda, who'd already posted the new roster, said it was a logical assignment for a second in command. If Karen could just keep away from Brick in the evenings and pretend to be asleep when he got home...yes, that might buy her a little time.

First thing tomorrow she would call a Realtor. Thank God they worked even on Christmas Eve! After that she'd come back to the office and volunteer to ride patrol for one of the guys who'd asked for time off over Christmas. She didn't want to think about the lonely holiday, anyway—when the loss of her father seemed so hard to bear—and there was no way she could join the other waifs who congregated at the Kelseys.

It was a great plan, but Karen knew that none of it would help her when she went home tonight. Brick hadn't been kidding when he'd said he would come to her after the party. She'd heard the need in his voice, felt the hunger in his hands. Worse yet, he'd felt her own raw need, seen it on her face.

He was all too sure she'd welcome him.

She hadn't come up with any scheme about of locking her bedroom door when Brick himself barged into the station house, exchanged a handful of words with Hedda, then stormed into Karen's office without so much as a preliminary knock. At once he filled the room with his great size, his barely capped anger and his potent desire. Furiously he slammed the door and locked it.

"Crawled into your burrow to hide, did you, Karen? Are you planning to sleep here, too? Maybe buy yourself a chastity belt and lock yourself in a cell for safekeeping?" He didn't give her a chance to answer before he roared on. "Funny, I didn't take you for a quitter. I thought you were the type to face life head-on."

He'd circled Karen's desk as he hollered at her, giving her no room to escape. She couldn't remember when she'd felt so small and helpless. Certainly not since she'd been a cop.

"I don't need to explain myself to you, Brick," she retorted as stiffly as she was able. "What I do is none of your business."

He edged closer still, his movements smooth and predatory. "Gonna buy a dead bolt for your door? Or are you planning to use that loaded gun you keep by your bed if I try to break in tonight?"

She knew he was angry, knew he had a right to be. She hadn't been honest with him. She'd given him every reason to believe she returned his own passionate feelings—and not just tonight—then had slunk away like a coward.

But she had the right to her feelings, too. A right to her own life! And she most certainly had a right to her own office. It was inexcusable for a subordinate officer to make her quail in this private room.

"Brick, I don't attempt to interfere in your off-duty hours. I don't know why you persist in meddling with mine."

"Oh, yes, you'd *never* meddle with my off-duty time! Hedda tells me that you've changed the roster this week so I'll work evenings while you're still working days. How convenient!" he burst out. He leaned forward, glaring at her as he grabbed the arms of her chair. "What a craven thing to do! Just like a woman, too!"

It was the last line that made Karen begin to sizzle—in a slow, angry burn that rose as Brick kept barking at her, revealing his disrespect for her with every word. It was obvious that he'd never come to terms with her captaincy or her inner strength as a person; even now, he expected her to turn tail and run at the first sign of danger. Yet Karen knew she'd done just that as a woman faced with the demands of the man she loved. Was Brick really so far off base, fearing she'd try to wiggle out of a tight spot the same way in her role as a cop?

"For your information, *Lieutenant*, I have moved you to swing shift because I need my best man to put an end to these ongoing break-ins," she informed him crisply, rising to her feet and pulling her courage tightly around her like a blanket. Brick didn't back off. He stood almost as close to her as he had on the dance floor. "We had three more tonight! No man on this force is better equipped to figure out what's going on in this town. But if you don't think you're capable of—"

"Stop it, Karen!" he ordered, his voice low and deadly. "Don't you *dare* 'Lieutenant' me! This isn't about my job or yours! This is about you and me and what we want when we're out of uniform."

Panicking, Karen cried out, "What I want out of uniform is the same thing I want when I'm in it! The knowledge that I'm working to the best of my capabilities! The respect of the community! The support of my men!"

Suddenly she felt two broad male hands on her waist. "None of that's going to keep you warm at night, Karen. None of it's going to put out the fire burning deep inside you."

It was in that moment that Karen made a deadly mistake. She was so stunned when he touched her—

right there in her office with Hedda outside the locked door—that she couldn't at once think of scathing words. And while she was wrestling with the sudden rush of longing triggered by his magnificent male hands, Brick cheated. He broke all the rules.

She didn't see it coming; didn't believe he'd be so bold. But suddenly she felt his lips on hers, lips she'd dreamed of for the past three weeks, lips that claimed Karen as Brick's woman and shook her, heart and soul. She tried to fight him, tried to remember all the escapes she'd learned for such a hold. But each and every one required the firm belief that her safety was in danger. A firm belief that what this man was doing to her body was all wrong.

And her body was singing loudly that Brick Bauer's flaming touch made the whole world seem damn near perfect.

Fiercely he pulled her hard against him, and for just a moment, Karen rejoiced in the heat of that hard male body, sought his mouth as he crushed her in his arms. She nearly buckled with the force of her own desire. It was so right, so incredibly, unbearably *right* to merge with him this way!

It was also incredibly, unbearably wrong.

She pressed her hands against his chest with some vague intent to push him away, but her fingers tugged loose his tie and stroked his throat instead. She told herself to hammer at his windpipe, to break his hold at the wrists, but her brain short-circuited the command. The captain in her could not put her arms around him and pull him close, but the woman, in her passion, could not bear to push him away.

And then, in the misty distance, Karen heard a voice squawking on the police radio. It was an ordinary message—there was no sound of panic—and Hedda, out in the squad room, answered the same way. But the simple exchange rocketed Karen back to reality. And reality meant that if she yielded to this turbulent emotion—if she let her love for this man break her iron will—she'd never trust herself to be a steely cop again. She'd never trust herself to be Captain Karen Keppler. And if she wasn't her father's daughter, who on earth could she be?

Resolutely she told herself that she was the captain of the Tyler substation of the Sugar Creek County Sheriff's Department. The captain could not allow a man under her command to kiss her in her office! Even at home, she could never yield to a man who had the power to bring her to her knees.

Bleeding inside, Karen wrenched away from Brick. It took all the strength she had. More strength, in fact, than she'd believed she had within her.

Brick was breathing hard, and she could feel the power of his longing in the hands that gripped her once again. She could see confusion and despair in his eyes . . . and love for her in his virile face.

"Baby, don't tell me this isn't right." His voice was low and ripe with passion. He didn't command her. He beseeched. "I'd never press you if I didn't know you loved me, Kare. I won't give up unless you swear this isn't what you want."

Karen stepped back. She had to look away. She was flailing, struggling for her life. She could not meet his haunted eyes. If she weakened now, he'd win this battle. And if he won this battle, she'd lose the whole war.

Summoning all the strength she'd inherited from her father, Karen faced Brick with a mask of ice. In sharply measured tones, she decreed, "Lieutenant Bauer, you are out of line. Get out of my office. Report to duty tomorrow afternoon at four o'clock."

Abruptly his despair flared into anger. "The hell I will! Kare, we can't go on like this! I know this isn't the place to be kissing you—" once more he reached out and urgently grabbed her hand "—but I had to make you see—"

"What you have made me see, Lieutenant, is that you are capable of totally unprofessional behavior and willful disregard of the chain of command." She jerked her hand away from his, then leveled him with the frosty expression she reserved for unruly criminals. "I'm only going to say this once, so I suggest you commit it to memory." She leaned forward and dropped each word like a rock tumbling off the edge of a riverbank. "If you ever touch me like that again, Lieutenant Bauer, *I will have your badge.*"

CHAPTER NINE

IT WAS ALMOST 4:00 a.m. by the time Brick got back to his room. He realized, with still-festering anger, that if he had a home of his own, he wouldn't have to worry about running into his nemesis or his overly protective aunt, both of whom he'd encountered in the past at this time of night. He'd saved enough money to start building a house on some property he'd acquired by the lake, but what was the point? He didn't want to live alone out there. He wanted a passel of children. He wanted a wife.

He sure as hell didn't want the woman in the next room.

He closed the door softly and tossed his overcoat on the bed, grateful for his only reprieve of the long, terrible weekend—returning unseen tonight. It had been a hellish few hours—he'd driven more than a hundred miles in light snowfall trying to calm down—but he was tired now. Most of his rage had burned out, and he was almost ready to face whatever happened when he encountered Karen in the morning. He sure as hell wouldn't be surprising her with philodendrons and a cat! Karen—make that *the captain*—would either write up that humiliating incident for his file or simply freeze him out from now on. Either way, she would make his life unbearable. And either way, she would still tantalize him, beckon to him, make him ache as he lay alone each night in this damn empty bed.

He wasn't sure how he was going to deal with that problem in the long run, but he was sure of three things. He would not surrender his badge to Karen Keppler; he would not abandon Tyler; and he would never, ever touch her again.

He knew Karen well enough to know that her vehement display of anger in her office might have been just for show. And he knew himself well enough to realize that maybe he hadn't given her very much choice. But knowing that he'd backed her into a corner didn't do much to mollify Brick's feelings. For weeks Karen had been giving him hints that she wasn't any more satisfied with their platonic relationship than he was. She'd given him every sign she was ready to surrender to him tonight. He'd followed her unspoken lead and she'd kicked him in the shins. It wasn't a scene he was likely to forget.

Brick had just pulled off his shirt when the knock came on his outer door: soft, apologetic, beseeching. Aunt Anna. Had to be. Uncle Johnny wouldn't bother him in the middle of the night, and Karen wouldn't come near him tonight for love nor money.

He didn't have much money to offer her anyway, and she'd made it excruciatingly clear that she didn't want his love.

"Come in," he called out irritably. He'd just finished tugging off his shoes when the door opened, revealing a beautiful face framed in long black curls. It was the first time in weeks Karen had used the outer door instead of the one through the bathroom. Dressed in her bright pink bathrobe, she hovered on the threshold, twisting nervous circles in a clump of her magnificent hair. Her party clothes and makeup had vanished—like Cinderella's trappings after the ball—but the mere sight of her filled Brick with every damnable emotion he'd spent the past two hours trying to eradicate.

The nighttime chill—or his instinctive reaction to Karen?—brought goose bumps to Brick's bare arms and chest. He was tempted to slip his shirt back on, but the audacity of Karen's invasion of his private space filled him with fresh rage. "Get out," he barked.

"Brick—"

"Unless there's a police emergency that requires my attention, Captain Keppler," he growled, "get the hell out of my room."

"Brick, I just want—"

"I mean it." His fury was growing now. "This is my home, the place I live my personal life, and you've made it abundantly clear that you'd rather die than have any part of *that*." He took an angry step toward her, surprised that she looked so small and frozen out in the hallway, unwilling to barge into his room. "If you still want my badge, you'll have to wait till I report for duty."

For a long moment, his eyes met Karen's eyes, beautiful gray eyes that had once been able to—dear God, could they still?—move him so profoundly.

She took a deep breath as her gaze dropped to his naked chest, lingering a shade too long, then to the braided rug on the floor. "I'm sorry I disturbed you, Brick," she whispered in a small voice he'd never heard her use before. Quietly she shut the door.

Brick listened to Karen start back to her own room, her footsteps rushed and faltering.

The last thing in the world he wanted at the moment was another encounter with that fickle woman, but everything about their brief conversation struck him as wrong. Under the circumstances, Brick was astounded that she'd waited up for him, astounded that she'd sounded meek as a puppy, astounded that she'd come to his room at all. Had something terrible happened? Did she need his help? After what she'd done to him this evening, she'd have to be desperate to approach him.

Angrily he yanked open the door and followed her into the hall. "What the hell do you want?" he barked, worried now but still too tense to sound civil.

"It doesn't matter," Karen answered without turning around. "It's too late, anyway."

As she pushed open her own door, Brick grabbed her elbow, releasing it quickly when he remembered her last threat in the office that should have been his.

"Captain," he growled, "there must be some reason you found it necessary to come to my room in the middle of the night. I won't get any sleep until you tell me what it is."

He watched her shoulders straighten, watched her struggle for composure as she turned around. She faced him squarely, but her eyes were shiny, pooling with tears. The sight touched Brick in a way that took him by surprise. He had only seen Karen Keppler cry once before, and that was when she'd been quite ill. Whatever had happened since they'd last talked was clearly tearing her apart.

"I came to apologize for my... outburst this evening, Brick. I don't want you to worry about your position in Tyler because of our... misunderstanding." She stopped, gulped once or twice and finished clumsily, "I shouldn't have threatened you like that. I just didn't know how else to make my position clear."

"You made your position crystal clear," he barked at her. "The only thing that confuses me is why you showed up at my room tonight."

She blinked rapidly. One tear spilled over. "I can't bear it when you're mad at me." Karen tried to say the words with dignity, but they came out forced and desperate. "I want you to know that I'll miss you terribly. I'm sorrier than you know that I can't risk being your friend."

She moved quickly toward the safe haven of her room, but Brick was inside before she could shut the door.

"I don't want you in here," she ordered, the tears flowing freely now. "It's not appropriate and—"

"Karen, stop it! You've waited for hours to talk to me and you're falling apart at the seams. You're not making any sense. We've got to get things straight between us so we can go on working together."

"I wanted to apologize. I did." Pain riddled every syllable. "Now I want to forget the whole thing."

He stood in the dark, barely able to see her face by the dim light of her bedside lamp. But he could smell the soft scent of her, hear the sound of her stifled sobs.

"So do I," he admitted slowly, hating himself for wanting her all over again. "But I can't."

For a long, terrible moment, Karen did not reply, but she kept on weeping. He longed to take her in his arms, but he didn't dare. He couldn't count the times she'd given him every reason to believe she wanted him, then pushed him away at the very moment he'd been certain she was going to give in.

"Dammit, Kare, did I really read you so wrong?"

To Brick's astonishment, Karen leaned forward and rested her forehead against his bare chest. It jolted him like the most erotic of skin-to-skin contacts.

"Of course you didn't read me wrong," she confessed, her moist lips vibrating against his skin. "But you only read part of the book."

Gingerly he touched her shoulder. "Karen..."

"I want you. I admit it."

The words electrified him. His whole body surged with need. But the moisture of her tears robbed him of any joy he might have taken from her confession.

"I tried so hard not to let you know it, but I failed over and over again. When you kissed me in the office with Hedda out there and the radio squawking, I knew I couldn't tiptoe around it anymore. I couldn't even risk being your friend."

"Cripes, Karen, I went in there mad as hell. Hedda wouldn't have risked poking her nose inside! Besides, I locked the damn door! It wasn't as though—"

"You *reached* me, Brick." She was sobbing openly now, pressing her wet cheek against his chest. "When you stomped out of that office, you took something with you that I don't think I can get back again."

Brick shed the last of his common sense and wrapped his arms around her fiercely. He kissed the top of her head, her temple, her ear. Karen clung to him, still weeping, her nails digging into his ribs.

She lifted her face to his and whispered huskily, "Don't kiss me, Brick. Don't ever kiss me again."

He kissed her. She kissed him back. Her lips felt hot, wildly urgent. His lips were hotter still.

Brick's hands slipped up to Karen's neck, cradled it, while she pressed herself against him. He could feel every intimate curve of her body seeking every ridge of his own. He sizzled. She burned. The kiss went from soft to hard, from loving to aching, from tentative offer to demanding claim.

A full minute passed before Karen broke away from him.

"I mean it, Brick." Her lips still grazed his even as she spoke. Her yearning tongue bathed his, *begged* his, and it was some time before she could plead for his mercy again. "I don't want this," she insisted, still hugging him close. "I can't bear it. There's nowhere for it to go."

There's a bed right behind us. What other destination could their be? he longed to say. But he was already well past words. This horrible night had robbed him of all patience, all discretion, all restraint. He pulled on her sash, slipped one hand inside her bathrobe, cupped the firm round flesh of one breast hiding beneath the soft blue flannel gown.

Karen gasped. Brick tensed, afraid he'd gone too fast, but suddenly she was pressing herself against his thighs with a moan. He kneaded her turgid nipple between his thumb and his forefinger, fighting the overpowering urge to press her back against the mattress. Every line of her body told him she was fighting it, too.

"Bunkie," he confessed, "you have no idea how long I've wanted this. You fill me. You make me ache. You make me want things I—"

"Stop it, Brick." Her voice was desperately pleading now. She was clinging to his waist, struggling to undo his zipper. "I can't do this. I can't stop if you won't help me. Please, Brick. Please."

Brick would have honored her plea, but there was no doubt in his mind that Karen desperately wanted him to make love to her. Still, it bothered him that she kept begging him to stop while she was doing everything in her power to seduce him. Was this part of her erotic technique? Had she been teasing him all along to make him this hot? Or did she really believe that her very selfhood would be compromised if she took him to bed tonight?

Somehow Brick managed to release her breast, managed to still the searching hands at the front of his slacks. With one trembling arm he still held her tightly. Gently he kissed her forehead.

"Time out," he whispered hoarsely. "Just for a moment. I want you desperately, Karen, and not just for tonight. Don't play games with me. Tell me straight. I know it's vital not to get you pregnant, if that's what's worrying you. And I know we have to keep this under wraps, at least for now, but—"

"No. No, no, *no!*" Karen took a deep breath. She was still trembling, but she no longer pressed herself against him with such vigor. Still, she did not pull away.

She kissed his bare chest just once, her tongue lingering. Then she vowed painfully, "I can't make love with you, Brick. I wasn't putting up a smoke screen before. I thought you understood. No matter how much I want you, I simply *cannot* have an affair with a man under my command. Not and live with myself."

He struggled to control his hunger, his disappointment, his sudden surge of fresh rage. "What are you saying? I'm not good enough for you because you outrank me?"

She took his face in both quivering hands. "I want you more than I've ever wanted any man in my life. I respect you. I ache for you." Her voice was so low he could hardly hear her now. "I love you, Brick."

Something in him broke. With tender urgency he cupped her head against his shoulder. "Oh, God, Kare, I love you, too."

She gave his chest a half dozen more fierce, nipping kisses, then lifted her lips to his once more. Brick kissed her again, and her mouth sizzled as he plunged inside it. Everything sizzled for another few moments, but Karen stepped back once more when he tried to move her toward the bed.

Ready to explode, Brick opened his eyes and stared at her. Her hair was wildly askew and her face looked flushed with fear and desire.

"Please, Brick." Her voice was husky with anguish now. "I love you, but I *can't.*"

Brick felt so hot and hard he could have entered her right then, without another kiss or fondle; he was trembling so violently he could hardly stand. He sure as hell couldn't make sense of her contradictory protests.

"Brick, don't you understand? This isn't your decision! This is my life, my job, my self-respect." Now she sounded like the Karen he knew. Captain Keppler. The tyrant who never wavered from her position.

Desperately Brick took her face in his hands once more, but this time Karen pulled away and drew her bathrobe sash up tight. "I mean it, Brick," she pleaded, anguish and desperation lacing the words. "I want you to go while you still can."

Brick was too angry to speak, too aroused to leave. A thousand devils wrestled within him. He loved her and hated her, tried to believe her and tried not to. He took three deep breaths, struggling to steady himself, struggling to crawl out of her room.

Still, he might have reached for her one more time if she hadn't whispered, "Brick, if you stay here tonight, I'll hate you when the men find out." She fought back a sob. "Worse yet, I'll hate myself."

"HE'S GOING BACK to his own room now," Anna said to Johnny, snuggling closer in bed. "Do you think he was in there long enough for them to make up?"

Johnny sighed, wrapped a fond arm around his wife and shook his head. "I don't know, Anna. All I'm sure of is that it's nobody's business but Brick's and Karen's. Can't you leave them alone?"

"If they're happy, certainly. But Karen was at the station house till three o'clock and Brick stayed out till four! You can't tell me that everything's just hunky-dory between them!"

He absentmindedly ruffled her hair. "I didn't say everything was okay. I said it was none of our business. If Brick wants advice, he'll ask for it."

"Well, he did. He asked me to find out what shook up Alyssa so much the other day when she and Janice took cookies to Worthington House."

"When she saw Eddie, you mean?"

"No. I know why she's upset about Eddie, especially after Marge stuck her foot in her mouth tonight. I could have wrung her neck!" She snuggled closer as Johnny patted her back. "But Brick said it was something else about Phil that seemed to throw Alyssa into a tizzy. Brick said she went pale when Phil called her some Polish word."

"I didn't think Phil still spoke Polish to anybody. He never did use it much after his parents died."

"I don't think he speaks it often, but I've heard him use an old Polish saying or endearment from time to time. Besides, I don't think Brick cares what he called Alyssa. What bothered him is the way she reacted." For a long moment Anna was quiet, recalling Brick's exact words. Then she said to her husband, "Johnny, he's never asked me to do this before. I don't think I can help him. The price of family loyalty is too high if it means spying on my friends."

SOMEHOW KAREN MADE IT through the next two days. Unable to bear the memories that cloaked her office, she spent hours prowling the streets in her cruiser, and the sight of the newly married Mr. and Mrs. Patrick Kelsey standing on the church steps increased her gloom. She made a few drunk-driving arrests and told herself that if she'd kept some Tyler citizens from being killed in senseless accidents, she could be proud of her job. But her pride didn't do much to ease the memory of what had nearly transpired with Brick in her room.

The only bright spot of the whole terrible time was that Hedda, who was also single and had volunteered to work, had baked Karen some brownies. "I know you don't approve of celebrating Christmas in the office," she'd told her boss, "but I thought you might like something special when you go home."

Moved by the undeserved act of kindness, Karen had surprised Hedda by giving her a hug and asking her to share some of the brownies right on the spot. Hedda hadn't asked any questions about Karen's obvious unhappiness, but the crusty woman had been exceptionally kind to her from then on.

It was Hedda who relayed Karen's request to Brick later in the week that she wanted to see him when he came on duty. She knew she wasn't ready to face him alone in the confines of her office, but she had a job to do.

For the past few terrible days since Brick had left her room that morning, they had danced around each other, exchanging cool, proper greetings when they reluctantly came face-to-face. Once or twice Karen had issued an order, and Brick had replied with a terse "Yes, Captain" that had wounded her to the core.

Still, she couldn't blame him. What she had done— leading him on, in essence, when she'd known she could not possibly make love to him—had been inexcusable. She should have waited till morning to apologize; she should have stayed dressed; she should never have let him into her room. But those were superficial problems. Her big mistake was not that she had let him kiss her, but that she had let him ignite her carnal desires. Long before the night of the Christmas party Karen had known that she loved Brick, known that his virility called to her every female pore. Still, she had not expected to be wrenched off her very foundation with a single kiss. No man had ever moved her quite like that before.

He had told her he loved her. She believed him. Not because he'd begged her to make love with him, but because when he'd finally realized how desperately sorry Karen would be if she gave in, he had silently left her room. She would always be grateful to him for that . . . and for so many other things. Karen wanted to believe that she would have found the strength to send him away if he'd fought her that blazing night, but it was a theory she never wanted to test.

"You wanted to see me, Captain?" His voice was civil but devoid of warmth as he poked his head in the doorway. Not a hint of passion lurked in his cold blue eyes.

"Yes, Lieutenant. Please come in and close the door."

He did so—warily, it seemed to Karen.

"I wanted to discuss this report with you." She plucked it from her desk but did not thrust it at him.

"What report is that, Captain?" he asked coolly.

"The report on the bullet that was found in Margaret Ingalls's old room at Timberlake Lodge," she retorted. "You knew I'd want to know about that right away. Why didn't you mention it?"

Brick glared at her, his body so stiff he might as well have been standing at attention. "I filed my report the minute I returned from interrogating the subject, in accordance with staff notice 2B. I used the new form 5–67 on the new computer using the new program, which I have mastered on my own time. If I have failed to follow the captain's orders in some minuscule fashion, she should feel free to write me up and add it to—"

"Dammit, Brick! All I asked was a simple question!"

"Of course, Captain," he said crisply, refusing to lose control just because she had. "You asked why I did not mention my report to you personally. The answer is that I have never seen a memorandum that requires personal interaction between the captain and subordinate officers. In fact, it is my understanding that the captain frowns on such fraternization."

Karen stared at him bleakly, almost too sad to be angry. Thank God she'd had enough sense to start looking for a new place to live! With any luck at all, her realtor would confirm her arrangements any day. "Is this the way it's going to be?" she asked sadly.

"I don't write the rules, Captain. I merely follow them."

Karen didn't answer that. She wanted something she knew she couldn't have—a free, friendly relationship with Brick that allowed them both to savor the joys of a platonic relationship without any of the risks of becoming lovers. She wanted to strangle her libido, but it was a hopeless task.

"Lieutenant, your report indicates that you went to the Forrester home in response to a request from Liza Forrester. Did that call come into the station for you in particular, or was it directed to anyone?"

"It was not a call, Captain. Mrs. Forrester herself told me at the Christmas party I attended at Timberlake Lodge that she had some information that might be relevant to an ongoing police investigation and asked me to continue our conversation privately at my earliest convenience. I went to see her the very next day."

He made this announcement without expression, but Karen knew he hadn't forgotten what he'd been doing in the wee small hours of that morning. Just the thought of it made her body twitch with a leftover pulse of passion. Desperately she hoped that her still-potent need of Brick didn't show on her face.

"So Liza wanted to talk to the police, and you took it on yourself—"

"Correction, Captain. Mrs. Forrester wanted to talk to *me*. She was quite precise."

Karen didn't press it. Instead she asked, "And she admitted that she'd been withholding evidence?"

Brick's eyes narrowed. "She did no such thing. She reported that a workman had located the bullet during the lodge renovations recently and turned it over to her. The party preparations pushed everything else out of her mind. Apparently seeing us at the party jogged her memory."

Thinking of the lodge jogged Karen's memory, too: sometime in that night of hazy passion and shame, she'd spilled a full glass of punch on the Ingallses'—or Eddie's—beautiful Oriental rug, and she'd forgotten to ask Anna to whom she owed both apologies and the price of the cleaning. Once, she would have asked Brick, but she didn't dare speak a word more than necessary to him now.

"Do you believe Liza?" Karen asked straightforwardly. She didn't. She suspected that her own recent visit to Liza—when she'd grilled the other woman about the old suitcase stolen from the potting shed—had caused her to decide to reveal some previously concealed information.

Brick's eyes were cold. "The facts are in my report, Captain."

"I read the report. I am trying to glean the impressions and opinions that a skilled officer can provide even though he cannot document them and therefore does not commit them to paper."

"Memorandum 6–C clearly states that personal opinions have no place in police science. I therefore have nothing but facts to offer orally or in writing. If my report is unclear, Captain—"

"It's clear. Liza gave you a bullet that we can't match unless we have a weapon. We can't find a weapon unless we have a search warrant, and we can't issue a search warrant unless we have enough evidence to bring somebody in.''

Brick did not reply. His eyebrows did not even twitch.

"I think someone close to Margaret did it. Probably her husband. But I'm a long way from proving it. If you have any reason to think that a member of the Ingalls family has additional pertinent information about this matter, it is your duty to tell me, Lieutenant.''

Brick's lips tightened. "I know my duty, Captain. Page 24.4 of the *Police Manual* states that—''

"All right! You win! Get out of here!'' Karen took a deep breath, slammed the report in the to-be-filed basket and grabbed a letter that had arrived in the morning's mail. She was just about to start writing a response when she realized that Brick hadn't moved toward the door. She did not look at him; she was still too angry to speak.

Surely he knew they couldn't carry on like this! She would have to give very serious thought to how to handle him in a way that would be both professional and fair. He had a right to be angry, but he was taking things too far.

"Captain?'' His voice was softer now...or at least more civil.

Her eyes met his defiantly. "What do you have to say, Lieutenant?''

"If there's some deep, dark secret that the Ingalls clan has been hiding all these years, I'm not privy to it. I think that finding the body has aroused a lot of slumbering memories that may or may not be related to the crime itself—I'm using my own sources to pursue that information—but I don't believe any of the family was directly involved in Margaret's death."

His voice was still low, still uncomfortable. But at least he was speaking to her as though she were a human being and not something he'd just scraped off his shoe.

"If Judson Ingalls killed his wife, I'm certain it was an accident," Brick vowed. "I know this man. He's not perfect. He might be capable of doing something stupid in a fit of rage—God knows that woman could have driven a saint to violence—but he loved her and grieved for her for decades. Under no circumstances would he have planned her murder. I'd stake my badge on it."

His unofficial report was a gift, and Karen took it as such. "Thank you for your input, Lieutenant," she said quietly.

"Just doing my job, Captain. When push comes to shove, I'll always be a cop."

There were any number of ways Karen could have taken his comment. Professionally, they all were positive. Personally, they all meant he'd finally accepted her decree. The realization should have made her happy.

Carefully Karen said, "Lieutenant, I don't want to make things difficult for you, and I'm sure you don't want to make them hard for me. As long as we don't let our personal relationship interfere with our professional obligations, I think we'll be able to work together just fine."

The brief illusion of camaraderie vanished in an instant. "Captain, we have no personal relationship,"

Brick answered tonelessly. "We have no relationship whatsoever."

He might as well have shot her right through the heart.

CHAPTER TEN

ANNA ANSWERED the phone on the fourth ring. She'd called out for Johnny to get it before she remembered that he was in the family room with Brick, Pam and Patrick, who were glued to the television while one brawny bunch of cleated fellows stomped over another brawny set. Normally it was a happy occasion for the group. Anna, who had no interest in football unless one of her boys was playing, spent the time preparing an enormous Sunday dinner.

But nobody was very happy in the family room today, because Brick had been acting like a bear with a sore paw ever since Christmas. That was a good two weeks ago, and the holidays were now behind them. But whatever had happened between Brick and Karen had clearly not been resolved.

Not once since then had Anna seen the two of them together. Poor Karen looked pale and Brick looked like death warmed over. Both of them had parried her attempts to get them to share their feelings.

It was obvious that they couldn't go on this way.

"Hello, dear." It was Martha Bauer's cheery voice on the phone. "I just heard a bit of news I thought you should know. I hope it won't be too distressing."

"Oh?"

"You know that little gal you've got staying with you? The one who plays cops and robbers with Donald?"

Anna knew Karen would shudder at the description, but she was too interested in Martha's gossip—and a little bit concerned—to take her mother to task. "Yes?"

"Well, Hobart Rameson was over here this morning when he brought Tillie back from church. He's such a good son-in-law, you know. Every Sunday—"

"Mother, what did Hobart say?" Anna was growing worried now. Hobart was a Realtor. If Karen had been to see him—

"She called him on Christmas Eve. Told him to find her a cute little house to buy or rent just as soon as possible. Tillie told me that Hobart says Karen sounded downright desperate to get out of your house. I know there can't be anything wrong with your hospitality, dear. I imagine she's had some sort of lover's spat with Donald."

Anna figured that was the understatement of the century. "Has Hobart had any luck?" she asked. "We don't have that many small houses for sale in Tyler."

"No, we don't. But Tillie's next-door neighbor had a stroke last month and may be in Worthington House to stay. Hobart got her to agree to lease the house to Karen with an option to buy if she can't go home in a year."

Anna closed her eyes as she waited for the news that would break Brick's heart.

"The lease begins on January fifteenth. She'll be moving out next weekend."

AUNT ANNA WAS GENTLE when she told Brick the news, but he still wanted to bang his head against a wall. Oh, he knew Karen had done him a favor. The Kelseys were his people. She was the one who had to leave. Hadn't he told her that the night she'd moved in? How he'd hated her then! Now he lay awake, night after night, listening to Karen toss and turn in the bed she'd so savagely denied to him. The days were even worse, when keeping the cruelest emotional distance from her seemed to be the only way Brick could survive. If he gave an inch, he'd be on his knees to her, begging her to surrender to him all over again.

If the problem had merely been sex, he could have tripled his workout time and found some way to ignore it. But it was so much more than that. He ached for Karen in a way he could not explain, because he'd never hurt for a woman quite this way before. He had grown accustomed to living with her, side by side, day by day, in a quiet kind of marriage that went far beyond the delights of sex or the demands of the job. It was pure hell to have her so near and yet so brutally far away.

Yes, he was glad she was going. But dammit, why did his grandmother's news make him feel like some giant sport fish speared through the heart?

ON WEDNESDAY NIGHT, Karen was still awake when Brick came in after his late shift. She was always awake, always listening, always worried about how much she'd hurt him, worried about how much he'd hurt her. And, because he was a cop, even in a little burg like Tyler, she was always worried that something might happen to him.

There didn't seem to be any solution to their problem. At first, when Brick became so stiff and angry, Karen had almost been relieved. Anything had seemed easier than fending off his incredibly potent kisses. But over time the relief had faded and the pain was growing worse. Karen was once more starting to seek some magical middle ground where they could each give some kind of platonic succor without unbearable guilt.

She was lying in bed, fighting a twinge of recurrent pain in her scarred left shoulder, when she heard Brick's footsteps on the stairs around 1:00 a.m. The tantalizing aroma of pepperoni wafted through the cracks under the door. Following her instincts, Karen jumped out of bed, taking a moment to pull on jeans and a T-shirt. After their previous middle-of-the-night fiasco, the last thing she wanted to do was go to his room in her bathrobe.

Karen reached Brick's door just as he was closing it. He spotted her and opened the door a crack, scowling. "What do you want? Trouble at the station house?"

She shook her head, hating his dry indifference. "I woke up to the smell of pizza," she declared with forced gaiety. "The temptation is killing me. Got enough for two?"

Brick looked surprised, but nonetheless tore off a couple of joined sheets from the roll of paper towels under his arm. Without a single wasted motion, he tugged three pieces of pizza out of the box, laid them on the paper towels and thrust them in her direction. Then he asked coldly, "Is there anything else that won't wait till I'm back on duty, Captain?"

Gravely she met his eyes, struggled for words to break the impasse. "When my father worked swing shift, he never could go right to sleep. He liked to watch TV or read for a while. He loved it if I was still awake when he came in. Then we'd sit and talk about all kinds of things.''

A wash of pain darkened Brick's weary features. Karen could see his stubbled jaw tighten.

He hasn't forgotten the passion that singed us the one time we broke all the rules. She hugged the thought to herself. *He didn't lie when he confessed his love for me.*

Darkly he warned, "I'm not your father, Captain." He started to close the door again.

"Brick—" he opened the door once more "—I wanted to tell you about some more evidence I found pertaining to Margaret Ingalls's death."

His eyes narrowed. "Evidence?"

"I think so." Actually, Karen wasn't sure whether she'd found any evidence or not, but her serendipitous discovery might keep him listening for a few more minutes. "Do you remember that I spilled some punch on that Oriental rug at the lodge on Christmas Eve?"

He winced as though the memory were one he'd like to forget.

"I remember."

"Well, by the time I thought to ask Anna who I should discuss it with, Alyssa had already sent it to the cleaners. So I called the cleaners to intercept the bill, and as soon as I mentioned the spill, this guy—"

"Joe Campbell."

"Right, Joe Campbell. He said that he'd had to send the rug to Sugar Creek for special treatment. The punch was no problem, but it would cost extra for the blood. And I said, 'What blood?' because I didn't remember anybody getting hurt while I was there."

"Nobody got hurt before I left, either."

"Exactly. Nobody got hurt at all. I asked Anna that after he told me that he thought the blood was really old and dried up."

Brick looked tired, frustrated . . . maybe even bored. "So?"

"So, Anna called Alyssa, and guess what?" This was the climax of the story. She didn't have any other tantalizing secrets to keep him from slamming the door in her face.

"What?" he asked irritably.

"I found out that the rug used to be in Margaret's room. It was rolled up years ago—not too long after she disappeared—and nobody even looked at it again until Liza started remodeling. I think—"

"I know what you think," Brick said coolly. "You think there's a good chance that Margaret's blood is on that rug, and you think the coroner in Sugar Creek can match it to bone marrow he can extract from her skeleton. You know what I think?"

"What?"

He stepped back into his room. "I think you could have waited until morning to tell me about it."

Karen couldn't stifle the terrible wash of pain his rejection caused her. Neither could she stop herself from grabbing the doorknob.

"Oh, Brick, I know you're tired. But can't we just . . . talk . . . the way we used to? When we were friends?"

He stared at her bleakly, looking more sad than angry now. "No, we can't." His tone left no room for argument.

Karen blinked back an unexpected tear. "Please, Brick. I hate this tension between us. I miss you."

His jaw twitched. He didn't say he missed her, too. "I hear you're moving out this weekend. That hardly sounds like you're longing for my company. You really hurt my aunt's feelings by not telling her up front."

Karen swallowed hard. "I told her the very day my plans were confirmed. It's not my fault that some old biddy beat me to the punch."

Now he positively glowered. "That 'old biddy' is my grandmother! You remember—the one who so lovingly made your little angel cop?"

He might as well have hit her with a baseball bat. The last thing she'd intended to do was insult his grandmother! "You know why I have to leave so quickly, Brick." Karen's voice dropped to a hushed whisper. "I'm doing it as much for you as for me."

His gaze fell to the floor. "Your living quarters are none of my business, Captain. I don't give a damn where you reside." Again he tried to shut the door.

"You can't have forgotten the friendship we once had, Brick," she pleaded, pushing the door open with her foot. Even his anger was better than this! "You can't tell me that you're that fickle a human being. One minute you're my colleague, then my friend, you say you want to be my lover and then...you hate me? What should I believe?"

"Believe any damn thing you want. It's got nothing to do with me!"

Karen pulled back as though he'd hit her. Then she handed back the pizza, knowing she'd never be able to get down a bite. "Forgive me for troubling you, Brick."

She was almost to the door before she heard him say bitterly, "Captain?"

She stopped, grateful that he'd called her back, even if he still refused to call her by her name.

"You can't have your cake and eat it, too."

Karen turned around and faced him. "I'm not asking for a miracle, Brick. Just a little civility, a little warmth. When I first came here you treated me like dirt, and I could bear it, because you meant nothing to me and I knew I meant nothing to you. But now that we've shared so much, it kills me when you treat me like Typhoid Mary."

For a long moment he was silent. A thousand demons warred on his rugged face. At last he said almost gently, "I'm sorry you're hurting, Captain. I wish I could help you."

The surrender in his low tone wounded her unbearably—how badly she'd hurt this wonderful man—but it also filled her with hope. Karen took a step toward him again, knowing she had to keep her distance, longing to pull him close.

"Please, Brick," she whispered, unable to hide the wrenching pain inside her. "I can't go on like this."

He jammed both hands deep into his pockets, as though he could not restrain himself from touching her. She waited, aching, while he slowly met her eyes. The anguish she saw there shook her to the core.

"Captain," he hoarsely confessed, "I can't go on any other way."

THURSDAY AFTERNOON Brick was getting ready to go talk to a woman whose store had been robbed—by the crooks in the blue van again—when Karen poked her head out of her office and called, "Lieutenant? I need you in here."

He moved toward her stiffly, wondering how to keep her at bay this time. Their encounter last night had been nip and tuck. The anger that had kept him going since Christmas had cooled to the ashes of despair.

As he reached the doorway, Karen whispered, "We've got trouble, Brick. For Tyler's sake, try to put aside your hatred of me for the next few minutes. You can always go back to being nasty later."

The plea shocked him. Put so baldly, it made him ashamed of the way he'd been treating Karen. It also made him wonder about the trouble she now faced. She must be pretty desperate to seek his help.

Brick was surprised to discover that the civilian in Karen's office was a man his own age dressed in a well-cut navy suit and a blue-striped tie. His dark chestnut complexion and angular features hinted at some Indian ancestry, probably Menominee or Winnebago if he was local. His thick black hair was clean and shiny, but too long for the current yuppie fashion. Either he'd been too busy to get a haircut for a while, Brick guessed, or he was deliberately letting it grow in the way of his people.

"Nice to meet you," Michael Youngthunder said pleasantly when Karen introduced him. He stood to shake Brick's hand.

"Likewise." Brick was about to ask how he could help the man when he remembered that he was number two on this totem pole. It would not do to wrest power from Karen's hands.

"Lieutenant, Mr. Youngthunder plans to seek a court order stopping the planned ground-breaking of the new wing of Timberlake Lodge. He is concerned that the expansion may encroach on a Winnebago burial ground."

Brick wasn't sure what to say to that. All his life he'd heard rumors of an Indian burial ground in the area, but Tyler had an impressive collection of tall tales about its past. Nobody took them seriously.

Unsure of what direction Karen wanted him to take, he offered, "The original lodge was built fifty years ago, Mr. Youngthunder. Surely if there was a burial ground in the area, someone would have voiced concern then."

Youngthunder shook his head. The shoulder-length hair moved with him, reminding Brick of a movie he'd seen starring a vigorous long-haired brave brandishing a tomahawk. This brave brandished his deep and powerful voice. He'd come armed with intelligence and conviction.

"Someone voiced concern, but no one listened. The Winnebagos were invisible to bureaucrats then." His words were quiet, but they seemed to lend inches to his already considerable height. "Now we have laws to protect us. Once again we have people with the will to fight for what is ours."

Brick sensed the quiet determination of the man and realized that he would not be easy to brush aside. Oddly enough, he didn't really want to. Hotheaded radicals always made him angry, no matter what their cause, and he'd assumed that Youngthunder was just another one. But now he had to reconsider.

Still, he knew why Karen was worried. This visit was not an idle act of a renegade. It was a probe, a first step, a symbolic act for a much larger group of people. If Tyler handled Michael Youngthunder well, no more might come of it. If somebody botched things badly, there would be hell to pay, with or without proof of a burial ground. It would make no difference to the Winnebagos, let alone to the press.

Youngthunder turned back to Karen. "I don't want to get arrested. I don't want to cause a scene. All I want to do is make sure that no sacred bones of my people are disturbed by this renovation. I want to stop the construction process legally, just long enough to verify that it won't impact the burial ground."

Karen moved around to her desk, sat down and gestured for the men to do likewise. Both followed suit.

"Mr. Youngthunder, what evidence do you have that there is a Winnebago burial ground in that specific area?"

A look of great sorrow passed over his face as he replied, "My grandfather says there is a burial ground north of Tyler."

Karen waited. Brick watched her closely. Paul Schmidt would have leaned back in his chair, lit up a cigar and said, "Now, son, my grandpappy had his fair share of stories, too. But me and you know . . ."

"Does he know for sure that it's on Judson Ingalls's—or, rather, Eddie Wocheck's—land?" Karen asked, as though Youngthunder's grandfather had produced voluminous evidence to verify his facts. Brick had to admit that when it came to this Indian, Karen's sober approach seemed to be more effective than Paul Schmidt's good-ol'-boy humor.

Youngthunder shook his head. "He is an old man, Captain Keppler, and very frail. He has not visited our ancestral land for many years. What he remembers is a cluster of oaks in the shape of a horseshoe. When he sees it, he says he will know. I am just the scout."

Karen met Brick's eyes. For the first time in days, he saw no anger there, no fear. He saw a police captain who trusted the instincts of her men. "Are there any clusters of oaks in the shape of a horseshoe at the lodge, Lieutenant?" she asked.

Brick thought a minute, then shook his head. "No, not that I recall."

"Are you familiar with the land surrounding Timberlake Lodge?"

"Yes, I am." He didn't see any point in mentioning that three years ago he'd purchased a piece of land in the area on which he planned to build his dream house—a house that he couldn't even design until he found his dream woman and was ready to start a family. He didn't go out there to visit much anymore. Nowadays it represented a dream that seemed to be slipping away from him.

Just like the woman before him.

"The trees are sparse near the buildings, but very dense around the lake. There's a nice meadow or two where we used to have picnics. As you circle out, it's mainly dairy country."

Karen's eyes were still on him, waiting, watching . . . trusting him. "What else?"

"Most of the former Ingalls land lies to the north. There are six or seven tourist cabins in that area. Due south is a dairy farm that belongs to the Gerhardts."

"That's it?"

He thought about it. "No. On the other side of the lodge is the old Meyer place. It pretty much went to seed when the old folks died off, but Renata still owns it. She checked in every now and then while she was in art school, back when I first started on the force. Last time I saw her she said she'd move back out here someday, but right now she's still in Milwaukee."

Youngthunder was watching him intently now. "I only want to look, sir. If I cannot find anything that resembles a horseshoe of oak trees, then I will know that the burial ground is farther west, or the trees have been cut down." He did not mention the possibility that his grandfather could be mistaken.

Now Karen said carefully, "What you're asking for is carte blanche to examine a great deal of private property without any legal authorization. I'm not certain that all the owners will approve."

Youngthunder's face darkened. A note of bitterness crept into his tightly controlled voice. "I am here to seek legal authorization. I could have come in the night. I could have invaded the privacy of these people who claim to own Winnebago land. Instead I came to the police as a law-abiding American citizen." He looked at Brick, then back at Karen. "Most things can be arranged with the right words in advance. Surely these people will let me search for the burial ground if they understand that I mean no harm."

Brick knew what the man was really saying: *I would prefer to do it legally, but if I can't, I will do it the other way.* He seemed too rational to take the risk. Brick almost had the feeling that searching for the burial ground was something he did not want to do. He spoke like a man who had no choice.

Youngthunder leaned toward Karen now, both elbows resting on her desk. In a low, unhappy tone he said, "Captain, please understand. I want no trouble, but I will not turn aside if trouble stands in the way of my duty. I promised my grandfather I would find that horseshoe of oaks and protect the dead who are buried there. He feels it is his duty to his ancestral clan."

It was obvious that his grandfather's conviction made it Youngthunder's duty, too.

Karen studied Youngthunder thoughtfully. "Surely most of your grandfather's clan are long since dead."

"Exactly, Captain," Youngthunder agreed, his dark eyes meeting hers forcefully. "They have no one left to speak for them."

An eerie silence filled the room, a silence that somehow bound the three people of the present with a thousand souls of the past. Brick saw Karen struggle with the problem Youngthunder had tossed in her lap. Her mournful gray eyes met Brick's sadly as she realized he was watching her. He had always known how much he missed her. Now, as he thought about her plea for his friendship last night, he realized how much she missed him.

Brick had dozens of close friends in Tyler. Karen didn't have a soul outside the warmth of the boardinghouse. She was going to miss casual dinners with Johnny, Zachary and Eddie. She'd even come to enjoy spunky Tisha. Anna was becoming her dear friend. And secretly Brick still believed that Karen loved him.

Suddenly he wanted to throw Youngthunder out of the room and seize Karen in his arms. He wanted to tell her that he loved her, loved her desperately, that he had a little patch of land waiting for the two of them to build a home on. Other men on the force dated professional women! Paul Schmidt had encountered no censure when he'd married after his first wife died. Surely—

Karen's phone rang, abruptly puncturing the silence and interrupting the bizarre trail of Brick's thoughts. She answered on the first ring, gave a short reply, then stood up. "If you'll excuse me for a moment, Mr.

Youngthunder, I have an emergency. Lieutenant Bauer, please make whatever quiet arrangements you can to help Mr. Youngthunder find his burial ground.''

Brick was surprised by the trust she'd placed in him; it was the first time she'd tacitly admitted that he knew things she didn't about Tyler's land and people. Bit by bit Karen had learned to trust Brick's instincts, but she'd never before acknowledged that he could, in his own way, be more effective than she in grappling with a given problem.

As Karen left, Youngthunder watched Brick with knowing eyes. ''Well, Lieutenant, she is the boss, but you and I both know that you are the only one who can help me. This is your town. These are your people. You can ask them for a favor. The captain can only order them to comply.''

It was true, but Brick felt a curious need to uphold Karen's authority. ''She outranks me, Youngthunder. I know it may be hard for you to imagine that a woman would hold such a position, but . . .''

To Brick's surprise, Youngthunder grinned. He had clear white teeth and a surprisingly boyish smile for a man with such sad eyes and such a sternly handsome face. ''It is obviously hard for *you* to imagine, Lieutenant Bauer, but it is easy for me.''

Brick was taken aback. ''Why is it easier for you?''

Youngthunder's grin widened. ''For two reasons. In the first place, my great-grandmother was a great Winnebago chief.''

''The Winnebago let women be chiefs?'' Brick asked incredulously, trying to imagine Martha Bauer wielding a tomahawk.

The dark eyes seemed to laugh at Brick's dismay. ''Each chief is determined by clan, and certain leadership roles within each clan belong to our women." He straightened with unmistakable pride. "We are Thunderbird."

Brick hadn't a clue as to why belonging to the Thunderbird clan was so important to the man, but he didn't think this was the right time to ask. He had a more important question on his mind. "You said there were two reasons why it was easier for you to think of a woman as a chief than it was for me. What was the second?"

Now Youngthunder chuckled, a warm and happy sound that made Brick hope he could get Eddie, Renata Meyer and the other folks who owned cabins out by the lake to let him search for the horseshoe of oak trees. "When I look at Captain Keppler," Youngthunder explained, "I see a competent police officer. When you look at her, her uniform keeps sliding off."

Brick's jaw dropped. He was too surprised to lie. "How did you know? Not that anything's ever happened—"

"Oh, I think a great deal has happened," Youngthunder corrected him. "At least in your heart." He stood up and headed toward the door, surprising Brick by handing him a respectable-looking business card with an admonition to call when he'd made the arrangements. "I don't know why the two of you are trying to hide what is obvious to a man with keen eyes. Everybody will know the lay of the land soon enough." He shook Brick's hand as he teased, "If I felt that way about a woman, I would take her to my lodge."

IT WAS ABOUT three o'clock on Friday when Steve Fletcher poked his head into Karen's office and said,

"Captain Keppler? Clayton and Franklin just found something kind of odd."

"Odd, how?" she asked, realizing with a curious sense of pleasure that his tone sounded almost friendly and respectful. In the beginning, the sergeant had opposed her almost as vigorously as Brick had. Nowadays Steve seemed pleased that she frequently turned to him.

With Brick barely speaking to her, Karen didn't have much choice. Cindy Lou still walked on eggshells around her, though since Christmas Hedda didn't seem to be giving her such a wide berth. Orson Clayton had lost so much weight that Karen had risked telling him how great he looked, and he'd grinned from ear to ear as he'd reported he'd had to buy some uniforms in a smaller size. The other men were respectful but restrained in her presence. She couldn't tell whether any of them suspected what was going on in her heart.

As she thought about the way Brick had looked at her during their meeting with Michael Youngthunder, she wondered what was going on in *his* heart. They had seemed perfectly in sync regarding the Winnebago's plea.

Michael Youngthunder was the sort of man who did not forget the values he'd been taught by his family, the sort of man to whom integrity was law. *Why couldn't I fall for a hunk like Michael?* Karen challenged herself. *He's handsome. He's deep. He's determined but respectful. The only thing wrong with him is that he's not Brick.*

But that was just the point. She couldn't fall in love with a man who did not move her profoundly, and she didn't dare yield to one who was ready to claim her soul. Ever since she'd met Brick, she'd felt her tough self-control slipping away from her. If he'd been a different sort of man, he could have—would have—destroyed her career by now.

"It's a suitcase," said Steve, snapping Karen back to reality. "Looks like it's fallen out of a car or maybe been tossed."

She watched him closely. "So?"

His eyes narrowed. "The clothes inside are totally rotted. Disintegrated. Like they've been soaked and left to molder in there for a hundred years. And here's the corker. It's got brass initials—M.L.I.—on the side."

"M.L.I.?" she repeated. It took a moment, but then Karen followed his line of thought. "What was Margaret Ingalls's middle name, Sergeant?"

He lifted his hands and grinned. "Lindstrom."

Karen grinned back. "Where is it?"

"In the evidence room. We were afraid to fuss with the insides much. Everything's so fragile."

"Good work, Sergeant," she praised him sincerely, pleased to see him glow. "Call Lieutenant Bauer and ask him to drop by and check it out when he gets a chance, would you?" It was Brick's day off, but Karen knew he wouldn't mind coming in. Besides, it would be a lot smarter to discuss the suitcase with him during the busy hour when the shifts were changing than in the isolated danger zone of her last night in their mutual home.

It took Steve a while to locate Brick, who showed up at the station house about seven. He went directly to the evidence room to examine the suitcase, then popped in to see Karen.

Under his ski jacket he was wearing his usual off-duty clothes—jeans and a Packers sweatshirt—but his skin had a vigorous glow that had been noticeably absent lately. He almost looked happy. Karen wanted to ask him how he spent his spare time these days, but she knew it was a personal question ... which made it off-limits. She certainly couldn't ask him if her greatest fear was true—that he might have found somebody else to take her place.

"Let me show it to Judson, Captain," Brick suggested. "I think there's a good chance it's Margaret Ingalls's. It looks like it used to be a very expensive piece of luggage. The clothes aren't fit for a rummage sale now, but they were once very stylish. There's a fancy felt hat with three gold feathers that I'm sure I've heard somebody mention before."

Karen wasn't wearing a feathered hat, but she'd dressed up in a crisp black suit today because she'd had to make a presentation at a local service club's lunchtime meeting. As she met Brick's eyes, she realized that she was searching for some sign of admiration for her posh look, and after a tense moment, she got it. Brick didn't say anything out loud, but his gaze took in her entire outfit, from her ruffled blouse to her fashionable boots, before he nodded once in silent approbation.

Suddenly Karen felt delicate and pretty—a warning, if there ever was one, that she should quickly send Brick on his errand. Still, she was tempted to go along with him to judge Judson's reaction to the suitcase herself.

Is that really why you want to go, Karen? an inner voice taunted. *Or are you simply losing the will to resist him?*

"If this is Margaret's suitcase, it would lend credence to Judson's claim that she left a note and was planning to leave him," Brick said thoughtfully.

"A note nobody ever saw," Karen pointed out, struggling to keep her mind on business. "An intention she never mentioned to anybody else."

"A logical intention if she was playing around, Karen."

Her eyes flashed up as she heard her name; it was the first time Brick had called her anything but "Captain" since the night he'd aroused her to the edge of no return. Struggling to forget the feel of his hands, Karen said, "If she was about to leave him for another man— not a bad theory, considering what we know of her— that only gives Judson a better motive for murder. He could have killed her and faked the note."

"He couldn't have faked the suitcase. It's been out in that potting shed for decades, all right. Nobody can fake that sort of mold and decay."

"Oh, I don't doubt that it's been out there all this time. But who's to say Margaret Ingalls packed that suitcase forty years ago? Judson could have done it to back up his story that she ran away. Think about it. It's possible."

Brick took a deep breath. *Anything's possible, bunkie,* his eyes seemed to say. *You're the one who wrote these awful rules. You're the one who can change them.*

Karen told herself she was imagining his mute message. They'd put all this behind them, hadn't they?

"It's possible that somebody else packed it, too," Brick continued prosaically. "Somebody other than Judson could have known that Margaret was planning to leave him and could have used the same logic to stage a cover-up when he killed her."

"Or she."

To Karen's surprise, he gave her a small smile, that damned dimpled smile that always rocked her. In spite of her firm resolutions, her heart did a tiny back roll, and in the emptiness of her secret woman's place she felt a hot rush of awareness of what she'd sacrificed when she'd turned this magnificent man away.

"If Margaret had a lover, he might have been married, too." Karen raised her eyebrows. "Hell hath no fury, and all that."

"Anything's possible," Brick agreed, leaning almost casually against her desk. *You and I, for instance. Haven't you had enough time to change your mind?*

Fiercely Karen told herself she was imagining his unspoken pleas tonight. Surely he wouldn't try to seduce her again after all this time!

Karen couldn't put her finger on it, but there *was* a change in him this evening. He seemed curiously content. Not exactly smug or hopeful, but somehow satisfied. His face wasn't marred by those deep lines of fatigue she'd grown accustomed to lately. Maybe he wasn't seeing somebody else. Maybe he was just relieved because she was moving out tomorrow.

As she studied his broad chest and tough-tender eyes, Karen sadly acknowledged that it would take a lot more than a change of lodging for her to get over Brick. She could change jobs, change professions, change *countries,* and it wouldn't make much difference. He'd burrowed his way deep into her heart where no man had gone before, and he was hunkered down to stay. What she'd give to find a way to have room in her life for police work and Brick Bauer at the same time! He wasn't a passing fancy, a mere temptation to indulge in a hot—

"Look, Karen, I don't know what you've got in mind—"

"About what?"

Her alarm seemed to surprise him. "About confronting Judson. Do you think it's important that you go by yourself?"

"I…intended to send you, Lieutenant," she told him honestly. "I once suspected that your intimacy with the family would impede this investigation, but I've come to see that it might be a useful key to solving it."

Brick looked touched. "I'm honored, Captain." His voice dropped a notch as he added, "Might I suggest that we go together when you wrap things up here? Even when we don't plan it, we seem to be quite effective playing good cop/bad cop. I think that might work to our advantage in this situation."

Karen stood up, met his eyes, then glanced away as she realized how clearly he could read her feelings. She was weakening again, wounded by the vision of moving to an empty house when they'd once shared such happy times in their tiny second-floor home. It was always dangerous to be alone with Brick…doubly so on this last night. But how much worse could a simple car ride be than sleeping next door to him every night, aching for the feel of his hands on her breasts?

Gingerly she offered, "I guess we do make a pretty good team."

Karen knew it was a mistake the minute the words were out of her mouth. Brick gave her that lazy, dimpled smile—broad and happy this time—as he drawled, "We do, Kare. We make a damn fine twosome."

His eyes told her he wasn't talking about police work. Her pulse told her he had something else in mind tonight.

BRICK DROVE UP to the Ingalls place at seven-forty-five with Karen by his side. He'd spent most of the afternoon secretly setting up his surprise at her new home. Tillie's neighbor's son had already moved all of the elderly lady's furniture into storage, which meant that Karen expected to move into an empty house. In her desperation to get away from Brick, she'd actually planned to spend her first night on the floor in a sleeping bag. She'd told Anna that she intended to purchase furniture over the weekend. Brick told himself he was just saving her a little time and money.

But his selections from the Kelseys' basement had not been made at random, and the extra touches he'd added would have been a surprise to his aunt. Michael Youngthunder had probably not been serious when he'd suggested that Brick take Karen to his lodge, but the Winnebago's comment had started him thinking—not about the dead ends that were closed off to him, but about the options neither he nor Karen had yet considered. Over and over again Brick had thought about their situation: the sense of home they'd once experienced in their virtual shared suite, the incredible emptiness that would assail him when she moved out tomorrow, the loneliness that would swallow her up in that vacant house tomorrow night. And in the wee small hours of the morning, Brick had suddenly realized that he had to find a way to keep her by his side.

If he couldn't take Karen to his lodge, he'd take his lodge to Karen.

He was glad to have some time alone with her tonight to spell out his long-term plans. Such openness would probably be a mistake, but some mistakes were unavoidable. And just about any mistake was preferable to losing Karen altogether.

Brick carried the decrepit suitcase up the well-shoveled walk and rang the bell, feeling guilty about coming to Judson's house as a cop in pursuit of evidence that might ultimately convict him. Karen stood perfectly still beside him but did not speak. She was so close he could smell her clean soapy scent. So close he could have leaned down and kissed her if she'd turned her head.

He wanted to kiss her. He wanted to kiss her desperately. But somehow he found the strength to face the other way.

"Why, Brick!" Alyssa said as she opened the door, her kind blue eyes lacking their usual warmth when she spotted Karen. "What a pleasure to see you."

"Good to see you, too, Alyssa. You remember Captain Keppler?"

Now Alyssa's eyes were definitely guarded. "Of course, Captain. Please come in—and let me take your coats."

After divesting themselves of this winter wear, they walked silently to the living room. Brick was still carrying the suitcase, but Alyssa didn't seem to have noticed it.

"Is your father here, Mrs. Baron?" Karen asked in a clipped, coplike tone.

"Well, yes, he is. He's upstairs reading at the moment."

"Would you please call him down here?"

Alyssa licked her lips. "Well, of course I can, Captain. Is something wrong?" Her worried gaze flickered back to Brick.

He felt terrible. He cared for this woman. He didn't want to hurt her. He wanted to tell Karen not to play bad cop.

"Please go fetch him, Alyssa," he said gently. "This won't take long."

"You're not going to arr..." She stopped, horrified at her own words.

She hadn't said it, not outright, but Brick knew exactly where her thoughts were heading, and he was sure that Karen knew it, too.

At that moment Judson appeared at the top of the stairs, waved a cheery hello and came on down. He was a strong, limber man, still clinging to the tail end of his prime. Alyssa turned to face him, visibly trembling. "Brick's here, Dad," she said. "And Captain Keppler wants to talk to you."

Brick watched the same look pass over Judson's face that he'd seen on Alyssa's when she'd first caught sight of Karen on the porch. He'd seen it on Liza's face, too, when she'd privately told him that she was turning the bullet over to him because she was scared to death that Karen was going to uncover something that would implicate her grandfather and shatter her mother's heart. It wasn't the look of guilt, exactly, but it was most certainly more than everyday fear.

"We found this suitcase on the outskirts of town today, Mr. Ingalls," Karen said in her sternest voice. "We think it might have belonged to your wife. We'd like you to identify it."

To Brick's intense relief, Judson's face relaxed. Whether he recognized the suitcase or not, he clearly did not think it held any secrets that could be used against him. He made no comment as Brick laid it flat and opened it, revealing the moldy remnants of leather shoes, silk blouses and a dramatic hat with three gold feathers.

It was Alyssa, to Brick's despair, who suddenly covered her face with both hands and began to cry. She'd been seven years old when she last saw her mother, but it was obvious that she still held that feathered hat in some secret part of her memory.

Brick wondered what else she remembered . . . and what she was trying so hard to forget.

CHAPTER ELEVEN

AFTER KAREN GRILLED Judson about the suitcase, she slid into Brick's truck beside him, wishing she'd insisted on driving the cruiser. But Brick had told her that he wanted to arrive at the Ingallses' looking like a friend. Besides, they were both off duty and in civvies. He'd repeated that last point twice. Now Karen wondered why.

"They're hiding something, Brick," she declared, partly to cover the eerie silence as they drove through the deserted moonlit streets of Tyler. "I think the suitcase was legitimate, but...that's not just leftover grief we saw in the house tonight."

He didn't answer right away, and when he did, his voice sounded haunted. "I know, Kare. The oddest thing is, I don't think they're just afraid of you. I think they're afraid of each other."

It was a keen perception, one Karen herself had missed. "How can you tell? They didn't seem to support each other much, but I figured that just meant they weren't very close."

"But they are, Karen. Alyssa adores her father, and ever since Margaret left, she's been his whole world."

That news took Karen by surprise. The two people she'd just observed had behaved more like members of a dysfunctional family.

Now, very quietly, Brick said, "I think Alyssa would do anything to protect her father."

"You've changed your mind, Brick? You think he did it?"

He shook his head. "I don't want to believe that. I don't think Alyssa believes it either. But she . . . I don't think she's sure."

It was the closest he'd ever come to admitting the possibility of Judson's guilt, and Karen knew it was hard for him. She wanted to slide over beside him, or at least touch his arm, but she knew she didn't dare.

"When you say she'd do anything to protect him . . . you mean conceal evidence? Lie under oath?"

"I'm not sure what I mean. I do know that when she was in high school, she gave up the boy she adored because her father didn't approve of him. He wanted to marry her. He worshiped the ground she walked on." He paused a minute, then added, "Maybe he still does."

"Still does? You mean it's somebody local?"

He gave Karen a smile. "I keep forgetting how little you know about this town. You've got to be the only one in Tyler who doesn't know that Alyssa was once secretly engaged to marry Eddie."

"Eddie Wocheck? Why, he's a nice guy, Brick, not to mention filthy rich and your uncle's best friend. What could Judson have against him?"

"He sure wasn't rich in high school, Karen, and he was a bit of a rebel to boot. He was Judson's gardener's son. The Ingallses are rather snobbish when it comes to what they call 'breeding.' Judson chose a husband for his daughter who was rich, well connected and willing to live under his thumb." When

Karen made no comment, he continued, "I bet you never dated a man your father didn't approve of."

"I never liked the wrong sort of man."

"Is that what I am, Karen? Is that why you can't let yourself love me? Because Daddy wanted you to out-man the boys and be supercop? And you'd rather be lonely as hell than disappoint a man who's long since dead?"

A deep wash of fury filled Karen's heart, followed by a piercing hurt. Worse yet was the suspicion that Brick was probably right. If she couldn't live up to the standards her father had set for her, she couldn't respect herself. That wasn't all bad, but maybe it wasn't all good, either. Maybe it was time to reexamine her dad's values and decide if they were best for her own life.

In that awesome silence, Brick said, "I didn't say that to hurt you, Karen. I said it to wake you up. When I look at Eddie and Alyssa, I think of you and me, thirty years from now, trying not to yield to a public kiss under the mistletoe." He turned to face her, his sorrowful blue eyes illuminated by the street lamps as he pulled up at the stop sign a block away from Kelseys'. "There's got to be a better way to go."

Karen could not answer. She knew it was a mistake to have gotten into his truck alone with him! Thank God they were almost home.

Brick drove right past the boardinghouse and headed out of town.

"Where are you going?" Karen cried out. "It's late, Brick. We both—"

"We both have things to talk about." There was tension in his voice, but the heat she heard there was not the heat of anger that had driven their conversation for so many weeks. This banked fire was more unsettling.

"No, Brick." Her voice was low. "Please take me home."

"Home," he said softly. "An interesting word for a boardinghouse. Why is it 'home' to you, Karen? Because of Anna? Johnny? Because I'm there?"

She swallowed hard. "It was just a figure of speech, Brick. It's where I've lived for a while, and I have no family."

There was a long silence. "I don't recall any clause in your job description saying 'singles only need apply.'"

She knew she'd hurt him badly, and maybe she deserved to suffer his revenge. But tonight, when it seemed as if they'd shared so much again, it was unbearable to have him bait her.

"Let's be realistic, Brick. When I decided to make law enforcement my career, I gave up any dreams of baby buggies and having dinner ready when hubby came home from the office." Karen turned her face toward the window and stared into the frosty night, feeling jumpy and afraid. She'd always feared yielding her power to another person, and marriage implied the ultimate surrender. She'd come closer to surrendering her soul to Brick than to any other man, and the memory still frightened her. "I think I asked you to take me home," she reminded him with all the strength she could still muster.

"Did you? I thought that was just the captain issuing idle commands. I got the impression that my woman wanted to spend some time alone with me."

The sore spot in her heart that bore Brick's name began to throb. Karen had to swallow back tears. She wanted to holler at him, to issue sharp orders that reeked of disdain, but she was too weary. And not just because it was late and she'd put in a full day. She was exhausted from the struggle of fighting her love for him.

"Please, Brick," she pleaded.

He kept driving. "Please, Brick, what? You don't really want me to take you home. Be honest with yourself, Kare. Be honest with me." Again he turned to face her. "What do you really want?"

She was silent for a long moment before she whispered, "I want you to stop hurting me."

Brick braked at once. The eerie moonlight played across his beautiful eyes, his dimples, the hard line of his jaw. The truck rolled to a stop near a snowbank at the edge of the plowed road as he reached for her hand and squeezed it gently. "Baby, that's the last thing I want to do. If you can't believe that, I *will* take you home right now."

The silence was overwhelming—the frigid stillness of a winter night. She knew there wasn't a soul for miles.

"I can't make love with you, Brick. Please don't ask me again."

He didn't release her hand. His fingers kneaded hers gently, urgently. "That wasn't what I was going to ask, Kare. I don't ever plan to."

Briskly Karen turned away, stunned at how much those gentle words wounded her. No wonder Brick's mood was different tonight. He *had* given up. He had done what she'd told him to do. He wasn't going to fight her, wasn't going to beg her to find a way that they could be together. She tried to feel relieved— hadn't she ached for this?—but her whole being felt battered and bruised.

Especially the fingers embraced by his hand.

"What do you want, Brick? What are we doing out here?"

He released her hand to turn off the ignition. "There's a spot up a few miles from here—" he pointed ahead and slightly toward the right "—that's my favorite place in the whole world. I used to play there when I was a kid and we'd come to Tyler to visit Aunt Anna and my grandmother. I bought it a few years ago so I could build a house. But I can't get started on the plans, can't even let myself dream, until I know there's somebody to share it with." Silence took over the truck once more before he said, "I've dated a fair number of women over the years, nice ladies, every one. But I never showed it to any of them, bunkie. Tonight seemed like the right time to show it to you."

She couldn't bear for him to call her bunkie. At first he'd done it to mock her, and it had made her angry. Then he'd called her bunkie in the middle of the night and the word had set her on fire. Now he used the endearment with the tenderest of inflections, and it made her ache for him anew.

"Karen, I love you." The quiet words echoed in the silent cab, setting off a tiny rocket in Karen's heart. "I love you in a way I don't think I've ever loved a woman before. I don't mean you're the first, but I do mean—" his eyes met hers and would not let her go "—I want you to be the last."

She struggled for breath. He couldn't mean—

"I know we've got some rough sledding ahead of us, on duty and off. But we're both strong people. We understand what it means to be independent, what it means to be loyal, what it means to be cops. I don't want to change you. I don't want your job or your freedom or your self-surrender. I just want your love."

Karen didn't speak—what could she say?—but she was listening tensely now, her heart battling tidal waves of adrenaline that were hard to ignore.

"If you stay here in Tyler, you may always outrank me, even if someday one of us is assigned somewhere else. I don't like that. But I can live with the situation better than I can live without you."

Karen closed her eyes, too moved to risk even a glance at him.

"There're one or two substations within commuting distance, and maybe I can earn my promotion at one of them someday, or even make captain here if you get bumped up the line. After all, County HQ in Sugar Creek isn't all that far away." The words seemed to come hard for him. His voice was thick with emotion now, husky and low. "Before the night we . . . got carried away, I saw you as my woman, not my captain. I didn't try to put myself in the shoes of some other man under your command. Now that I've had plenty of time to think it over, I understand why you can't have an affair with any one of us. As the man who's getting shut out, I hate it, but as a cop assigned to the Tyler substation, I wouldn't have it any other way."

Brick slid over until he pressed against her, thigh to thigh, and gently laid one hand on her face. "I'm not leaving Tyler, Kare, and neither are you. We can't go on like this. People are talking about us as it is—"

"What?" She pushed his hand away. "How could you—"

"Hey, I haven't said a word to anyone about the night of the Christmas party. But Uncle Johnny and

Patrick have both guessed how I feel about you, anyway. I can see the questions in their eyes."

Karen writhed with fresh humiliation. "Your aunt suspects something. She grills me about you every day."

Infuriatingly, he smiled. "And yesterday Michael Youngthunder told me that I was looking at you as though I wanted to tear off your uniform. Now if that doesn't—"

"Michael Youngthunder!" she squealed. "He doesn't even know us!"

"He doesn't need to know us, Karen. That's just my point! He's a man and he's got eyes. Do you think everyone else in Tyler is blind? I'm telling you, all this suffering isn't going to help your reputation. The whole town can feel the fire between us. The local gossips are probably already spreading word of things we haven't even done."

Karen felt ill. Her career seemed to be slipping through her fingers. In her panic she lashed out at the bearer of bad tidings. "So what's your point? Everybody thinks I have no professional ethics so I might as well prove it? Honest to God, Brick, I thought you had more—"

"Dammit, Karen! You're impossible." He slid away from her and slammed the steering wheel with an angry hand. "Don't you have any faith in my integrity?"

"Integrity? You're using every trumped-up reason in the world to convince me to cast aside my self-respect just so you can have a few minutes of carnal pleasure! Can you deny it?"

He grabbed her by the shoulders and made her face him. "Yes, I can deny it! I haven't the slightest interest in a few minutes of carnal pleasure with you, Karen Keppler. I'm in the market for a lifetime of them.''

Karen froze, not at all certain she understood him. If she'd been watching a movie, she would have said that the hero had just proposed to the heroine. But this was Brick Bauer, her own real-life hero, and he'd never even hinted at marriage to her before.

And she herself had never dared to think of it.

Angrily he turned away again, pounding the dash with a killing blow. ''I was trying to ask you to marry me, Captain, but I'll be damned if I'm going to drag you kicking and screaming to the altar!''

Brick turned on the ignition before Karen could speak. He swung the truck in a wide arc and flew down the road back to town. Karen knew she had to stop him. She couldn't possibly accept his offer—could she?—and she didn't dare throw herself in his arms. But she couldn't let him throw a left-handed offer of marriage in her face and just drive off! She couldn't just pretend he'd never brought the subject up!

She reached out and grabbed his arm. ''Brick, stop the truck,'' she begged him. ''Talk to me.''

''I don't have anything else to say. It's obvious that I've said far too much already.''

''You asked me to marry you,'' she reminded him, ashamed of the desperation in her voice. ''If you were serious, you'd want to hear my answer.''

''I heard your goddamn answer! I knew it before I even got the words out. God knows you tried to stop me. I should have listened.''

Karen's stomach lurched. She relived all the terrible days since she'd sent him from her room, remembered the anguish of each empty night. She couldn't let him bolt up the stairs in anger now; she couldn't go through it again. She couldn't marry him, of course, but she couldn't let him go until she knew they were friends.

"Brick, I want you to stop the truck. I want to talk this through."

"I'm freezing, and it looks like it's going to snow."

"Please, Brick."

"A few minutes ago you were begging me to take you home."

"Brick! Stop the damn truck!"

"Is that an order, Captain?" His voice was fierce and low.

She wanted to tell him it was an order that he'd damned well better obey, but she knew that if she did, she'd lose him forever. Besides, it wouldn't have made any difference. He hadn't asked his captain to marry him; he'd asked the woman he said he loved. That was the woman who would make him stop the truck.

Karen laid one hand on Brick's upper thigh and squeezed his tense flesh. She knew she was starting downhill in a toboggan, but she couldn't help herself. In her softest voice she pleaded, "Bunkie, stop the truck."

In an instant Brick braked, slowed, pulled over by the side of the road. Tiny snowflakes were drifting down against the windshield. Karen shivered despite her winter coat.

Brick took a deep breath, but he did not look at her. He stared out the window, bent, defeated. She knew she'd scraped his pride to the bone.

For a long, quiet moment the truck was silent. Not a single sound drifted into the cab from outside. Brick didn't move, even when Karen found her grip tightening on his quadriceps.

"I do love you," she finally admitted, her voice painfully low. "And I am deeply touched by the fact that you actually want to marry me."

He didn't answer. He didn't stir.

"I can imagine snuggling up each evening with you before the fire. I can imagine curling up beside you every night in bed. I can't imagine myself as a mother, but I feel warm inside when I think of your baby in my arms."

He slumped forward. He seemed to know what was yet to come.

"I want you so much, Brick. More than I have the courage to show you. And if things were different, I would rejoice in your love for me." She reached for his hand, still on the gearshift, but he didn't respond. "But I can't imagine going into the squad room and telling those men that I'm your lover. I don't have the courage to face that. I could never stand up to them again."

There was no answer, no motion, from the other side of the cab.

"Can't you understand that?"

He did not face her, but at least he finally spoke. "I'm not asking you to tell them you're my lover. I'm asking you to tell them you're my wife."

He said the words so wistfully Karen wanted to cry, but somehow she clung to her convictions. "Brick, it's the same thing to them. They'd chortle, they'd laugh—"

"No, they wouldn't. You can make fun of a man's bedmate. You can't laugh at his wife."

She took a deep breath. "Okay, maybe it's different for you. But for me...it means that I'm...surrendering to a man." She couldn't explain how dangerous that would be for her. To admit the risk to Brick would be tantamount to surrender. "A man under my command. How would it look—"

He pushed away her hand. "I don't give a damn how it would look. Matrimony is an honored tradition in this town. Every head cop we've ever had in Tyler has had a spouse. Why shouldn't you?"

"I'm a woman, Brick. You know that makes a difference."

"Yes, it makes a difference. Yes, it means that some of the men will wonder who holds the reins in our personal life. Some of them will laugh at *me*. You'll still be the boss. They won't dare to laugh at *you*."

"I don't want any man to hold my reins, Brick. I'm my own woman, offstage or on." It was hard enough to remain tough and hard when she was all alone and could devote herself to her work. When she was with Brick, she didn't feel cold; she felt sweet and helpless and demure. She couldn't be a demure captain, and she didn't want to be a tough wife. If she couldn't even balance the two images of woman in her own mind, how would she ever juggle them in real life?

"I'm sorry, Brick," she whispered. "More sorry than you'll ever know."

He turned on the ignition again. Karen turned it off. She just couldn't let him go.

"What's the point, Karen?" he snapped. "You've carved out your own little niche, full of power, full of pride. It may be lonely as hell in there, but there's no room for anybody else. You aren't even willing to consider the possibility that you and I could work out some sort of domestic compromise. I know I'm not the world's most liberated fellow, but if I can learn to work beneath you, I think I can learn to live by your side. You won't even give me a chance to prove it."

"I can't give you a chance," she told him desperately. "We can't date. We can't live together. We can't experiment and adjust. We'd just have to run off and get married overnight and then work out all our problems later. It could be a disaster."

For a long time, he didn't answer. Then his beautiful blue eyes bathed her face once more as he whispered, "Bunkie, it could be bliss."

An instant later Karen was hugging Brick, glorying in the strength of his arms and the pillow of his massive chest. She didn't plan it, didn't choose it, knew it wasn't wise. But it felt so good to hold him, so good to toss the anger and fear and emptiness of the past few terrible weeks aside. "Oh, Brick, you don't really think—"

He swallowed her hopefulness in a kiss that rocked Karen to the bone. She relished the feel of his fingers in her hair, felt the flame of his hands as he pulled her closer.

In a second she was burning. Brick's tongue was plunging deep within her soft, moist mouth, foreshadowing the merging yet to come. It was as though their urgency had been put on hold the night he'd left her room—an action picture left on freeze-frame. Now the barriers they'd erected then collapsed with a resounding bang. The unquenched coals of the fire that had once burned between them instantly exploded into flame.

Karen stifled a cry of need as Brick pulled her onto his lap. Instinctively she straddled him. She was wearing panty hose, but she might as well have been stark naked from the waist down. Brick opened her coat, dropped a flaming kiss on her throat, then buried his face between her breasts. She whimpered in joy at his urgency. She knew she had to stop him, but she didn't know how.

In a moment Karen felt Brick fumble with the buttons of her blouse. His fingertips were erotically cold as they slipped inside her bra, rousing her nipples to pinpricks of wild craving. She could feel his stiff body surging upward, hotly pressing against the center of her woman's core. Everything was happening so fast she had no time to think, no time to make rational decisions. Desperately she wanted to tear off her clothes.

But she was hemmed in between a dashboard and a gearshift, crushed against the door. She knew it was unseemly, dangerous, insane. She almost didn't care. She felt like a sixteen-year-old parked in a car at night. As a teenager, she'd always been afraid a cop would catch her . . . a cop who knew her dad.

Suddenly, Karen knew that Brick was thinking the same thing. And she knew that it was her well-being, not his own, that forced him to still his trembling hands and push her bodily off his lap. He took a great breath, then forced himself out the door.

Despite the freshly falling snow, Brick jerked away from the truck, banging on the hood with his fist, heaving and breathing hard. Karen thought she would burst from desire; she knew he was ready to explode.

It was crazy! They couldn't stay away from each other. But they couldn't get married, either. What kind of a solution was that to a sexual problem? And it was a sexual problem, wasn't it? She couldn't get married just to avoid an affair! If she ever took such a permanent step, it would be because nothing in this world meant more to her than her husband.

A frightened voice inside Karen warned her that she already felt that way about Brick.

CHAPTER TWELVE

AFTER HE RETURNED to the truck, Brick drove Karen home without a word and dropped her off at the curb. He kissed her one more time, a devastating kiss of love and longing...a kiss that was more shattering than any they'd ever shared before.

He was still shaking when he drove off. So was Karen. Hours later, when she crept out of bed and left Anna a goodbye note, she was still trembling.

And Brick was still not home.

Karen had only one suitcase to pack...all she had to show for her personal life in Tyler. Oh, there were still a few boxes of her books in Rob's garage, but there was nothing that spoke of home.

She drove to the station house at dawn because she could not sleep. She could not bear to lie in bed wondering why Brick had not returned. She had no right to expect him to report to her, but she couldn't keep from worrying, either. At least at the station, she could listen to the scanner without alarming Anna. If he was in trouble, she would be the first to hear.

But nothing seemed amiss at the station house. Cindy Lou was chewing on a doughnut and seemed glad to see another human face—even Karen's. Within an hour, the night shift wandered in. The day people showed up and started to take the cruisers out. They were friendly. They were efficient. They were oblivious. Not one person seemed to notice that Brick Bauer had ripped their captain's heart out by offering to make it whole.

Not once all day did Karen hear from him. Not a whisper, not a word. She ate breakfast, lunch and dinner at Marge's and lingered there far too long at each meal, but there was no trace of Brick. No rumors, no gossip, no casual jokes that featured his name.

She drove past the Kelseys' three different times and finally called Anna on the pretense of having left something at the house. When she probed, Anna revealed that she hadn't seen Brick either. By nightfall, when Karen finally forced herself to head to her own cold little house—the haven from Brick she'd been so eager to claim—she thought she'd lose her mind.

All her life Karen had wanted a little house like this. It was red with white shutters, with withered rosebushes poking out of the snow heaped up on either side of the front porch. It was so close to the station house she could walk if she wanted to, but far enough away that she could shut out the world.

But she could not shut out memories of Brick.

How could she willingly hide from a man who not only inflamed her with his touch, but loved her enough to push her away when she herself might not have found the strength? How could she run from a man who begged her to marry him? How could she reject a man who made her long to share her life in a way she'd never done before?

Brick did not know that she had told him only half the story. He did not know that more than her reputation and her career was involved. Her craving to merge her life with Brick's threatened her very essence as a competent human being.

Today was a prime example. Since dawn Karen had been as fluttery as a schoolgirl in the throes of puppy love; she was not sure she could ever be an iron-hard cop again. Somehow she'd stumbled through her professional responsibilities, but they had all been routine. It wasn't safe for her to be so distracted. It wasn't fair to her men.

Maybe it would be more intelligent to marry Brick. Maybe it's the only way to save my career. Maybe it's the only way to put myself back together again. After all, if the whole town thinks I'm sleeping with him anyway...

Karen knew she was rationalizing, that she was desperate for a way to end her inner torment, desperate for a way to cling to her self-respect when she bowed to the inevitable.

It was almost eight o'clock when she finally turned the key in the door of her new place, dragging her sleeping bag in from the car. *You'll have time to make it feel like home tomorrow,* she told herself, bracing herself for the dusty, empty rooms she'd seen last week. She planned to spend Sunday afternoon in Sugar Creek buying the essentials. Once, she'd eagerly looked forward to decorating a house of her own, but she didn't have the heart for solitary living anymore.

As she unlocked the side door to the kitchen, Karen suddenly realized she was not alone. She'd walked into a strange, deserted house at night without even loosening the safety catch on her holster! Her mind was so full of Brick that she'd forgotten the most basic laws of self-preservation.

She was bracing herself for an attack when she suddenly felt a nudge at her ankle. Simultaneously a small feline voice cried, "Meeeeow?"

Heart pounding, Karen fumbled against the wall for a light switch. When she flipped it on, she spotted a small calico cat at her feet. "How on earth did you get in here?" she asked, heart pounding in relief. Granted, she'd always longed for a kitty to warm her hearth, but she hadn't expected one to show up like this!

The half-grown cat cried again and rubbed against Karen's leg. She leaned down to rub the tiny nose, suddenly delighted to find a friendly face waiting to greet her. "I don't have a thing to feed you, sweetheart," she told the cute little creature, "and I'm not going shopping till tomorrow. But maybe Tillie's neighbor left something in the kitchen we could share. Some soup, you think? Or some tuna? At least something in a can?"

Karen picked up the cat and opened the nearest cupboard. To her surprise, she found a dozen cans of soup in the cupboard—and bags of candy bars, too. She didn't find any tuna for humans, but there were ten cans of the feline variety lined up on the floor next to a bag of dry cat food. Some of it filled a tiny bowl. Nearby was a saucer of water.

She didn't recall cat food or water in the kitchen last time she'd been in this house. She didn't recall the gleaming philodendron hanging over the refrigerator, either . . . or the two Boston ferns on the counter. How the greenery helped chase the loneliness from this empty house!

Karen might have missed a sleeping cat, but she knew she couldn't have missed three plants in an empty kitchen. Somebody had been here since she'd last visited the house. Somebody had tried to make her empty little house feel like home.

Recalling the sweet note Anna had left her the night she'd moved into the boardinghouse, Karen rushed to the back bedroom on a hunch. On the way she spotted a half dozen other plants, and old-fashioned furniture that somehow seemed familiar even though she was certain she'd never seen it before. The house had been layered with dust the last time Karen saw it, but now it was so clean it sparkled.

It was not until she reached the bedroom—and spotted the beautiful old Blazing Star quilt on the bed—that she realized Anna couldn't have moved this furniture here without help. Besides, she couldn't possibly have hidden so much of her own old furniture in her basement. The Kelseys' basement was full of tables and chairs that belonged to Brick.

And then Karen remembered that she'd never told Anna she'd always wanted a calico cat. She'd never told her how she felt about plants warming a home.

Karen fought a rush of tears as she realized what care had gone into this project. Not just time but loving attention to every detail that reflected her personal dream of home. Details she'd told to only one person in Tyler.

The person who could have been waiting here to greet her every night.

Then she saw the note. It was by her nightstand, in the perfect place for her father's picture, right next to a beautiful silver vase with a single red rose.

Shifting the cat, Karen picked up the note and read it quickly as she sank down on the bed, unable now to hold back the tears that had battled for release all day.

Dear Bunkie,
I left this space empty for your dad's picture. I know that's what will really make you feel at

home. Keep the furniture as long as you need it. I hope the kitty will be a good friend to you.

Now that you're gone, I think I'll be able to keep my distance, if you're still sure that's what you want. But if you ever need a friend, I'm as close as your radio or your phone.

At the bottom of the page was a postscript that caused Karen to smother so forceful a sob that the kitty stopped purring and jumped out of her arms. In Brick's tense, masculine scrawl the tender words were written: "I won't change my mind, Kare, but I won't ask again."

JANICE ARRIVED for lunch at the diner a few minutes after twelve, wearing a blue pantsuit that showed off her slim figure but somehow managed to dim the beauty Anna remembered from her younger days. Janice had never been a bold, assertive person, but she'd always had a sweetness about her that had made her shine with life. Nowadays it seemed that everything about her was subdued.

"Sorry I'm late, Anna. Kurt wanted to go play handball today and he couldn't find his new sweat suit. I had to look everywhere. He'd left it in his suitcase."

"Oh? He's been out of town again?"

"He's been out of town a lot lately, Anna." A ghost of frustration darkened her loving tone. "He works so hard. It's not like we're starving or anything. The kids and I would rather have him home more than have another car or stereo. I wish he'd slow down."

Anna expressed her sympathy and swallowed her questions about Kurt. She wasn't indifferent to Janice's feelings, but today she had another agenda. Her beloved nephew had looked so distressed since Karen moved out that she simply had to do something to cheer him up! Poking around for a little information seemed like the least she could do.

After Marge came over to take their order—smiling radiantly as she told Anna to give her "personal best" to George—Anna didn't have much trouble bringing Alyssa and Eddie into the conversation. She and Janice had talked of little else since Eddie had first come back to town.

"I could have killed Marge for forcing Eddie to kiss Alyssa under the mistletoe at that party," Anna declared. "If there's any future there, they need to go at their own pace."

"Oh, do you really think they might get back together?" Janice asked, her eyes aglow. "I'd give anything to see Alyssa happy again. She hasn't really had much joy in her life since Ron...well, since she lost Ron."

In some ways, Alyssa hadn't been too happy since she'd lost Eddie thirty years ago, but Anna decided that this wasn't the time to say so.

"Brick said he ran into the two of you at Worthington House just before Christmas. He didn't get the impression that Alyssa was all that glad to see Eddie. Did you notice anything amiss?"

Janice sipped her coffee and pondered that a moment. At last she said, "Well, now that you mention it, Anna, there was something sort of odd. But I don't think it was Eddie who upset her. I think it was Phil."

"Phil? Why, how could that old dear disturb Alyssa? He's adored her ever since she was a baby. Remember how he used to call her all those cute Polish things?"

Janice leaned forward, her eyes intense. "That's just it. I don't remember the exact Polish words, but I know she always sort of liked the way he fussed over her. She was like the daughter he never had, you know?"

Anna nodded.

"But this time when he said *'maduska'* or *'maluska'* or whatever it was, she looked at Eddie, not at Phil." Janice shook her head. "She looked so upset that after we left, I asked her what was troubling her. I mean, other than just seeing Eddie."

"And?"

"At first she didn't want to talk about it, but finally she told me that Phil used to call her that word—it's a Polish endearment—when she was a little girl. She said that in those days, Phil looked the way Eddie does now."

Anna wrestled with that for a moment. "I guess that would make sense. I mean, Johnny looks the picture of his father taken when he was in his fifties. But why would that realization upset Alyssa?"

"I'm not sure, and I don't think she is, either." Janice gazed out the window for a moment before she went on. "But she said to me, 'It was like a ghost brushed my spine. I felt as though I was watching an old black-and-white movie, starring Eddie as Phil.'"

Anna wanted to know what else was playing on the screen of Alyssa's mind.

BRICK HAD MADE arrangements to squire one healthy young Indian to each of the likely spots where a Winnebago burial ground might still lurk beneath a horseshoe of oak trees. But on Monday afternoon, when Michael Youngthunder was scheduled to arrive, he did not come alone.

He walked into the station house beside a denim-clad fellow who looked as though he'd been limping over the earth for about three hundred years. His sun-leathered skin looked as though it had been bronze to start with; his nose was like an ax head planted in the middle of his face. The old man's eyes, the blackest eyes Brick had ever seen, were full of compassion, pain and wisdom. His hair was gray and wispy; here and there it stuck straight up on his head. Around his neck he wore a beaded leather pendant.

"Lieutenant?" Michael said as Brick approached the two men. "This is my grandfather. He insisted on coming along. He won't get out of the car at each cabin, but he feels that he'll be able to sense when we're close to the burial ground."

Brick wasn't sure what to say. At the moment he had no faith in instincts; his own had told him that Karen loved him and only needed to be assured that he wanted her for more than a pleasure cruise. Three whole days had passed since he'd battled her desire and his own to let her cling to the illusion that nothing sexual had actually transpired between them. It was a technical distinction, in Brick's view. Their touching had been pretty damn intimate! Only Karen's panty hose and Brick's self-control had kept them apart. Both had been equally thin.

Dammit, Karen, I love you so much. I want you to be my wife! he wanted to holler at her. He'd almost gone back to her little house over the weekend to do just that. But he'd already made his feelings painfully clear, and he would not grovel. It was time to accept the fact that Karen meant what she said. It was not going to be easy to forget his love for her—hell, it was going to be impossible—but somehow he had to learn to do just that.

It took Brick a moment to realize that the ancient man was speaking, perhaps had been speaking for quite some time. His voice was low and shaky, slightly accented by his native tongue. Brick had to listen closely to follow him.

"If the spirits want us to find the burial ground, they will tell me when we are near it. I am not certain they will tell my grandson. He is not sure he believes."

Brick cast a quick glance at Michael, who didn't look pleased with his grandfather's opinion. But Brick had the feeling that the old Winnebago's assessment was right on target. Michael Youngthunder seemed to be a man torn between two worlds.

"When was the last time you saw this oak horseshoe, sir?" Brick asked gently.

The old man shook his head. "I was a boy. I was with my father. I was...lost...when I should have shown it to my son."

Brick turned to Michael for a translation. "He left Wisconsin for seven years," he said, as though that explained it.

"Michael's father is lost to us. For a long time, Michael was lost to us, too."

Brick wasn't sure he wanted to pursue these family secrets, but he was truly curious. What exactly did "lost" mean? Dead, at least in spirit? Falling apart? Or simply rejecting the Winnebago way and happy in the white man's world?

Someday, if he got the chance to speak to Michael alone, he would ask. It wasn't something he wanted to go into with the old man. It was obvious that the senior Youngthunder was quite frail, and this afternoon was going to be hard on him.

For the next three hours, Brick told the two men everything he knew about the history of the area north of town, drove them to every piece of property that might hide an old burial ground, answered questions about standing trees and trees that had been cut down. It was not until they reached the old Meyer place that the old man straightened and said, "We are near the burial ground. I can feel it."

But they circled Renata's old house and sometime art studio for half an hour and never found a single oak. After Michael convinced him that they'd done their best, the old man slumped silently in the cruiser.

Brick felt like slumping himself by the time he returned to the station house, knowing he'd have to report the day's events to Karen. He tried to get Michael Youngthunder to talk to her with him—they desperately needed a chaperon—but he was clearly worried about his grandfather, who looked sad and a bit bewildered that the "spirits" had given him a false clue. Michael thanked Brick profusely for his time and his kindness, then took the old one home.

The police-station door had barely closed behind them before Hedda said, "Better put on your helmet, Brick. The captain's asked for you three times. Something about paperwork that just won't wait."

He couldn't remember any paperwork that he'd botched up recently, and anyway, he was surprised that Karen was in a hurry to see him. Considering the way they'd last parted, he wasn't sure it was safe to risk even being in the same room with her.

Deciding to get it over with, Brick marched quickly to her office, rapped once on the door and stuck his head inside. Unless Karen ordered him to close the door, he was going to stay in the hall...or at least keep one hand on the doorknob.

Apparently Karen had other plans. She stood the moment she spotted him. "Would you come in and close the door, please?"

She was all spit and polish in her uniform today, her braid tight and flat on top of her head. Brick remembered how her hair had brushed his face the night he'd nearly made love to her in her room; he remembered how it had slipped loose from its clips Friday night in the truck. He remembered how her full breasts had filled his hands with warmth, how his body had swelled when she'd straddled him, how desperately he'd tried to believe, for the split second she'd given in to him, that she really did love him enough to be his wife.

It was a dream he knew it would be hard to abandon.

"Uh, Hedda said you had some paperwork for me to do," he stalled, hoping she'd just hand him something so he could dart out quickly. He didn't want to stand here, studying her magnificent curves; he didn't want to see the anguish in her eyes or the tension in her forced smile. He didn't want to remember the flush of passion on her lovely face.

To his surprise, Karen shook her head, loosening a few enticing wisps at the nape of her neck. "Hedda misunderstood. I've already done all the paperwork in question. I just need for you to sign your name."

Brick tried to remember what report would require both of their signatures. He'd already written up his account of Friday night's visit to the Ingallses, and he figured Karen had, too. There was no reason for either of them to add a John Hancock to each other's docu-

ment. The only thing likely to require both signatures
was a personnel review or complaint. Karen had
warned him more than once that making a pass at her
could cost him his badge. Had she finally decided that
he'd gone too far?

Was she actually *insulted* by his offer of marriage?

"Why do you need my signature, Captain?" he
asked carefully, trying not to sound combative.

She gave him a tight, frightened smile, unlike any
smile Brick had ever seen on Karen's face before. Then
she held up a piece of paper—it didn't look at all like a
departmental form—and said shakily, "I got all the
other information I needed from your personnel record, but I can't sign your name. I arranged for my own
blood test and made an appointment for us at four
o'clock Friday at the Sugar Creek Courthouse. The rest
is up to you."

Brick was lost. What was she talking about? Blood
test? Courthouse? Why was she trembling? Why did
she look so scared?

Karen stayed behind her desk as she faced him, her
eyes alert and wary. Then she handed him the form. He
read the title three times before reality set in: Applica-
tion for Marriage License, State of Wisconsin.

The blanks were filled in with his name and hers, and
other information that was required by the state.

The room seemed to swerve sharply around him.
Brick felt so dizzy he had to grab hold of the desk.

"Karen?" He struggled to catch his breath.

Her eyes were huge. "You promised not to change
your mind," she whispered. "I thought you really
meant it. I thought you were leaving it in my hands."

"*Karen!*" He gasped again.

"Please?" This time she sounded as frightened as a child, not at all like the assertive captain who so coolly bossed the other men. But at the moment he wasn't about to dwell on incongruities, not when a miracle had just occurred in this very room.

Brick longed to reach for Karen's hand or kiss her, but he knew it wasn't an accident that she'd remained on the other side of her giant desk. "You're not jerking my chain? This isn't some kind of a joke? You're sure you want to be my wife?"

She didn't answer his questions. She bit her lip and fought back tears. Her voice was low and haunted when she pleaded, "Brick, I don't want to see you alone until then."

"I understand." Until he was sure she wasn't going to pull the rug out from under him again, he didn't want to be alone with her, either. It was a miracle he'd made it this long without making love to her. Now that he knew she truly wanted to marry him, he knew he couldn't hold back if things got steamy again.

"I don't want anyone to know until it's done. Not even Rob or your family."

He didn't like that idea—Aunt Anna and his grandmother would never forgive him—but he was not about to argue over a technicality. "I promise, Karen. Maybe we can have a private family celebration afterward, once we get settled in." When she did not reply, he pressed on, "You want me to live with you? In your little house? At least until we can build—"

"We can worry about these details later. I just wanted to get the basics settled now." Now her tone was clipped. The captain giving orders again.

Brick wasn't comfortable with the way the conversation was going. He was still in shock, stunned and overjoyed. And he didn't expect Karen to swoon all over him in her office, but he'd never seen a less enthusiastic bride.

"I'm game," he said a bit guardedly, "but I think the basics include a few things we haven't discussed. We're not talking about holing up somewhere for the weekend. We're talking about..." He broke off, watching the uncertainty that still haunted her beautiful face. "Do you really want to be my *wife*, Karen, not just my lover? Do you plan to love me for the next sixty years?"

"A hundred and sixty," she whispered, a dozen lifetimes of love shining in her aching gray eyes.

When Karen fought back a shaky sob, Brick forgave her for all the pain she'd caused him.

THE DOCTOR'S APPOINTMENT on Friday afternoon was over all too soon. Armed with everything she needed to postpone pregnancy, Karen arrived early for her appointment at the beauty salon, then checked into her hotel. She spent an hour getting ready...soaking in the tub, fussing with her makeup, slipping into brand-new satin undies and a Victorian lace dress with a striking cranberry sash. It said "wedding" all over it, but it wasn't a wedding dress in the classical sense, and she could wear it again. Along with the baby tea roses in her hair, it made Karen feel soft and fragile, stripped of all her thorns.

That pretty much summed up how she'd felt ever since Saturday night, when the kitty had reminded her of how Brick made her purr. She'd only mentioned that calico cat once, and she and Brick had been at loggerheads most of the time since then. Under the circumstances, it was a miracle that he'd remembered something so special.

It was a miracle that she'd ever resisted him.

By the time Karen had finished reading his "Dear Bunkie" note, she'd realized that she belonged to Brick Bauer, heart and soul, and a thousand years of sexual denial would never change a thing. She couldn't carry on without him anymore. It was as simple as that.

At least, it seemed that simple until she reached the courthouse at three-thirty to wait... and fret. As the minutes ticked past, Karen's stomach experimented with all kinds of knots. She reminded herself a dozen times that she was early; there was no reason why Brick should arrive ahead of time.

At four o'clock she started to look for him, hopping up from her marble bench to check the steps out front every five minutes. By four-fifteen she started getting nervous, recalling the challenges of parking and traffic snarls in downtown Sugar Creek. By four-twenty she was remembering how heavily the snow had been falling on the road; she was remembering the risk a cop took each and every day and night. By four-twenty-five she'd chewed off all her lipstick and was trying to decide whether she should call Tyler to see if something terrible had happened or consider the possibility that Brick had done the unspeakable and changed his mind.

It wasn't impossible. He hadn't—oh, dear God, surely he hadn't been stringing her along right from the start! Was this some sort of bet for the station pool to see which one of the guys would conquer Captain Curvaceous? No, it couldn't be that! He loved her. He wouldn't deceive her! But it was one thing to hope desperately for something you were sure you couldn't have, to ache for a woman you thought you'd never get into bed, and another to marry her. Maybe once Brick knew he'd gotten Karen for life, he'd started having second thoughts. Maybe he was facing up to the challenges of the two-cop marriage, playing second fiddle to his wife on the job. Maybe he didn't want to live with a woman who'd hurt him so much.

Karen checked outside at four-thirty, then studied herself in a rest-room mirror. She looked white-faced, terrified, ridiculous in her ornate hairdo and exquisite dress. She looked like a debutante, not a cop! How could a woman who looked so frail be a police captain? How could a police captain be a police lieutenant's wife?

Karen, calm down! she ordered herself as she returned to the lobby feeling weak and frazzled. *You're overwrought. Everything will be okay when Brick shows up. Every bride falls apart at the last minute. It's par for the course.*

The elderly clerk at the window gave her a sympathetic smile when Karen asked if there had been a message, then asked if she'd see if the judge could wait.

Karen was starting to tremble by then. It was four-thirty-five. "I'll wait for him a few minutes longer," she said, ashamed that her cheeks were turning pink.

With rising panic, she checked the front steps again, trying to remember what Brick had said in her office the last time they'd talked, trying to remember love in his eyes the last time she'd seen his rugged face.

At four-forty-five the clerk told her they had to start closing up for the day. For the weekend. Was there someone she could call? Anything at all she could do to help?

Karen thanked the clerk for her kindness, then headed for the courthouse steps, feeling like a tiny cork in a wind-tossed sea. She had never felt so foolish, so helpless, so alone. Was Brick dead? Was he injured? Had he blatantly stood her up?

She couldn't think; she could take no action. Was this what her life would be like when she married him? Would she be angry with him one minute, terrified the next? Totally dependent on one man for happiness and peace of mind? It was crazy! Even if Brick still wanted her—oh, God, what would she do if he didn't still want her?—how could she carry on this way? If she had a police emergency in this state of mind, could she perform her duty without making a fool of herself? Or worse yet, endangering the lives of her men?

Karen desperately wanted to be Brick's adoring wife *and* hard-as-nails Captain Keppler, but she was afraid she could never be both women in the same life.

CHAPTER THIRTEEN

ANNA LEFT the Hair Affair feeling edgy, partly because she felt guilty about trying to pump Alyssa for Brick and partly because it was obvious that Alyssa had not been quite herself today. She'd spent a good deal of time during her manicure staring at Tisha's parrot. Twice she'd ignored Tisha's cheerful jokes and several times she'd responded so vaguely to Anna's comments that Anna knew she wasn't really listening. By the time they'd said goodbye, Anna had decided it was time to tell Brick she hadn't found out anything worthwhile for him and wasn't going to. Something was deeply troubling her friend, and she was considerably more interested in helping Alyssa sort things out than she was in proving who'd killed her mother.

She was both surprised and relieved when Alyssa showed up at the hospital office three hours later, just as she was getting ready to close up for the weekend. George was already gone—he usually took off early on Fridays—and Anna was just about to grab her purse when Alyssa wandered in.

"Alyssa? What is it?" It wasn't that unusual for Alyssa to show up at work to see her, but not a few hours after they'd had their hair done.

"Anna? Do you have a few minutes?" Her voice was soft and uncertain. "I'd really like to talk to you alone."

It wasn't a comment that needed further explanation. Between the boarders at the Kelseys' and the family at the Ingallses', neither house provided much in the way of privacy. An empty office on a Friday night was as good a spot as any.

"Sit down, Alyssa," she warmly urged her friend, relieved that she could finally be of help. "What's troubling you?"

Alyssa sank down in a vinyl chair by the door, twisting her purse handle as she hugged it to her lap. She didn't even unbutton her coat. "I think...I think I'm..." Her haunted blue eyes met Anna's. "There's something wrong, Anna. Something wrong with my father or my memory or..." She took a deep breath. "Have you talked to Brick?"

Anna wasn't sure how to answer that. "Brick has been working evenings lately, and when he's been home, he's sort of kept to himself," she said truthfully. Ever since Karen had moved out, he'd been as surly as a bear. The last day or two, he'd seemed more cheerful, but there was still a tension in him that she couldn't ferret out the reason for. And he'd offered no explanation whatsoever when he'd told her he wouldn't be coming home tonight. Surely he couldn't have found another girl so soon!

Of course, Alyssa wasn't asking about Brick's relationship, or lack thereof, with Karen. But Anna couldn't bear to tell her friend that Brick was using his own family connections to investigate her father. She hoped Alyssa wouldn't ask her outright. She'd do almost anything for her nephew, but she would not repeat anything Alyssa told her in confidence or tell Alyssa a bald-faced lie.

"Brick's been out to the house a couple of times with that...that woman. That captain. She...thinks Dad killed Mother," Alyssa whispered, as though the words were too terrible to speak out loud. "I know she does! Brick's trying to protect him, but I know he's got a job to do."

Anna circled around her desk and sat beside her friend. "Alyssa, I don't for a minute believe your father killed Margaret, at least not on purpose."

Alyssa's eyes flashed open. "Not on purpose?" she murmured. "You think maybe somebody didn't mean to hurt her...?" Again her voice trailed off.

"I don't know what happened. Neither does Brick. But Karen's made it clear that she won't stop digging until she finds some answers."

"I know!" Tears filled her eyes. "Liza says we've got to figure out the truth before the police do!"

Anna took her hand. "What do you mean, Alyssa?"

Alyssa started to tremble. "I know something. I don't know what it is, but...I was there, Anna. I mean, I lived at the lodge. I was just a little girl, but...I remember telling you that my mother was gone. Do you remember that? When we were small?"

Anna nodded. "Of course I do. I felt so awful for you."

"You offered to share Martha with me."

Anna hadn't remembered that, but she was glad she'd been so kind.

"If I remember that much, isn't it possible that, deep down, I remember...something else?"

Anna took a deep breath. "Like what?"

"I don't know! All I know is that I've started having dreams. Waking up in a cold sweat. There's always some noise, like people nearby having a fight, but when I wake up there's nobody there! And once I heard a gunshot—in the dream, you understand, not in real life. At least, I don't remember it in real life. At least, not when I'm awake. And the last time I saw Phil..." She stopped. She almost looked frightened. "Surely that didn't mean anything."

"Tell me," Anna urged, and not just for Brick. "You need to get this out of your system, Alyssa. I had no idea this was tearing you up."

Alyssa started to cry. "The last time I saw Phil, he called me *maluska*. It's what he always called me when we lived at the lodge. It's Polish for 'little girl.'"

Anna waited.

"It's been years since he called me that. So what made him think of it the other day?"

"Maybe all of this discussion of Margaret just got him thinking about life back then."

"Maybe. But why did the word strike me so hard?" She fought back a heart-shaking sob. "I looked at Eddie—not like Eddie now, but like...well, Anna, he looks so much like Phil did back then!"

"Yes, he does at that. But much more dashing."

"I don't usually think about it," Alyssa persevered. "But when Phil called me *maluska* and Eddie was right there...it was like, I don't know, a great wave came over me. A sense of memory."

Anna squeezed her hand. "Alyssa, what is it you remember?"

"I don't know!" She all but shouted the words. "All I'm sure of is that there's an ugly memory locked inside of me that I've...turned away from all these years. It's alive now, trying to get out, and it's killing me!"

Anna took her friend in her arms and held her while she sobbed.

For a few minutes, Alyssa was beyond speech. Then she whimpered, "Liza's been hammering at me to talk to Dad. She says we've got to figure out what happened before that new captain does. It takes a lot to scare Liza, but she's afraid of that woman. She knows Brick will try to help us, but he's such a straight arrow! When push comes to shove..."

She let the sentence trail off, but Anna knew what she meant. Brick would do what he could, but he wouldn't turn away from hard evidence in a murder, even against a friend or family member.

"Alyssa, I think you should sit down and talk to Brick. Alone," she counseled kindly. "Or maybe with Amanda. At some point your dad may need a lawyer, whether he did anything or not."

Alyssa pulled back, her eyes so miserable that Anna wanted to cry herself. "Anna, I've got to make Dad talk to me! Ever since they found Mother's body we've been tiptoeing around each other, afraid to ask questions, afraid..." She gulped back one last sob. "Afraid to know the truth."

Two HOURS after the slapdash wedding ceremony, Brick knew he'd made a terrible mistake. He'd suspected it even as the judge had asked the lifetime-commitment questions...which Brick had answered with feeling and Karen had answered as though she'd mistaken her wedding for a wake. Not once during the brief exchange of vows had she met his eyes. Her lips had offered not a trace of response when the judge had told Brick to kiss his bride.

He knew she understood why he'd been so late; she had no call to be angry. As the first officer on the scene of an accident on the highway, he'd instinctively stopped to do what he could for the young mother and her two small children, even though he was off duty and out of his jurisdiction. By the time the first Casner unit had responded, Brick was already quite late, and the heavy snowfall had further impeded his progress.

Karen had not bawled him out for his tardiness. She had hardly greeted him at all. Rather stiffly she'd informed him that it was too late to get married. If the clerk hadn't rushed out to the foyer to tell her that the judge could wait another minute now that her "young man" had finally arrived, he might have given up trying to persuade her to hurry inside.

With no visible enthusiasm—with no expression of any kind—Karen had trailed Brick to the judge's chambers and gone through the motions of committing herself to him for life. Once she'd signed the mandatory forms, she had marched out of the courthouse with terse directions to the restaurant where she'd made reservations for dinner. Brick had followed her in his truck, hoping that all she needed was a little bit of time.

But all through dinner Karen had chattered about police business and her plans to furnish "her" new house. He looked in vain for the tiniest bit of joy on her face. She looked numb with regret.

By the time she paid for dinner—refusing to let Brick even leave the tip—he knew his honeymoon plans were shattered. When she scrambled up to the hotel room before he could park the truck and join her, he made the hardest decision of his life.

A few moments later he knocked on the door. When Karen opened it, Brick met her eyes sadly, but did not step inside.

She looked so beautiful, so magnificently sad. He'd never seen her look so delicate, so feminine...so frail. She didn't look like the tough woman he'd learned to love and respect. That he didn't mind—he loved her tough; he loved her gentle. What broke his heart was that she was now his wife, and it was obvious that the knowledge filled her with despair.

"Karen?" he said softly, when she started to march away from the door.

She turned back, her lips pursed apprehensively, as she realized he was not coming in.

"This is all new to me, so please forgive me if I do this badly." His voice was low and hoarse. Every word felt like a load of cement. "But it seems to me—fōr God's sake, Karen, correct me if I'm wrong—that you might be more comfortable if I...took another room here tonight." He swallowed hard; he had to look away. "Or maybe just drove back to Tyler."

When Brick heard her gasp, his gaze rushed back to hers. At last he saw true feeling in her eyes again, but he still could not understand it. It wasn't joy, nor was it irritation. It was fear.

Her voice was a fragile wisp as she asked, "Is...is that really what you want to do?"

"Oh, Karen." He closed his eyes and leaned against the door, plunging his hands in his pockets to keep from touching her. "I had such plans for tonight. I had such plans for our life together! I would give anything to make them still come true." He opened his eyes and managed to face her again. "But I bulldozed you into marrying me. I won't steamroll you into sharing a bed with me, too."

She looked shaky now. "Brick, nobody bulldozes Karen Keppler. I don't do anything I don't want to do."

For a moment he took heart. The words belonged to the police captain he knew, even if the tone of voice belonged to a stranger. "Karen, what *do* you want? What's going on? Will you just . . . talk to me like I'm not a stranger?"

She blinked a few times, then shook her head. "So much for my efforts at nonchalance. I thought I was doing pretty well over dinner. You knew I was faking it, huh?"

The vise on his heart tightened its grip. "I knew."

For a moment she stood there staring at him, obviously fighting tears. "I didn't mean to be cruel or rude. I didn't mean to be unfair to you. I was doing the best I could."

Brick didn't know what to say to that. He'd never felt quite so helpless in his life.

Then she whispered, "I think it would be easier to talk about this if you came inside. I don't want to tell the whole hotel what I'm feeling. It's going to be hard enough to say it to you."

With sinking hopes, he stepped inside, unable to speak while Karen shut and locked the door. He could hardly breathe while he waited for her to tell him what he could expect. He didn't know whether he should rejoice or start grieving.

Karen's face looked like a Madonna's in the softly lit room. She was hurting—she could not hide it—and it wounded Brick that he could do nothing to ease her pain. If he touched her now, he would only make things worse.

For a long, tense moment she merely met his eyes, and her own were full of unshed tears. Then, to Brick's astonishment, she pleaded, "Please hold me. Please tell me it'll somehow be all right."

"Oh, baby." Instantly he gathered her up close; fiercely she clung to him. When he heard her smother a sob, he pulled her closer yet. "Karen, I love you so much. I desperately want you to be my wife. Tell me why everything's going wrong!"

She kissed his throat, then hungrily met his lips when he leaned down closer. It was the kiss they should have shared at the courthouse—long, hopeful...hot.

Then she was babbling, "I'm so frightened, Brick. I feel so disconnected. I don't feel whole without you. I've never felt anything like this before."

He kissed her again, his courage growing. "I'm listening, Karen. Tell me what's going on."

She wasn't crying so hard now, but she was still weeping some. "When I thought you were late, I was afraid you'd changed your mind. I was afraid you'd won a bet on the station pool. I was afraid you'd played games with me all along."

"Karen! You can't really—"

"Then I was afraid you were so sure of me you didn't care if I was scared or embarrassed. I was angry, a thousand times more angry than the situation warranted—a man being late for an appointment, even for a wedding."

He kissed her again, deciding his own words wouldn't add much to the conversation. But she pulled back again, still gripping his waist.

"And then I realized that I was furious because I was terrified. I knew you loved me. I knew you hadn't forgotten me. That meant the only reason you could be so late was that you were injured...or dead."

He pulled her closer. "Baby, I couldn't call. If I'd been in Tyler I could have sent a message—"

"In all the years I've been a cop, I've never felt that kind of panic. Irrational, out of control. I started thinking how it would be if I was on duty. I started thinking about what you believed about women cops—that they lack courage, that they freeze, that good men die because they can't hold their own."

"Karen, I was wrong. You taught me that Mark died because of one weak woman. It wasn't you."

"But I don't know anymore! Don't you see? Ever since I started falling for you I've been struggling to hold on to the core of myself, losing my strength little by little. It's the real reason I was so afraid to love you, even when I realized that you wanted to marry me and my rules about never dating subordinates didn't really apply anymore."

Brick reeled inwardly as he tried to digest this news. He'd always believed that it was what other people thought of how Karen did her job that had kept her from surrendering her heart to him. No wonder she'd battled him so fiercely! From her point of view, her very core as a person was at stake.

"You're right about the rest of the men adjusting sooner or later to our marriage. I know they will. But I don't know what it's going to do to me. *Inside.* I need to be hard to keep the men under my control, Brick. I have to be tough to survive." She brushed back a new wave of tears. "You make me feel sweet and soft and silky. I've cried more since I met you than I have in the past three years!"

Brick kissed her temple. He didn't know what to say.

"I fell apart at the courthouse. I've never felt so helpless in my whole adult life. And there wasn't even an emergency!"

"Karen, your own wedding is an emergency! Aunt Anna says that every bride falls apart over something on her wedding day. This is a unique set of circumstances that won't ever occur again."

"But how do I know that, Brick? How do I know that sometime you'll be on duty, and I'll hear there's trouble, and I'll have to make a decision—"

"You'll make it, Karen. I'm sure."

At last he seemed to reach her. She pulled back, her eyes finally dry. "Are you, Brick? Are you really?"

Slowly, he nodded. Even if he hadn't believed it, he would have told her the same thing. This was not the time to air his own reservations...reservations he'd long since buried, or at least put on hold. After all, they were in a hotel room on their honeymoon, not in the middle of a shoot-out. "You're tough as toenails, bunkie," he assured her with all the confidence he could muster. "We'll look back and laugh about this a few years down the road."

At last Karen smiled. It was a small smile, but a smile nonetheless. She was starting to look more embarrassed than depressed. "I felt as though I were losing a grip on myself for a while there, Brick. When you showed up, I had to keep you at a distance to make sure I didn't...get *us* confused with *me*."

"Karen, I warned you we'd have some adjustments to make in the 'us' department," he reminded her, wishing they could have made them without Karen's becoming so rattled. "We're going to have our ups and downs. But nothing's going to happen that we can't handle as long as we're honest with each other. You're not the only one who's never been married before, you know. You're not the only one who's been scared to death tonight."

That was when she laid both hands on his face, her gray eyes meeting his with love and a whole new brand of tenderness. "I never meant to hurt you, bunkie. I've loved you almost from the start."

Brick took her hands and kissed each palm. "Likewise, Kare. Flipping me on my backside isn't the only way you took me off guard."

Her smile was broader this time. He decided to brave the next step.

"I'm sorry I forgot to pick up flowers for you in all the fuss. At least I brought the ring, even though I left it in the truck."

"It's all right."

He kissed her again, more slowly now, more intimately. As her lips parted to welcome his seeking tongue, her breasts pressed against him, soft and warm. "I had the ring in my pocket all through dinner, but it didn't seem quite appropriate to bring the subject up."

Karen snuggled closer. Her hands slipped down his back and kneaded the base of his spine. "Do you think it might be appropriate now?"

He nodded, fighting the hunger her hands incited in him. "I hope so, Karen Bauer."

She grinned. "You can call me that off duty, but two Bauers at the station house might get confusing."

"I suppose. Especially someday when we'll have two Captain Bauers in the family."

Her grin widened. "We will, Brick. I'm sure of it."

Brick took her hand and led her toward the huge bed. He sat down and pulled Karen onto his lap, then dug out the ring box and handed it to her without fanfare. When she opened the box, true pleasure lit her lovely features.

"Oh, Brick, it's just right."

He touched the artistic ring of roses engraved around a wide gold band. "I knew you wouldn't want anything fancy, but I didn't want it to look like it belonged on a man's hand."

She have him a thank-you kiss that foreshadowed a long night of poignant gratitude. "Brick, it's perfect. Really."

He took it out of the box, lifted her left hand and slowly, gingerly, slipped it on her finger. He kissed her once, very gently, then whispered, "With this ring, I thee wed."

When Karen's eyes met his, Brick saw fresh tears, but they weren't the same kind of tears she'd shed before. He held her hand tightly and said, "I don't remember just what we said in front of that judge, but I'm telling you here and now that I'm proud as hell to be your husband, and I'm going to love you forever."

Karen swallowed hard, then touched his face with the gentlest of hands. "And I'm proud to be your wife, Brick Bauer. I'm even willing to issue a memo to that effect." He was about to kiss her when she added soberly, "Even if I can't make a big fuss publicly, you need to know, for now and for all time—" her voice grew choked with sincerity "—that I belong to you irrevocably."

Brick knew what the words cost her, and he was ready to spend the rest of his life making her glad that she'd taken the risk. He was struggling to find the right words to tell her just that when Karen stood abruptly and marched away from the bed.

Brick fought a fresh wave of fear until he realized that she was unzipping that magnificent Victorian dress, stepping out of it, hanging it up in the hotel

minicloset. Underneath she was wearing a delicate pink
slip, slathered in lace, low-cut and high-slitted. The
satin all but begged for Brick's hands to explore what
it concealed. The bullet scar on Karen's left shoulder
only heightened his desire for her. It was proof that she
was the woman he'd come to love—courageous cop
and still all female.

He stood, struggling for breath, as Karen returned
to the bed. Her walk was different now, fluid, sexy,
openly inviting. She grinned provocatively as she slid
her hands over his chest, then slipped them under his
suit coat and pushed it off along with his heavy overcoat. She didn't bother to hang up either one, just
tossed them on the bed. Slowly, tauntingly, she undid
his tie and unbuttoned his shirt, leaving his quivering
chest naked as she slowly pushed him flat on the bed.

"If memory serves," she teased as she straddled
Brick's lap, "I think this is where we left off." She
leaned forward and bit his chest, ever so lightly, just as
she had the night she'd begged him to leave her room.

Brick growled; he couldn't help himself. Then he
pressed his hands against the satin. Down her back,
over her hips, up the front of her perfect body until
they cupped those deliciously full female breasts. He
was still tense, not quite certain she wouldn't change
her mind again, afraid to let himself get too aroused
until he was sure this was really what Karen wanted. If
she needed him to do nothing but hold her this first
night, he would find a way to do it.

But dear God, let her want more.

He rejoiced when Karen's greedy hands slid down his
chest and tugged on his buckle, rejoiced when the circles his thumbs drew around her nipples made her
squirm. Brick savored each moment as he tapped and

kneaded the tight buds through the slinky satin, listening to Karen whimper.

"Oh, God, Brick! I used to lie awake at night and fantasize about this," she confessed.

"So did I." Brick was already on fire before Karen slid down over him and squeezed him with her thighs. Quickly he tugged her slip over her head, then discarded the lacy bra beneath it. Karen's breasts fell back into his eager hands, and she cried out as he took possession of them.

Brick sucked one nipple into his mouth, teasing it mercilessly with his tongue. Karen gasped, then gasped again, struggling with his belt in fresh frenzy.

She was shaking too hard to do the job right, so Brick helped her with his buckle as she slipped off to one side. Together they dragged down his slacks and her panty hose. Then Karen plunged both hands into his briefs.

Brick was already so hot that he didn't think there was much more she could have done to inflame him, but when she seized the swelling core of his manhood, he lost all control. He whispered her name as she rubbed and tugged and stroked him. He couldn't stifle an aching groan.

The pleasure was so intense Brick could not bear it for long. Abruptly he grabbed Karen's shoulders and pressed her back into the mattress, his knees locking with hers as his manhood probed the entrance to her secret woman's place. Only the tiniest wisp of satin still lay between them.

When Karen moaned with deep, aching hunger, Brick knew it was nearly too late to stop; nearly too late to ask again if he'd correctly read every sign of passion and caring. When he pulled off her satin undies and replaced them with his kneading hand, Karen seemed as desperate for their union as Brick was himself. She was crying out his name now, a veritable litany of sexual desire: *"Brick, Brick, Brick, Brick, Brick!"*

But he'd heard her beg for him before, then beg for him to stop. He still wanted proof that this ultimate merging was truly what she wanted, not another mistake she'd blame him for at daylight.

Karen was tugging on his hair, whispering disconnected syllables of incoherent passion. Brick wanted her so much he thought he'd burst if she turned him aside now. Still, he forced himself to murmur, "Bunkie, are you sure?"

Karen's eyes flashed open as though she'd just landed from a distant flight. For a long moment her blazing gaze met his, reading his desperation to please her, his desperation to please himself. She took a deep breath, as though words were beyond her. Then she found one, just one, as she scraped her nails down his arched back and clawed erotically at the quivering base of his spine.

"Husband," she vowed.

Joyfully he claimed his bride.

IT WAS A WONDERFUL, marvelous, magnificently erotic night. Karen could recall nothing in her entire life that came close to it. Brick wrapped her up in a blanket of tenderness and passion that shut out the entire world. She could not remember police work. She could not remember Tyler. She could not remember fear.

The terrible snowstorm had ended in the night.

It was not until they left the hotel about noon the next day that she came face-to-face with reality again.

As Brick walked her down to her Toyota, his arm possessively draped around her waist, he asked casually, "Should I meet you at our new house? Or do you want to stop by home and break the news to Aunt Anna and Uncle Johnny first? Remember, I have to go on duty at four o'clock."

Karen didn't answer him at once. She had told herself that she would call Commander Harmon right after the ceremony, but she hadn't been able to think of anything but Brick since then; she still felt like cookie dough in his hands. He'd even convinced her to put on her wedding dress again so he could admire her in it over a casual lunch. Now she said slowly, "I meant to call Harmon before I told anybody else."

"There's no reason you can't call him from here. Or from Kelseys'."

"Well, no, I guess not."

He studied her quietly for a moment. "I think we should make this announcement together. If it's just up to you, it's like...you're the queen bee and I'm one of the drones."

Karen flushed. "Hardly that, Brick. Although if I ever decide to have a baby, I'll be glad to have such a skilled worker bee to help me in that endeavor."

"If *we* ever decide to have a baby," he corrected her. "And I hope it's a decision we'll make someday."

It was a small reprimand, but Karen knew he was reminding her that she might be his boss on the job, but he'd never tolerate a secondary role in her private life. She understood his position, but it still made her uneasy.

She was more uneasy still when he said firmly, "If you want to call the commander before we make an announcement in Tyler, that's fine with me, Kare, but

I want you to do it today." His voice was calm, but he was still giving her an order.

An order he could never have given his superior officer until today.

Karen took a deep breath. She wanted to fight him, but she knew he was right. "Okay, Brick."

His face seemed to relax a bit. "My captain's put me on duty till midnight," he reminded her, "but when I'm done I'm coming home to my wife."

Her eyes met his. She could almost feel him reaching for her once more. She could also hear Commander Harmon say, "You *married* the man I sent you to investigate?"

"I'll go try to reach him now, Brick. You better get on back. You know how your cranky boss berates you when you're late."

He gave her a dimpled grin, then kissed her lovingly and lazily. For a minute everything seemed to be okay.

"See you at midnight, Captain," he whispered in her ear, "and then we'll see who's boss."

The next kiss lasted so long that Karen almost forgot they were standing in a freezing public parking lot.

The memory of that kiss kept up her courage when she found a phone and called the commander, who was gone for the weekend. Karen wasn't sure whether to be angry or relieved. It was great that she didn't have to face him. But it wouldn't be easy to face Brick.

Should she stall announcing their marriage until Monday, when she could talk to Harmon? Or should she call back and leave a message now? Even drive by his office and leave a note? Or was she merely looking for excuses to postpone the inevitable? When she thought about telling anyone in the police world that she'd gotten married, her blood turned cold. But when she was with Brick, there was only. . . Brick.

After a few weeks or months or years under his spell, she wondered, would there be any Karen left at all?

Karen's uneasiness began to grow and spread roots as she drove back toward Tyler a good two hours later, after shopping for some household essentials in Sugar Creek. As she reached the outskirts of Tyler, she listened for trouble on her scanner. At first everything sounded routine, but suddenly Clayton's excited voice reported a robbery in progress.

Instinctively Karen picked up speed, listening to Hedda exchange data over the radio with Franklin and Clayton. It was the van again. The same damn pair of crooks! She listened to the cars going out. Hamilton and Ross. Farmer and Smith backing them up.

And then, a few minutes later, Hedda reported to Clayton that Sergeant Fletcher and Lieutenant Bauer were on the way.

It was at that moment that Karen began to feel worried. It was always a big event when a whole Tyler shift converged on a pair of suspects. She wanted to join her men, to back them up, to take charge as captain, even though she knew Brick could handle everything. But she was still a good fifteen minutes away.

Fifteen minutes from the men under her command. Fifteen minutes from her husband. By the time she got there, it would be all over. There was nothing she could do to help her fellow officers. Nothing she could do to help Brick. She felt helpless, impotent, gripped with a brand of disquietude she'd never known before.

Karen knew she'd never get there in time to help, but she flattened her accelerator anyway, desperately wishing she was driving a cruiser with a siren and a lot more horsepower.

Suddenly Clayton hollered, "Send an ambulance! Send an ambulance to Gunther and Third!"

Somebody had been shot! she realized in paralyzing panic. A vision of her father flashed before her, followed by the memory of the night she'd nearly lost Rob. She didn't want Clayton to be injured, or Steve or Franklin or any of the other men. But if Brick... Brick... Brick...

Karen's mind short-circuited. Then all her senses simply shut down.

CHAPTER FOURTEEN

THE MEN SPREAD OUT and covered the downtown district where the two punks had been spotted, but a good ten minutes passed before Brick flushed them out in the open. He chased them for a block and a half, his fingers wrapped tightly around the butt of his gun as he ordered them to stop.

But he was a guard, not a quarterback, and they were too fast for him. One feinted to the left while he fired at the one that slipped right. In the blink of an eye they'd both disappeared into an empty warehouse. In his haste to catch up with them, Brick tripped over an old shovel and fell with a crash that pinpointed his exact location and left his shoulder bloody from a gash. It was a superficial flesh wound that bled profusely, but he was too angry to feel much pain.

By the time he reached the alley in back of the warehouse, the van was squealing away.

"Dammit!" Brick swore to himself, adding a few unsavory epithets he figured a man in his situation was entitled to. How many times were these damn punks going to raid Tyler and get away with it? He'd launched into this mess without time to review last night's log completely, but he knew they'd hit an empty tourist cabin while he'd been honeymooning with Karen. Granted, she'd left her hotel phone number with Steve just in case anybody needed her, but he knew she felt a little guilty—as he did—at being out of town overnight.

He didn't have time to worry about Karen as he headed back to the squad car at a lope. He'd seen Franklin clutch his elbow as he went down, but he wasn't at all sure that an arm wound was his only injury. Mark had been shot in the arm, too. He'd also been shot right through the chest.

Brick was gasping for breath as he rounded the corner, trying to rub out a stitch in his side. An ambulance was just pulling in, siren crying. Two more cruisers had arrived.

So had Karen's Toyota.

The other men looked grave and worried, but it was obvious that they knew the worst was over. It was Karen, who bolted toward him with the speed of a gazelle despite her heels and lacy dress, who looked like the worst was yet to come.

He'd only seen that look on her face once before—when he'd shown up so late at the courthouse. He remembered those long and awkward hours after that, before Karen had broken down and told him how afraid she was of losing him...to his indifference or to some criminal's bullet. Now he saw that fear again. When her gaze fell on his bloody shoulder, all strength seemed to leave her.

"Get a stretcher over here!" she shouted at the attendants. "This man is injured!"

Brick shook his head, trying to calm her down. "It's nothing, Karen," he called out. "Just a scratch. And not even from a bullet."

She didn't seem to hear him. She was still running toward him, her gaze riveted on his shoulder.

"Is it your arm? Your chest? Can you breathe all right?" Deftly she fitted under his arm to help him walk, oblivious to the fact that he was doing just fine on his own steam. "Don't try to talk, just—"

"Karen, I'm all right," he explained again. "I just tripped over a shovel. Don't make a big deal of it, all right?"

Beneath his arm, he could feel her shaking. "A shovel?" she said numbly, as though it were a foreign word.

Brick stepped away from her, embarrassed at the fuss she was making. He didn't want any of the men to think he was falling apart over a little flesh wound.

"Are you sure? You're not just being proud? You're not—"

"Captain!" he snapped, almost past embarrassment now. "I'm all right! Now call off the paramedics and get yourself together!"

It was the order a lieutenant gives to his men. But Karen wasn't one of Brick's men; she was his woman. She was also his superior officer.

A superior officer who was so distraught with fear for his safety that she seemed incapable of making intelligent decisions.

It seemed to take an awfully long time for Karen to pull back and look into his face. "You fell over a shovel? You're not shot? You're going to be all right?"

"Yes." His voice was stony now. *He* was going to be just fine. But he was no longer sure he could say the same for Captain Keppler.

KAREN WENT BACK to the station house after things settled down and the paramedics hustled Franklin off to the emergency room at the hospital. The bullet was lodged in his arm but hadn't shattered any bones. Alyssa's son, Jeff Baron, had assured them that it wouldn't take long for Franklin to be as good as new.

Jeff had also given Brick a tetanus shot and cleaned out his gash, which hadn't even required stitches. Karen felt red-faced every time she thought of how she'd fussed over him. Worse yet, she was worried about that brief paralytic moment in the car when she'd first suspected that he was the man who'd been injured.

It was only for a moment, but she knew she'd panicked like a civilian. Brick—not her husband, but the judgmental Lieutenant Bauer she'd met when she'd first come to town—would have said she'd panicked like a female. She didn't want to believe that she would have indulged her fears if she'd been called to perform in the line of duty, but she couldn't rule out the possibility either. Ever since she'd fallen in love with Brick she'd felt increasingly unsure of herself, like a child trying to run through deep sand. Brick certainly hadn't needed to reprimand her, though. She hadn't been behaving *that* badly.

The instant he reached her office an hour later, Karen knew he didn't see it quite that way.

The man she'd made love to the night before had vanished. It was Lieutenant Bauer, the man whose job she'd "stolen," who marched into the room.

He closed the door without asking permission to speak to her. He filled the space across from her desk.

"Karen, you lost it," he said bluntly. "You lost it altogether out there."

She met his eyes with all the strength she could muster. "I was afraid for my husband. You were doubled over and covered with blood."

"I told you I wasn't hurt. I told you three damn times before I could get you to listen."

"My adrenaline was talking louder than you were."

"Karen, you were in the middle of a police crisis. You reacted like a woman, not like the leader of men."

Slowly she stood up, belatedly hearing the terrible tension underlying Brick's dark calm. It had been a long time since he'd criticized her position. He didn't sound angry; she couldn't tell him to cool down. He sounded profoundly concerned and disheartened.

"I arrived after the crisis was over. The only thing I could do was respond to an injured warrior, a man I promised to love forever."

He studied the desk, his eyes refusing to meet hers. Fresh fear bloomed within her. A new kind of fear.

"Karen, you were lucky we were out of earshot of the other men. If they'd seen you crack up like that, if they knew you'd lost control—"

"They'd think I was human. Aren't you the one who's always telling me to admit my true feelings and not act like a robot? Besides, what man in my position wouldn't have felt a moment's panic if he found his wife covered with blood?"

Now his eyes met hers. "He would have hidden it better."

"On zero hours of sleep in the middle of his honeymoon? For Pete's sake, Brick, this isn't exactly an ordinary workday for me! I'm tense. I'm upset. I'm exhausted!"

"Sometimes cops are frazzled on the job, Karen. But they can't afford to lose their stuff."

She straightened, wishing desperately that she was wearing something other than this delicate lacy dress that reminded them both of how totally she'd submitted to his strength the night before. It made her feel like the most feminine of creatures, not like a crusty cop.

"I had a moment's panic when there was nothing I could do to help. Half of my frustration was because I was so far away when I first heard the officer-assist call that I knew I'd never reach the scene in time to help anyone."

"To help *me*," he said coldly. "You didn't give a damn about the other men."

"That's not true!" she flared. "I cared about all of them. You know how strongly I reacted the night you told me Clayton was injured, and I considered him the weakest man on this force! Oh, I won't deny that I was more afraid for you than for the others, but what officer doesn't have people he cherishes more than others?"

"Franklin was shot tonight. You ran straight to me."

"Franklin had three officers and two paramedics fussing over him when I got there. You were all alone."

"I wasn't hurt!"

"I didn't know that!" Suddenly she stopped, realizing that they were hollering at each other. What had happened since they'd kissed goodbye in Sugar Creek? It had been only a few hours ago. This wasn't a scrap that occurred just because two people were tired and edgy. Something was troubling Brick deeply. Remembering his patience with her withdrawn behavior the night before, she tried to return the favor.

"Brick, why don't you sit down and tell me why you're really so upset. I'm sorry if I embarrassed you, but—"

"*Embarrassed* me? You think that's what this is all about?"

Honestly, she said, "I think that's part of it. What cop wants his buddies to know he let two suspects escape because he tripped over a shovel?"

"Karen, this is far more serious than that."

She disagreed; she really thought the odd collection of circumstances had contributed to make Brick so upset. He hadn't had a lick of sleep, either; he was hardly at his best. If he'd just been her lieutenant, she would have told him he was out of line and tossed him out of her office. But he was her husband, and she owed him more than that.

"I'm listening," she said stoutly.

He shook his head. "I'm sorry, Kare. I'm really... very sorry."

It wasn't an apology, at least not for anything he'd already said. There was another reason for those words, and whatever it was, the somber tone of his voice put Karen on edge.

"I don't—" he seemed to choke on the words "—think I can forget this, Karen. If you'd given me an order out there—captain to lieutenant—I don't think I could have obeyed you in good conscience. I would have given my own commands based on the needs of the men."

Her skin began to crawl. "I don't think I follow you."

He tried to meet her eyes and failed. "I told you once before that I wouldn't stab you in the back, Karen. I gave you a chance to prove yourself. In a lot of ways, you're a splendid officer. I know there's a place for you in the county system... out of the line of fire in administration." At last he met her eyes. "But you're not cut out to run a substation. You don't have the hard edge you need to lead and protect this group of men."

Karen was struck dumb.

"You made your own report to Commander Harmon based on your vision of me as an officer," Brick continued darkly. "I understood. Now I'm asking you to understand that I have to let him know what I think, too." His eyes looked flat and hopeless, almost sick with grief. "Mark's memory won't let me turn away from this, Kare. I have to tell Harmon I don't think you're fit to command."

At last she found her voice—a thin, reedy version of her regular voice, but the voice of Karen Keppler nonetheless. "*You* don't think *I'm* fit to command? Based on the honest expression of my fear that you were mortally injured?"

"It's more than that," he said, his voice low and aching now. "Last night, I just wanted to be supportive. I wanted everything to be all right between us. I wanted—"

"You wanted to get me into bed!"

Brick recoiled as though she'd hit him, but still he pressed on. "Dammit, Karen, when you were telling me that you'd lost yourself, that you were too wound up in me to think, I was...honored. As a man. I wanted you to be so crazy in love with me that you were off base. I didn't want you to be unhappy, but...having you feel so helpless made me feel like a stronger man." He ran one hand through his thick black hair. "Now I'm hearing those words again as a police officer under your direction. It gives me the willies."

A deep, volcanic anger was growing inside Karen now. Her worst fears had tracked her down, converged upon her in this moment. And Karen Keppler was a fighter. When she was cornered, she came out fighting.

"I didn't share my innermost feelings with Lieutenant Bauer. I shared them with my husband!"

"Karen, I know that. And I'm not going to repeat them to—"

"How dare you judge my performance in this office by my performance in bed! How dare you use our marriage as an excuse to justify every prejudice you've ever harbored against women cops! How dare you assume that because I bared my soul to you in one or two shaky moments I won't be there for my men when the chips are down and we're dodging bullets!"

"Karen, we *were* dodging bullets! We were counting on each other. We sure as hell weren't counting on you!"

"That's not my fault! If I'd been ten miles closer, I would have gotten there in time to help, and I would have pulled my weight, Brick Bauer! How dare you assume otherwise just because I wasn't thrilled to see you bleeding!"

"Karen, it's over!" He leaned forward, jamming both heavy fists down on her desk. "You gave it your best shot. Your dad would be proud. But you can't keep pretending that you can do this job. You've been lucky so far. But how are you going to feel if somebody dies because of you?"

She faced him coolly. "I couldn't possibly feel as guilty as you would. If you're honest with yourself, you'll admit that the main reason you're so afraid to trust me is because you still blame yourself for what happened to Mark."

"I can't trust you because I know how soft you really are, Karen! It makes you a wonderful woman and a wonderful wife. But it makes you an inadequate cop."

Karen shook her head, too deeply hurt for anger now. "The woman you married—the one you said you wanted—isn't a helpless female, Brick. In bed she may be sweet and passionate, but on the streets, she'll always be a police officer as tough as they come." Suddenly, for the first time in twenty-four hours, Karen *felt* tough again. Brick's words had hit her in the face like a bucket full of ice. The bridal hysteria had vanished. Once again she was a police captain who would unhesitatingly do what must be done.

"I knew it would be a challenge for you to live with my two roles, Brick, but I thought—I convinced myself—that you were a big enough man to cope with it." Despite Karen's unwavering resolution, it wasn't easy to utter the next horrible words, and for Brick's sake, she said them softly. "Deep down inside, I always knew it was a mistake to marry you."

"No, Kare!" His voice was hoarse and low. "I don't need a captain for a wife. All I want is you. No matter what profession you choose or—"

"You don't get it, do you, Brick? You can't report me as a washout to the commander and expect me to be your wife! Nobody knows yet, and as rushed as that slapdash ceremony was, we've probably got grounds for annulment without all the hassle of divorce. Besides—"

"No, Karen, no!" The pain in his voice was ripped from his soul. "You know you'd do the same thing in my place! I can't turn my back on what I believe is right! You wouldn't want me to."

Slowly, sadly, she shook her head. "No, I wouldn't want you to."

A moment of hope lit his beautiful blue eyes. "Then you can forgive me? You'll forgive me in time?"

Karen tugged at her lacy sleeve, wishing she could throw the dress in the trash. Why had she violated all her instincts and given herself to this compelling man? She'd known right from the start that loving him would devastate her. "Brick, don't you see? It doesn't matter whether I forgive you or not, or even whether Commander Harmon takes any action on your complaint." She was too full of despair to be angry. Not since her father's death had she felt so totally devoid of hope. "I can't live with a man who doesn't have any faith in me without losing faith in myself. If I ever grow to believe that I failed here—that you're right, that I'm a coward, that I'm not fit to be the captain of these men—then there won't *be* any Karen Keppler, Brick. There won't be any *me* left to be your wife."

Brick lifted one hand beseechingly, but he couldn't seem to speak. Karen had never seen him look so bowed by sorrow.

For a long, terrible moment Karen just stood there, knowing it was over, but too sad to say goodbye. It wasn't the first time a male colleague had tried to ax her career by reporting her to somebody up the line and she didn't think it would be the last. But Karen had always gotten over it before. This was different. Brick's betrayal would haunt her for the rest of her life.

She was about to ask him to leave her office when the door burst open and Hedda cried out, "It's another officer-in-need-of-assistance call! Steve spotted that van on his way home to Belton and chased it out to Timberlake Lodge. He's going to end up out there all alone! Clayton's still at the hospital with Franklin, and I can't raise Smith and Farmer—"

"Bauer! You're with me!" Karen snapped as she grabbed her gun from her purse and bolted out the door.

Brick didn't hesitate for even a second. Instinctively he responded to the voice of command.

ANNA WAS JUST CARRYING in a load of groceries when she heard the phone ring. It took five rings—almost six—before she reached it.

"Hello, Kelseys'," she said cheerfully.

"Anna?" It was Janice, Janice sounding like a frightened child, lost and all alone. "Anna? Are you there?"

"Well, of course, I'm here, dear. Whatever is wrong?"

There was a silence. A silence that slithered eerily from Anna's back to her shoulders; a silence that lasted far too long.

"Anna? Can you come over here?" There was a terse, terrible pause before she added, *"Right now?"*

Anna stifled a shiver of panic. Not once in the forty-odd years that she'd known Janice Eber had she ever sounded quite the way she did now.

"Of course I can rush right over there, Janice, if you need me. But tell me—"

Suddenly she heard Janice gulp back a sob.

"Janice?" Anna's heart was now slamming bitterly against the walls of her chest. "Janice, for pity's sake, tell me what's wrong!"

"It's Kurt!" Her voice was breaking now. "He collapsed playing handball! They've rushed him to the hospital. I can't . . . I don't think . . . Anna, I've got to get to him, but I don't think I can drive!"

Anna could hardly breathe. Kurt was Janice's whole world. She didn't take a step without her husband's say-so, saw no life for herself without him as the center. Surely Kurt would recover quickly! There was no way her dear friend could carry on without him.

"Wait for me out front, dear. I've got my keys in my hand. I'm leaving right now!"

She dumped the perishables on the counter and bolted back to the garage. In less than three minutes she reached the Eber house. Janice ran full speed to the street when she saw the car.

All the way to the hospital she clung to Anna's hand, her grip so hard that Anna's bones ached. Janice wept softly, but she never said a word. Anna talked nonstop, trying to quell her friend's panic. Her promises glistened with ungrounded hope: "He'll be fine. George Phelps and Jeff Baron will take care of him. He'll be up and around in no time."

But the instant she pulled into the hospital parking lot, Anna knew she'd been lying to herself . . . and to Janice, too. George Phelps was waiting outside the emergency-room doors. His kind face was full of sorrow as he walked very slowly toward Janice, who had bolted from the car.

Janice didn't seem to notice the evidence that Anna read on George's face. By now she was shaking convulsively. Desperately she whispered, "Is Kurt going to be all right?"

George took Anna's hands in his and squeezed them gently. Then he said in his most soothing doctor's voice, "He didn't suffer, Janice. He had only a moment's pain, no time to be frightened." He put his arms around her and finished gently, "He was gone before he hit the ground."

As BRICK RACED Karen to the cruiser, he didn't have time to think. He'd exchanged gunfire up close with the two punks, and he knew they were ruthless—cornered as well. Without some help, Steve didn't have a chance. Even with help...

Desperately he hoped they could reach him in time.

Karen got into the car first and jumped into the driver's seat before Brick could stop her. Karen had driven with him in the cruiser before, but never, in all the time he'd known her, had they ever rushed to a scene together with the certain knowledge that they were going into danger.

Going into danger with their future utterly haywire. Going into danger when Karen might take foolish chances to prove her courage to him.

Brick wanted to warn her not to be stupid. He wanted to tell her to go home. But those were the things he longed to say to his wife, not his captain. And he wasn't sure if the woman carrying the .38 Smith & Wesson still belonged to him. All he was sure of was that—for the moment—she outranked him.

They roared into the parking lot of Timberlake Lodge with the siren wailing, bolting out of the cruiser the moment it came to a stop. Brick heard a gunshot off toward the potting shed. Then he heard a body hit the ground.

He ran full out toward the gunfire, with Karen right behind him. He took a position to the right of the potting shed; Karen turned off to the left. Ahead of him he could hear popping sounds. Shots. Then Brick nearly tripped over a man lying on the ground.

It was one of the punks he'd chased that afternoon. He looked dead. His chest was bloody. He certainly wasn't moving. Brick forgot him an instant later when the other punk bolted through the narrow space between his position and Karen's.

"Hold it right there!" Brick hollered, firing a warning shot. "You're under arrest."

When the man froze and dropped his gun, Brick felt a keen relief that all but drained him. It was always great to know he'd caught the criminal, great to know he'd escaped with his life. But he'd never felt almost giddy with relief before. Only now that it was over could he allow himself to realize how terrified he'd been that Karen would be injured.

Quickly he crossed the narrow walkway, pulling his handcuffs from his belt. "Turn around and put your hands behind you," he ordered. "You have the right to an attorney. You have the right to remain silent. Anything—"

"I have the right to shoot you in the back, pig," growled a dark, ugly voice from the ground behind him. "So why don't you put down that piece real slow."

Brick's heart hammered into overdrive. How could he have been so careless? The man on the ground had looked dead—certainly harmless—but obviously he was still alive and kicking. Did he have a gun? Did he know Karen was out there, or did he think the gunshots from the left had come from another uniformed cop? Why was Steve still so silent? Had he been shot, too?

Brick heard the pistol's hammer cock, inches from his ankle. "Drop the gun, fuzz!"

Slowly, he did as he was told. There was a chance—a slight chance—that they wouldn't kill him. They were break-and-enter punks, not professional killers. They could still take their loot and run.

As he made a mental calculation of Karen's whereabouts, Brick realized that she could not get the drop on the punk without revealing her location prematurely. He didn't want her to risk helping him, anyway. All he wanted her to do was stay out of sight. If she slipped back to the cruiser and drove off or called for help, she might still get out of this alive.

If only this had happened an hour ago, when she could have lived with the memory of their one marvelous night together! Brick didn't want to die without telling her he loved her. He didn't want her last memory of him to be that terrible fight.

The punk he'd been about to handcuff turned around and glared at him smugly. "Well, well, the tables are turned now, aren't they?" He grabbed Brick's gun from the pavement. "You want to shoot him, Earl, or should I?"

"You do it," said the bleeding man on the ground gasping for air. "I got to shoot the other one."

Brick's last hope died in that instant. He prepared to face his end like a man.

And then, incredibly, he heard a frail female voice call out, "Oh, Donald! Where are you? I heard all those nasty bullets and then—"

Brick turned sharply, sickened and stunned, as Karen came sashaying into view. In her lacy dress and heels, she looked sweet and feminine and utterly helpless. Had she completely lost her senses? The punks hadn't known she was back there. She could have escaped! He'd thought she was safely out of harm's way by now!

"Get over here, sister," the first man said, grabbing Karen roughly around the waist. The gun that had been aimed at Brick now was pressed against her temple.

"Looks like we're going to have a party. Do you think we should kill him first, or make him watch and wait?"

Brick was so full of dread for Karen that he could hardly think. There had to be a way to save her! He knew he could disarm the injured guy on the ground, but not before the other one shot Karen. He had never been so willing to die, so willing to risk anything at all to save another person. But his love for his wife paralyzed him. No miraculous escape plan leaped to mind.

Desperately Brick met Karen's eyes, longing to give her comfort. At the very least, he had to let her know he loved her. He had to say goodbye.

But the moment he glanced at Karen, Brick realized that she had a completely different agenda in mind. Her eyes held not a glimpse of surrender or regret. *Trust me, damn you!* they ordered, glittering with careful calculation.

Brick was overwhelmed. While he'd been writhing in helpless panic, Karen had done what he'd been unable to do—set a plan in motion! She hadn't been able to draw a gun in her position, so she'd darted in to save him armed only with her hands. She'd called him Donald, for Pete's sake. What an obvious clue!

Despite the delicate dress and heels, Captain Keppler was joining him in battle. His *wife* might be sweet and harmless, but suddenly Brick realized that his *captain* was still competent and shrewd.

"Ooh, what happened to that poor man on the ground?" Karen simpered, her eyes still on Brick. Then—ever so quickly—her glance fell toward the pavement. A moment later she bent forward as though to look at the unfortunate fellow, and Brick went into action.

He could not have explained to anyone how he knew what Karen was going to do in that instant. He didn't have time to think it through, to remember her past or the tiny details of her history. He did not know whether it was his captain or his woman that he trusted so completely, but he knew instinctively—without doubt or hesitation—that he could count on her to disable the punk who thought he held her in an unbreakable grip. And he knew that she was counting on him to disarm the other one.

The next two seconds went like clockwork. Brick couldn't see Karen as he whirled on the prone man with the gun, already injured and taken by surprise. Brick had him pinned in an instant. By then he heard the sound he'd been subconsciously waiting for. The thump of a big male body hitting the dirt.

Karen had maneuvered into her favorite self-defense position and flipped the man right over onto his back. When Brick glanced up at her, she was standing above the stunned crook, pointing his own gun at his head.

She looked like an angel but she sounded as tough as Dirty Harry when she ordered, "Don't move a millimeter. Touch me again and you're going to lose a vital portion of your anatomy."

No words ever sounded sweeter to Brick's ears. Captain Keppler was back on duty! Karen had reclaimed her soul.

He was terribly afraid that it might be too late to reclaim her love for him, but he would sleep a thousand times better knowing he hadn't caused her to lose herself. How could he have misjudged her so completely? Had his own wedding passion blurred his common sense?

Was that why he'd blundered into this situation in the first place? Had he done precisely what he'd accused Karen of doing—losing his grip when faced with the possibility of losing his beloved spouse?

Karen rolled the punk over, handcuffed and frisked him while Brick did the same to the other one. "Where's the other cop?" she demanded, without so much as a glance in Brick's direction. "You want to live, you tell me now. I won't ask again." She didn't sound a bit like the fragile jewel who'd wept in his arms last night.

The bewildered criminal croaked, "He went down over there." He jabbed an elbow toward the main lodge. "My partner punched him out."

"Steve!" Karen called, poking her gun into the man's neck. "Are you conscious? Are you all right?"

Deep concern colored her voice... the proper concern of a captain for all her men.

Then Brick heard Steve call out, "I'm all right, Captain Keppler. Dizzy and winded, but I'm not hit."

Brick felt a sudden wash of feeling so powerful he was hard-pressed to contain it. He was thrilled to hear Steve's voice, thrilled to see Karen safe, and thrilled to be alive. But it was more than that. He was...dammit, he was humbled. He was *impressed*. He was damn proud to be part of the Tyler substation that rose to the call of such a leader.

A leader of men.

Steve wobbled around the corner, belatedly brandishing his gun. The rueful look on his face made Brick wonder how long he'd really been out. Steve seemed to be avoiding his eyes. Was it possible that he'd had a moment of panic after he came to? Had he decided to lie low when things looked so grim... cowering while

Karen had used a uniquely feminine tactic in order to save Brick's life?

Suddenly Brick was sure that was what had happened. But he couldn't hold it against Steve. He was a man who'd been there for Brick a dozen times. So he had feet of clay. He was human. A shaky moment could be forgiven between men.

In a wash of understanding, Brick realized that Karen had been right all along. He never had given her a fair chance as a captain, not really. She *had* started out with two strikes against her. If she'd been a man, he would have given her the benefit of the doubt during her rough patch.

The man Karen had flipped on his back was now looking pitifully at Brick. "Don't let her shoot me," he bleated. "I didn't know she was a killer cop. I thought she was just a woman!"

"Are you kidding me?" Brick warned with all the ferocity he could muster. "She's a black widow. Eats slimes like you for breakfast. You think they'd put a woman in charge of the Tyler substation if she wasn't twice as tough as any of the men?"

Following Brick's cue, Steve chimed in, "You don't mess with Captain Killer. You don't mess with our Captain K!"

A fresh wave of tenderness swept over Brick. How Karen had longed for a nickname that spoke of the men's respect and affection! By morning every man on the force would know about the innovative courage she'd displayed tonight. Every man would know that "Captain Killer" had saved Brick's life with her own bare hands while those punks had rendered him helpless.

Thank God none of them would know that Brick had gotten his soft, sensual wife mixed up with his captain earlier today and almost blackened this splendid police officer's fine career. At least he hadn't ruined her self-confidence. She was strong enough to survive any challenge life threw at her. She'd sure as hell proved it today.

Karen loaded the two men in the cruiser by herself, leaving Brick with little to do but crawl in the front of the car to sit rather sheepishly beside her. For the first mile or so she was busy cracking commands over the police radio, but when silence finally enveloped the car, Brick found himself desperately longing to beg for her forgiveness.

It wasn't until they'd reached the station and jailed the suspects that Brick dared to approach her. He entered her office and found her sitting behind her desk in her raggedy wedding dress, looking more beautiful, more distant and more angry than he'd ever seen her before.

"Karen?" he began softly, struggling to face her. He didn't know what to say to her. He couldn't imagine what words would be powerful enough to win her back, but somehow he had to find them. He was willing to do anything. He was willing to beg.

"This afternoon I said some things... jumped to some conclusions...." He took a deep breath. "I'm sorrier than you can ever know, Kare. And more grateful. You saved my life today."

Karen glared at him with about as much warmth as she'd glared at the two punks. "You blew it out there, Lieutenant. You let your personal concerns interfere with your professional judgement. It's inconceivable to me that an experienced officer could turn his back on a suspect just because he was on the ground.''

Brick took a deep breath. He wasn't talking to his wife. This was hard-nosed Captain Keppler he was facing. Would she write him up? Report him to Harmon? Get back at him for what, an hour ago, he'd threatened to do?

"I'm human," he said simply. "You are, too."

Her eyes were cold. "My personal strengths and weaknesses are none of your concern, Lieutenant. If you feel that my performance is inadequate and you wish to lodge a complaint, that is your business, but you do it on your own time."

Brick found himself staring down at his hands. He'd never felt so helpless, so stupid, so lost. "Karen, I was wrong. You want to hear me say it again?" Bravely he faced her once more. "I'm groveling here, okay? I'm on my knees. I made a terrible mistake today—and I don't just mean out there at the lodge. I know I wouldn't have judged you so harshly if you'd been a man who had a weak moment, and I wouldn't have been so afraid for you if you weren't my wife. I'm sorry. I'm a heel." He took a step closer, aching to touch her face and terrified that it was a liberty she'd never allow him again. "But I love you, dammit. Please don't ax me out of your life."

Karen responded to his impassioned plea by picking up the phone. "I have to call the hospital and check on Franklin, Lieutenant," she informed him coolly. "You have a report to write."

Brick felt sick. Desperate. There had to be a way! He couldn't just let her turn her back on him. Now that he'd known Karen Keppler's love, he knew he could never live without it.

"Bunkie, please! I'm begging you . . ."

She didn't tell him to leave again. She simply ignored him and started speaking into the phone.

Battling a wave of nausea, Brick turned to leave her office. He felt shell-shocked as he groped for the door, moved by instinct to his own desk. He tried to focus on his paperwork; he tried to feign interest in the celebratory noise in the squad room. Swensen and Harold, roused by all the news on the scanner, had drifted in from home. Steve was regaling them with the story of Captain Killer's dramatic performance, embellishing the tale along the way. Hedda interrupted twice to remind Steve that the captain had praised her level-headed dispatching throughout the tense afternoon.

Nobody seemed to notice that Brick wasn't talking, and for that he was glad. He couldn't bear to let his friends know what he'd been through today. How high his expectations had been at sunrise! How they'd plummeted with the fall of night! He'd been so certain that today Karen would announce their marriage and tell the world she was proud to be his wife.

Now Brick was going to be the man who'd been her husband for a single night. And out of deference to the woman he would cheerfully have died for, he could never tell a soul.

An anguished hour passed before he suddenly felt a familiar hand on the back of his neck, a hand that was gentle yet strong and curiously possessive. He caught a whiff of the soapy scent of the woman he loved.

"Don't bother to dot your i's and cross your t's, Lieutenant," Karen ordered in a sultry voice Brick remembered from last night. "It's your honeymoon, after all, and it would be bad form to make your bride wait up for you tonight."

The office went dead still. Nobody moved; nobody breathed. Brick thought he must have died because his heart had simply stopped beating.

Slowly, with desperate hope raging in his heart, he turned to face his woman. Had a miracle occurred? Was there any chance—any chance at all—that now that she'd had time to cool off she might be able to forgive him? Was it possible she was announcing their marriage right here and now, so sure of herself and of his newborn understanding that she knew he would never question her strength on the job again?

When their eyes met, Karen smiled, a magnificent smile that promised Brick every dream he'd ever longed for. Her beautiful face was full of love and hope and forgiveness . . . for all the ways they'd hurt each other and all the ways they might accidentally hurt each other again. On Monday she'd told Brick she had enough love for him to last for 160 years of marriage. How could he have doubted that she had enough to get through the first terrible day?

Karen looked around the squad room, proudly facing her people one by one. She waited until their shocked expressions turned to stunned but happy grins, then took Brick's hand and purred, "It's been a long day, husband. Let's go home."

And now,
an exciting preview of

SUNSHINE

by Pat Warren

the sixth installment of the
Tyler series coming in August

When homebody Janice Eber's husband,
Kurt, dies of a sudden heart attack, she must
learn to cope with her loss, the responsibility
of his business and some shocking facts she
discovers that shatter her illusions about her
perfect marriage. Kurt's old friend, David
Marcus, teaches Janice to become her own
woman, as well as to let go of the past and
learn to love again.

Watch for it next month, wherever Harlequin books are sold.

CHAPTER ONE

EMPTY. She felt empty inside, lost and bewildered. And alone, despite all the people she'd left sleeping back at her house. The big, two-story house she and Kurt had lived in together for all but two years of their twenty-three-year marriage. The house that she would now occupy alone.

Janice Ingalls Eber gathered the collar of her winter coat closer about her throat and stared out at the icy center of Lake Waukoni. She'd awakened early and driven out here to one of the peaceful places she and Kurt had visited often. Only half an hour's drive from Tyler, the small lake wasn't nearly as popular as Wisconsin's Lake Winnebago, which was one reason they'd liked coming here to fish, to picnic, to lie on the thick grass in the summertime.

In her mind's eye, Janice could picture Kurt rowing away from shore, his strong, tan arms moving rhythmically, his dark eyes laughing at her because she'd insisted they wear life jackets. She'd always been the cautious, careful one, while Kurt had loved the excitement of challenges, physical and otherwise. As a young man, he'd raced cars, learned to fly single-engine planes and skied every chance he had. He'd had a restless energy that seemed to drive him to swim regularly, even late into the season, to jog daily and to compete fiercely in tennis matches with friends.

At forty-six, slim and wiry with not an ounce of spare flesh, Kurt Eber took care of himself and was the picture of health. Or so Janice thought until five days ago when she'd received the call. Kurt had died of a massive coronary while playing handball.

The rising sun shimmered on the surface of the lake and would probably melt much of the accumulated snow on this unseasonably warm January day. The day she would be burying her husband. Despite the mild morning, Janice shivered and thrust her hands deep into her coat pockets.

Fragmented thoughts drifted through her dazed mind. The frantic phone call from Kurt's office manager and handball opponent, Tom Sikes, urging her to rush to the hospital. Her best friend, Anna Kelsey, offering to drive, her solid presence keeping Janice from falling to pieces. Dr. George Phelps, an old friend and their family physician, holding her hands, as he gravely told her that Kurt had been dead almost before he'd hit the floor. She should cling to that, George had said— that Kurt hadn't suffered more than a moment's swift pain.

Janice had wanted to lash out at him to shriek a denial that surely he had to be wrong. Kurt couldn't be gone so quickly, so unfairly. He wouldn't leave her like that. He'd always been there for her. Always, since they'd met at the University of Wisconsin so long ago. Just after she'd finished her sophomore year, Kurt, newly graduated, had persuaded her to quit college and elope with him, to leave her father's house and become his bride. Surely this had to be some cruel joke.

But it hadn't been.

Hunching her slender shoulders against a sudden gust of wind that swirled powdery snow at her, Janice turned and walked slowly back to her station wagon. She'd best return, for her children would be wondering about her absence. She'd left a brief note on the kitchen counter explaining that she'd gone for a short drive, but they'd worry anyhow.

Kurt, Jr.—K.J. as he'd been affectionately labeled as a youngster—a junior at his father's alma mater, undoubtedly would be pacing the kitchen and drinking black coffee as Kurt so often had. His sister Stefanie, only two years older and believing herself to be much more mature, would be calmly making breakfast for everyone. In her disoriented state, Janice had insisted that her father as well as her sister and brother-in-law, Irene and Everett, stay at the house, and now she regretted the impulsive invitation. She dreaded being alone, yet she craved it, an odd dichotomy of emotions. Perhaps they would sense her mood and leave right after today's funeral service.

Janice got behind the wheel and turned the key. After a few rumbles, the engine caught. She and Kurt had talked about going shopping next month for a new car for her. With a trembling sigh, she wondered if she would be able to make such a large purchase on her own. She'd never picked out furniture or anything major without him. Swallowing back a fresh rush of tears, Janice headed for home.

SHE WAS SHAKY, but holding up well, Anna Kelsey thought as she stood studying Janice Eber across the funeral bier. Her long auburn hair was coiled under a black felt hat and her wide gray eyes were hidden behind huge sunglasses. Anna's heart went out to the slim, fragile woman who'd been her close friend for more than twenty years. It was difficult enough burying the very elderly; to bury a husband in the prime of life was a travesty, Anna believed.

Needing a moment's reassurance, Anna slipped her hand into her husband's, and felt his strong fingers tighten in response. The death of a friend was a stark reminder of everyone's mortality, she thought. Of course, Johnny and Kurt had not really been friends, not the way she and Janice were.

With his thriving insurance business and his near-obsession with competitive sports, Kurt was quite different from Anna's husband. Johnny was a foreman at Ingalls Farm and Machinery and preferred quieter activities such as fishing, camping and a game of touch football with their grown children and expanding family. With Anna's help, Johnny also operated Kelsey Boardinghouse, while Kurt had owned a large Victorian-style home, driven a Mercedes and worn five-hundred-dollar suits. Quite a difference.

A chill wind blew across the snow-covered hillside cemetery where the large gathering of mourners stood by the grave. Anna had known the townspeople would come in droves, for Tyler was a friendly place to live, a supportive community. Though Janice Eber had never worked outside her home, through the years she'd volunteered at her kids' school, the library and the hospital, and she was well liked.

She was a sweet woman, Anna thought, a good wife, caring mother and wonderful homemaker. Anna had never heard Janice raise her voice nor give a dissenting opinion. She simply didn't like to make waves, which often annoyed Anna, who felt Janice ought to speak out more, be a little more assertive.

Anna watched the solemn-faced minister move to the head of the casket and begin reading the Twenty-third

Psalm. Shifting her gaze, she saw Janice's face turn even paler as her son gripped her hand on one side and her daughter gripped the other. Kurt had been from Boston, an only child whose parents had died some years back, so there were no Ebers to mourn his passing. But the Ingalls clan was well represented, flanking Janice on both sides under the dark green canopy.

The Ingalls family had been involved in the early settling of Tyler. Inventive and industrious, they were still the wealthiest folks in town. Janice's father, Herbert, ran the company lab in Milwaukee and seemed friendly and down-to-earth to Anna. His wife died years ago and Herbert had raised both Janice and Irene. No two people could be less alike than Janice and her sister, Anna thought as she watched Irene clutch her full-length mink coat more tightly around her ample bosom.

Then there was Janice's uncle, Judson Inglass, Tyler's patriarchal figure at nearly eighty. Tall and dignified, he stood next to his widowed daughter, Alyssa Baron, and her three children. In truth, they were no longer children. The oldest, Dr. Jeffrey Baron, was thirty and already being mentioned as the next chief of staff at Tyler General Hospital.

Next was Amanda, a couple of years younger, sweet and unaffected and a practicing lawyer in Tyler. And the youngest, Liza, a fun-loving, spirited young woman, a decorator who'd recently married a somewhat reclusive fellow named Cliff Forrester. A striking family, attractive and intelligent and, with the possible exception of Liza, dignified in their bearing.

Had the Ingalls family, with their wealth and style, made Kurt into the man he'd become—a restless superachiever and self-made businessman who'd never quite felt accepted despite his best efforts? Anna asked herself that question as she heard the minister winding down. Kurt had married Janice when she was very young, obviously wanting to exceed her family's achievements, to make her proud of him. Anna wondered if Kurt ever knew that Janice would have loved him just as much if he'd been a used-car salesman.

Stepping back with Johnny, Anna stood among her own children, watching the many citizens of Tyler file past to say goodbye to Kurt and offer a word of comfort to Janice. She saw her two married daughters, Laura and Glenna, walk over with their husbands to talk with their cousins.

Looking up at her husband, Anna squeezed Johnny's hand. "I think you should phone the office for an appointment," she said quietly. "You haven't had a checkup in a long time." As Dr. Phelps's receptionist, she knew the health history of nearly everyone in town, yet she had trouble persuading this stubborn man to take care of himself.

"I will," Johnny answered in the vague way he had when he didn't want to argue the point. Obviously he had no intention of complying. "Are you going to Janice's when this is over?"

"Yes, of course. You remember last night, all that baking I did? I had Patrick run it over to Janice's earlier."

Johnny frowned. "What about the rest of the town? You have enough to do without—"

Anna stopped him, raising a hand to caress his cheek. "Lots of people are bringing food. It's already done, so don't fret. We *wanted* to do it this way. Alyssa dropped off several platters already and Marge Peterson sent two boxes of covered dishes from the diner. You should stop and have something to eat.''

"I can't. We've got a lot of people out at the plant with this damn flu bug.'' Johnny glanced up at the early-afternoon sun. "Freezing one day, then almost sixty the next. Half the town's sick with it.''

"It's still the middle of winter,'' Anna commented as she frowned at her only son. "Patrick, why aren't you wearing a topcoat?''

Patrick Kelsey smiled at his mother. "I'm married now, Mom,'' he answered as he slipped his arm around his wife's slim waist. "You can't boss me around anymore.''

"As if I ever could,'' Anna muttered. "Pam, you need to take a firmer hand with your husband.''

Pam Casals Kelsey looked up into her husband's vivid blue eyes. "I try,'' Pam answered. "I insisted Patrick bring his coat and he insisted we leave it in the car.''

"That's because my son thinks he's a macho man,'' Anna responded with a smile. But then her gaze shifted back to Janice.

There was a weary slump to her friend's shoulders and her hands fluttered nervously as she accepted the condolences of a well-dressed man Anna had never seen before. Obviously Janice was still struggling with the shock of Kurt's sudden death. Maybe if they got her home now, she'd have time for a short rest before having to put up a brave front during the luncheon.

Quickly, Anna said goodbye to her own family and moved unobtrusively until she was next to Janice. Taking one of her cold hands, she smiled gently. "Why don't we move along to the house now? You can talk with the rest of the people there.''

"Yes, yes, fine." Janice sounded tired. Slowly, she turned for a last look at the coffin that held her husband's remains.

She hated to leave, yet she wasn't certain how much longer her legs would hold her. She was so cold, cold clear through. Her feet, her hands... It should have rained today, Janice thought irrelevantly. You shouldn't bury someone on a sunny, crisp day but rather on a gloomy, rain-filled one. Much more appropriate.

Her thoughts were rambling, disjointed and a little frightening. She needed to get out of here, to be home, to be safe and warm again. She would not cry here in this grim, desolate place. Moving woodenly, as if she were sleepwalking, Janice placed the rose she'd been holding on top of the casket, then closed her eyes a long moment, fighting the quick flash of pain. When she felt her son's hand on her arm, she straightened and let herself be led to the waiting limousine.

SHE LOOKED TIRED, David Markus thought as he stood at the far end of the living room watching Janice and the seemingly endless stream of neighbors and friends who kept coming up to her. Women with reddish-brown hair usually looked good in black, but today Janice's pale skin was too stark a contrast. Yellow was her color, a preference he'd shared with her years ago.

Sipping his coffee, he studied her from his unobtrusive corner. The dress was somewhat shapeless and not terribly flattering to her willowy figure. She'd wound her thick hair into a haphazard upsweep that was nonetheless appealing. Her face was oval, with high cheekbones, a small nose and a generous mouth. By far her best features were her wide-set gray eyes. Without the sunglasses, they appeared huge and terribly vulnerable, fleetingly reflecting a myriad of emotions as they settled on first one person, then flitted to another. He doubted if she'd remember much of what was said today.

She'd changed, David decided as he settled himself on the arm of a nearby chair. But who hadn't in the past twenty-plus years? Changed, and yet she was in many ways the same. A little hesitant, her voice still low and husky. He'd been enamored of that voice back when he and Kurt and Janice had all three been attending the University of Wisconsin at Madison.

David had just started his junior year when Janice had arrived as a bright-eyed yet shy freshman. In a bevy of sophisticates, she'd stood out as a guileless innocent. He'd gravitated to her and they'd started dating. It wouldn't have taken much for him to have gone off the deep end over Janice, and he'd recognized that quickly. But he'd been nearly penniless then, financing his education with scholarships, and on what his mother managed to scrimp together. He'd had nothing to offer a girl from a moneyed background.

She'd come from a sheltered home and a watchful father. Finding herself suddenly on her own, she'd gradually moved out of her shell, and David knew she'd dated others besides him. After a while, he'd stopped asking her out, telling her he had too many obligations to allow much time for dating. She'd accepted his news calmly, though he'd thought she looked disappointed. Or had that been wishful thinking? The next thing he knew, she'd been all wrapped up in his roommate, Kurt Eber.

Kurt's parents had died, leaving him with a decent nest egg that he hoped to parlay into even more money.

The Ingalls family didn't seem to intimidate Kurt, though he'd mentioned to David that they appeared to disapprove of his brash confidence. David had wondered if Janice would succumb to Kurt's heated pursuit of her, and indeed, she'd been overwhelmed by his charm. Over her family's objections, she'd run off and married him. David had chosen not to go along to stand up as Kurt's best man.

So much water under the bridge since then. Finishing his coffee, David stood and set the cup aside as Herbert Ingalls walked over to him, squinting through his bifocals.

"I know you from somewhere, don't I?" Herbert asked, extending his hand.

"Yes, sir," David said, shaking hands. "We met some time ago. David Markus."

"Ah, yes. You were involved in a government program that my lab was working on about five or six years ago." Herbert ran long fingers through his unkempt white hair.

He was a big man, tall and thick through the chest, even though he had to be in his mid-to-late sixties. Compared to his well-groomed older brother, Judson Ingalls, Herbert in his baggy tweed suit looked a little like an unmade bed, David thought.

"You still with the Feds?" Herbert asked.

David shook his head. "Twenty years was long enough. I've got my own firm now. Financial adviser."

"Out of Milwaukee?"

"No, sir. Chicago." He nodded toward Janice. "I went to college with your daughter. And Kurt, of course." Janice had taken him to her family home once, but David was certain her father didn't remember meeting him then.

"Football, right? You played college ball. Pretty good, as I recall."

So he did remember. A sharp old man. "That was a long time ago."

Herbert wrinkled his brow as he glanced over at his daughter. "Damn shame about Kurt. A quick heart attack like that—easy on the victim, hell of a thing for the family to handle."

"Janice looks pretty shaken up."

"She is, for now," Herbert went on. "She's stronger than she looks, though. I've been telling her for years to get out of that man's shadow. Not healthy. Janice has this stubborn streak. But now she's got no choice."

David's gaze took in the crowds of people filling the downstairs. "It looks as if she's got a lot of supportive friends and relatives."

Herbert's shrewd eyes moved to study David. "Always room for one more, son." He clapped David on the shoulder. "Good to see you again."

"You, too, Mr. Ingalls." David watched Janice's father wander over to a small cluster of people by the door. Was he reading too much into their brief conversation or did Herbert seem less than grief-stricken over his son-in-law's death? Perhaps the family's early disapproval of Kurt had lingered through the years. How, he wondered, had Janice coped with all that?

Reaching for his cup, David strolled to the dining room for more coffee. As he poured, someone spoke from behind him.

"Excuse me, sir. Are you David Markus?"

David turned and looked into the dark brown eyes of the young man he recognized as Kurt's son. He was taller than Kurt had been, his shoulders broad in a dark sport jacket. "Yes, I am. You're K.J., right? Your father mentioned you to me often. He was very proud of your excellent grades."

The young man flushed with pride. "Thank you. I've wanted to meet you. You're kind of a legend around school. They've never had a running back as big or as fast as you."

It had been the only sport, the only diversion from work and his studies, that he'd allowed himself. The young man before him seemed as intense as he'd been in those days. "I used to love the game."

K.J. jammed his hands into his pants pockets. "I sure wish I could have made the team. Dad wanted me to in the worst way. I'm big enough, but I don't have the feel for it, I guess."

"Not every guy's meant to play football." David sipped his coffee. "What do you like to do?"

His expression became animated. "I'm interested in art. I like to draw. Cartoons, mostly. Political satire, that sort of thing. I've had a couple published in the university press. Dad said drawing was okay as a hobby, but that I'd never make a lot of money at it."

David leaned back against the buffet. "Is that what you want to do—make a lot of money?"

"Well, yeah, that's important, isn't it? But I just wish I could make a good living doing what I like to do best."

"Maybe you can. Are you majoring in art now?"

"No, business administration. Dad thought that would be best. But I take as many extra art courses as I can squeeze in."

"Well, K.J., I'm not sure I'm the right one to advise you, but it's been my experience that the most successful men are those who work at doing what they like best. Your dad was a success because he honestly loved business—making deals, beating the competition. However, that may not be for you."

"I think he wanted me to follow in his footsteps. You know, take over when he was ready to retire and all that."

David nodded. "My dad owned a butcher shop and loved what he did, cutting the meat, joking with customers. I worked there after school for a lot of years and hated every minute. We're all different. Maybe you should talk this over with your mother. She might be in favor of a change."

K.J. cast a hesitant glance through the archway at his mother. "I don't know. She always went along with my dad."

David laid a hand on the boy's arm. "She's going to have to make several important decisions without him from now on."

Swallowing, K.J. nodded. "Yeah, I guess so. Anyhow, it was good meeting you finally. Dad talked about you a lot, told me he saw you often in Chicago on his business trips. How come you never came to Tyler before?"

David shrugged. "I have a client in Whitewater, and whenever I'm in this vicinity, I usually end up there rather than Tyler."

"You know my mom, too, don't you?"

"I did, years ago." David hoped he didn't sound as nostalgic as he suddenly felt. Gazing into the eyes of Kurt's son, he also felt a pang of regret for opportunities lost and things that could never be. "Good luck, whatever you choose to do."

K.J. smiled at him. "Thanks."

As the boy walked away, David searched the room, his eyes drawn to Janice, deep in conversation with the buxom woman who'd been introduced as her sister. He vaguely remembered Irene from their college days, though her hair color was different now and she was carrying an extra thirty pounds. Wishing he could take Janice aside for a talk, even a short talk, he carried his coffee over to the window seat and sat down.

TRAILING A CLOUD of expensive perfume, Irene Ingalls Bryant came up to Janice and hugged her. "I really hate to leave you, but it's a long drive home and Everett has to stop in at his office."

Stepping back to rub at a spot above her left eye, Janice nodded. "I understand."

Not satisfied with the natural reddish highlights in her hair, Irene had gone to cosmetically enhance them, winding up with a brassy look. She patted the lacquered curls and frowned. "You really should get some rest. You've had a terrible shock."

Janice wanted everyone to leave, *everyone*. But that would be rude of her and ungrateful. She put on a small smile. "I'll be fine. Thank you for coming."

"What is family for?" Irene asked rhetorically. "Hayley wanted to make the trip with us, but I wouldn't hear of it. Her baby's due any day. She sends her best." Irene and Everett's only daughter was expecting her first child.

Janice nodded again. She'd been nodding all day, it seemed.

"Maybe, after you rest awhile, you should come to Milwaukee for a nice long visit. We can catch up."

It occurred to Janice that people said a whole lot of things at awkward times like this. She and Irene had never been close and had rarely exchanged long visits, but she supposed her sister's invitation was heartfelt. Fortunately, she was saved from answering as Everett joined them, already wearing his topcoat and carrying Irene's mink. Everett was a successful stockbroker in Milwaukee, a big man who liked sailboats, silk ties and smelly cigars.

"You ready to go, Mama?" he asked in the clipped tones of a man with a cigar clamped between his teeth.

Janice could recall few instances when she'd seen Everett without one of his imported cigars. She'd once remarked to Kurt that she wondered if Everett showered with his cigar, slept with it, made love with it in his mouth. They'd laughed over the foolish thought. She swallowed past a lump.

"You're looking pale, Lady Janice," Everett went on as he helped his wife into her coat. "Got to take care of yourself better. Those two fine kids, they need you now more than ever."

Janice ground her teeth and hoped he wouldn't notice. Everett's habit of giving everyone a pet name annoyed her suddenly. Had she lost her sense of humor and her level of tolerance, as well as her life partner? Everett was nice enough and she was being unfair. With his florid face and his excess fifty pounds he seemed a more likely candidate for a heart attack than Kurt. Was she reacting so badly because Kurt was gone and Everett was very much alive?

In a rush of remorse for her thoughts, she placed an apologetic hand on Everett's arm. "I'm sorry we didn't have more time to talk today." Her glance took in Irene. "Perhaps I will drive to Milwaukee soon."

Irene gave her a smile and another hug. "Take care of yourself and call me if you need anything. *Anything.*"

"I will." Janice watched them leave, then paused a moment to catch her breath. The crowd was thinning out at long last. Her father had left some time ago, walking out with his brother, Judson, the two of them deep in conversation. Now if only the others would leave.

She turned to find her cousin Alyssa's concerned eyes studying her.

"How are you holding up?" Alyssa asked softly, slipping her arm around Janice's waist.

"All right." Janice drew in a deep, steadying breath. "It's odd but I never once pictured this scenario." Alyssa's husband had died about ten years ago, and though she'd not given it much thought before, Janice now found herself wondering about many things. "How on earth did you cope after Ronald's death?"

Alyssa shrugged her slim shoulders, her expression unchanged, though there was a hint of sadness in her blue eyes. "You just do somehow. One day at a time. You have your private moments, and the nights are very long, very lonely at first. It helps to stay busy." She smiled then, trying for a lighter note. "I have loads of committees I can use your help on. In time, my dear."

Charity work and volunteering. She'd done her fair share of all that, Janice thought. More of the same held little appeal. Yet what would she do when there was no one to cook a special meal for, or redecorate a room for, or plan an outing around? She would find *something,* but this wasn't the day for decision making.

Janice indicated the dining room table, still laden with food. "The luncheon was lovely. You and Anna did a wonderful job."

Alyssa shook her head. "You didn't eat a thing, did you?"

"I'm not hungry, truly." She squeezed Alyssa's hand. "I need to say a word to Tom Sikes. Excuse me a moment, please."

She found him in the dining room at the dessert bar. She'd known Tom, Kurt's office manager, for years and found him to be earnest and honest, if a shade pedantic. He also seemed to feel a measure a guilt, since he'd invited Kurt to play handball with him at his apartment complex on the outskirts of Tyler on that fateful day, though she'd tried to reassure him that Kurt's heart attack had been no one's fault.

Janice touched his arm. "Tom, I'm sorry we haven't had more time to talk."

From behind thick, horn-rimmed glasses, he blinked at her. "I want to say again, Janice, how very sorry I am. I'll really miss Kurt."

"I know. Thank you."

"And I want you to know that I'll be at the office every day, at your disposal, when you're ready. I know this isn't the time or place, but..."

Janice frowned. "I'm not sure what you mean. At my disposal for what?"

Tom stroked his thinning blond hair. "To go over the books. Some decisions will need to be made about the business, about who will run things. What about the satellite office Kurt had set up in Chicago, the plans he had for expansion? We have several large policies coming up for renewal soon. We need to work up bids, since...well, since Kurt's gone, some of our clients may not automatically renew with us as they have in the past."

Rubbing her forehead, Janice felt light-headed. She hadn't given a thought the past few days to Kurt's work. "I...we didn't discuss the business much, Tom. I know very little about how the agency operates."

Tom nodded understandingly. "It's all right. I can update you when you're ready. In the meantime, I hope you'll trust me to keep things running smoothly."

Tom had been with the firm almost from the day Kurt had opened Eber Insurance Agency. He and Kurt had also become jogging buddies and had gone skiing together often since Tom's divorce. Looking at him now, Janice realized she hardly knew the man. But Kurt had trusted him and that was good enough for Janice. "Yes, I do trust you. And I'll be in as soon as I...well, soon."

"No hurry. Take your time."

She watched Tom walk away and turned to get herself a cup of coffee. But when she picked up the cup, her hands were shaking so hard that the cup rattled in its saucer.

"Here, let me help you with that." David Markus poured coffee for her, then led her to the window seat where he'd been sitting watching her.

Gratefully, Janice took a bracing sip, closing her eyes briefly. "Thank you," she whispered.

Up close, he saw a light sprinkling of freckles on her nose that he remembered from an earlier time. They gave her a youthful look that touched him. "Rough day. I know you'll be glad when we all leave."

She opened her eyes to look into his steady blue gaze. She saw empathy and concern and something else she couldn't identify. Having David Markus appear at the

cemetery after so many years had surprised and unnerved her. He was so big, his shoulders in his pin-
striped dark suit so broad, his hand as he took it from
her elbow large and tan.

He'd changed from boyishly handsome in his college football days to a deeper, more mature attractive-
ness. She'd dated David as a freshman, but she'd
quickly learned that he had goals, commitments and
obligations, and he wasn't about to let a woman side-
track him. Yet he was looking at her now with a
warmth she couldn't help responding to.

"It's been a very long time, David," she said.

"Yes, it has." He indicated the house, the people.
"Good years for you, I see."

"They have been, until now."

"Your daughter is lovely. She reminds me a great
deal of you when we were in college."

"Oh, she's far prettier. Stefanie lives in Boston now
and just became engaged to a Harvard law graduate. I
still miss having her around."

"I can imagine. I had a talk earlier with your son.
Nice young man."

"I think so." She paused, trying to remember. "Your
wife died some time ago, isn't that right?"

"Yes, twelve years ago."

Janice's expressive eyes reflected sympathy. "An
accident, I believe Kurt said."

David nodded, angling his body on the window seat
so he could look at her better. "She lost control of the
car on an icy road." He decided to change the subject,
to probe a little, hoping he wasn't getting too personal. "Will you be all right?" A man who spent his
life in the insurance business probably had good cov-
erage on himself. But as a financial adviser, David was

well aware that many men had all the trappings of wealth, yet were mortgaged to the hilt. And, though Janice's family had money, he didn't know if she had an interest in their holdings.

Janice finished her coffee and set it aside, deciding that his politely worded inquiry was about her financial situation. "I'm embarrassed to tell you that I haven't any idea. Since you were his friend, you're probably aware that Kurt was the kind of man who liked to run the show, to take care of everything. And I let him." She glanced over at Tom Sikes with a worried expression. "Now I wish I'd at least asked more questions about the business. But I never dreamed...I mean, he was only forty-six." Her voice ended on a ragged note.

David took her hand, threading his large fingers through her slim ones. "Life takes some funny turns, doesn't it, Sunshine?"

For the first time in days, she felt a smile tug at her lips. Sunshine. She remembered going on a hayride with David back when she was a starry-eyed freshman thrilled to be asked out by a football hero. They'd all been singing, and one old song, "You Are My Sunshine," had been given a particularly rousing rendition. After that, David had often called her Sunshine.

"That sure takes me back," she told him.

"You remember then?"

"Of course. We had some good times together."

"That we did."

He was so solid, Janice thought, his presence so calming. For a fleeting moment, she wished she could lay her head on David's broad chest, to let him comfort her and ease her fears.

Instead, Janice shifted her gaze out the window. The wind had picked up in late afternoon and the sky was gray, the clouds heavy with snow. She felt a chill skitter down her spine, reminding her of the reason they were all gathered together today. "It's so very hard to accept that he'll never come home again." She spoke softly, almost to herself. "Kurt traveled a great deal, but I was seldom lonely because I knew he was coming back. Being alone and knowing there'll be no one returning ever again is very different."

David had lived alone most of his adult life, yet there were times he felt the same. "Fortunately, you have your children, family, friends."

Yes, there were people, plenty of people. But would they be enough? Surprised to find her hand still in his, Janice pulled her fingers free and stood, suddenly uneasy. "I have to talk with a couple of others. David, it's good seeing you again."

He did something then that he'd been wanting to do since he'd stood watching her at the cemetery. Rising, he placed a hand at her back and drew her close to his body for the space of a long heartbeat, then pressed his lips to her forehead, finding it cool to the touch.

Her hands rose to his chest in surprise, then lingered a moment. She inhaled the clean scent of soap and smoke mingled with the outdoor smell of a wintry day, a decidedly male combination. Stepping back, she realized she was trembling.

David took a card from his pocket and pressed it into her hand. "If you ever want to discuss a business matter, or if you just need to talk, my office and home numbers are on here. Call me."

Janice nodded. "Thank you."

Brushing a strand of hair back from her forehead, she watched him make his way to the door and find his overcoat. In moments, he was strolling down the snowy sidewalk toward a long gray Lincoln.

David Markus had been widowed for years and seemed to be coping fine. She would, too, Janice thought as she slipped the card into the pocket of her black dress. Somehow.

With a weary sigh, she turned back to mingle with her remaining guests, wondering if this very long day would ever end.